MAGICAL MIDLIFE
MADNESS

ALSO BY K.F. BREENE

LEVELING UP
Magical Midlife Madness
Magical Midlife Dating (coming soon)

DEMIGODS OF SAN FRANCISCO
Sin & Chocolate
Sin & Magic
Sin & Salvation
Sin & Spirit

DEMON DAYS VAMPIRE NIGHTS WORLD
Born in Fire
Raised in Fire
Fused in Fire
Natural Witch
Natural Mage
Natural Dual-Mage
Warrior Fae Trapped
Warrior Fae Princess

FINDING PARADISE SERIES
Fate of Perfection
Fate of Devotion

MAGICAL MIDLIFE MADNESS

BY K.F. BREENE

CHAPTER 1

THIS WAS NOT the fresh start I'd had in mind.

I sat in my idling car in front of my parents' house, going over my life choices.

When the—*now ex*—husband had told me he was moving on and that he wanted a divorce, I was pretty sure he hadn't expected me to exclaim, "*Awesome!*" I'm positive he didn't think I'd start packing right away. And when I pouted at his "concession" that I could stay in the house until it was time to sell, I definitely confused him.

He had found someone else. Someone he had more in common with, apparently. Someone who shared the same life goals and liked to hold hands like we used to.

I'd told him that I hoped she was young, because if she was my age—tiptoeing past forty—and had any relationship experience at all, the second she learned that he liked his boxers ironed but wouldn't do the ironing himself, she'd be gone-skies. Only uptight guys ironed their boxers, and only self-absorbed, entitled dickheads had someone else do it for them and then negatively critiqued the creases.

Our life goals had only diverged because I'd gotten tired of supporting him through all of his endeavors without being allowed to achieve anything for myself. Somewhere along the way, when I was cooking, cleaning, ironing, changing beds, changing diapers, working, doing the bills, cooking—oops, I said cooking twice—I had started to wonder when *my* life would begin. When *I'd* kick butt and take names. When I would be recognized for my merits instead of looked down upon for the untidy laundry room.

I wanted more than this provincial life.

Matt had done me a favor by cutting me loose. He'd pushed me down the first step to my freedom. With my son starting college, thereby taking away any excuse to stay, I could finally start my own adventure. Create some *her*story.

I stared at my parents' house through the car window.

My jump-off point needed a little work.

I put my ten-year-old Honda into park.

I could not believe I was doing this. At forty years old, I was moving back in with my parents in a city just north of L.A. What had I been *thinking?*

But I knew what I'd been thinking. I had money

from the divorce, but no home, no job, and no idea where I wanted to find those things. My son didn't want me following him to the East Coast where he was going to college—another relief because I didn't want to spend my weekends doing his laundry—and I was tired of L.A. I needed to go somewhere new, but it wouldn't be sensible to waste money on hotels during my time in limbo. Which was why I'd taken my mom up on her offer to crash at my childhood home for a while.

Crash? What was I, twenty?

Midlife ladies did not crash. Not unless there was a lot of wine involved and a rogue set of stairs jumped in front of her.

I climbed out slowly, surveying my parents' mud-brown house. Nails were sticking out from the siding in places, randomly trying to flee confinement, and while the front lawn was perfectly manicured, it was sur-rounded by weed-choked bushes, fallen leaves, and a couple of rusty wagon wheels for decor. It couldn't look weirder if they'd actively tried for it.

Home, sweet home.

I grabbed a couple of suitcases out of the trunk and walked to the front door, the funeral march playing in my head. An old Wagoneer Jeep and an older truck sat in the driveway, both of them mainstays of my child-hood. They were still on my dad's "projects list." He intended to fix up the former to its past glory, which would be quite the job since the roof was cracked to hell, the wooden siding was multicolored and fading, and weeds were literally growing up out of the floorboards, and the latter would become a dump truck (just you wait!). It would get a new motor, the back would be taken off, and a dump truck bed would be installed (no problem!). There was even already a motor or ten in the garage. Stacked on the floor. With rats living in them…

The porch groaned under my weight, in dire need of some new boards. The door, once stained a deep brown with lovely stained glass, now had deep scores at the base where the last dog had made its own doorbell. Someone had painted the damage a lighter mustard-brown, not even close to matching the original mahogany hue. At least the stained glass was still lovely. There was that.

"Hello?" I asked, letting myself in the front door.

Two pairs of shiny, black-marble eyes looked at me from the deer heads mounted on each side of a painting of a deer.

The TV blared, the sound filling the living room to bursting. My dad sat on his recliner with his hand tucked into the waistband of his sweats and his chin lowered to his chest, sound asleep. Cars streamed across the screen, some Nascar race or other.

Grimacing, I edged farther into the house. I set my bags down, closed the door, and headed to the kitchen, the first place I always looked for my mother. She stood at the sink, suds covering her yellow gloves, ear buds in her ears, and her phone tucked into the back pocket of her jeans.

"Hey, Mom," I said, raising my voice over the sound of the TV in the other room. They had a circular open floor plan, in which a wall separated the kitchen from the living/dining room combo, but there was plenty of air and sound flow between the two spaces.

"Mom!" I said, just a little louder. I knocked on the dated cream square tiles climbing the wall to my right. It didn't help.

I walked closer as she bobbed her head to the music. She scrubbed a pan with gusto.

"Mom," I repeated, this time tapping her shoulder.

She jumped, screamed, and let go of the pan. It clanged into the sink, throwing up a *sploosh* of water that covered her front. She rounded on me with wide eyes.

Not turned to me.

Not flinched from me.

Rounded on me, as though this seventy-year-old woman was about to beat the ever-lovin' crap out of me!

"Oh, Jessie, it's you!" A smile replaced her look of *crazy*. She pulled her ear buds from her ears. "How are you?"

Her hug soaked the front of my shirt, and her gloves wet my back.

"Martha, what are you doing in there?" my dad hollered. "The race is on. I can barely hear a thing!"

My mom rolled her eyes. She didn't bother to reply.

"Let me just finish this up and I'll show you to your room," my mom said, gesturing at the sink.

I scanned the loaded dish dryer perched over the second sink…and the dishwasher beneath it. "You have a dishwasher, why are you doing these by hand?"

"Your father never wanted to waste the electricity on the dishwasher, remember?" She turned back to her task. "I've always had to do them by hand. Well, since I retired, I've had just about enough of chores. He barely earns any money any more, did he tell you? He doesn't take a paycheck most of the time. I don't know why he doesn't retire. Anyway, we're living off of my retirement. So I thought, you know what? If I want a machine to make my life easier, I've earned it." She nodded adamantly. "But the thing was so old, it broke after the second wash." She sighed. "So I went to Wired Right down on the square there. You know the place. With the green awning?"

She turned back to make sure I was on the same page so I nodded even though I had no idea.

"Well, I bought the very best they had," she said. "With all the bells and whistles. Cost me an arm and a leg, but you know what? To heck with it. And he can't say anything, because he spent all that money on that new motor. So there."

"Right…" I leaned against the counter. "So where is it?"

"Delivers on Tuesday. Boy will I be glad to get these dishes out of my hair. Then I can go upstairs to my sewing room and shut the door. You can barely hear yourself mutter down here."

"Cool. I can just head up to…my old room, right?"

"Just wait there. You want a beer?" She paused and drew her hands out of the soapy water, white bubbles shivering on her yellow gloves.

"Sure," I said, because that's what this house did. If people came over, everyone drank a beer. What else did I have to do? The future stretched wide open ahead of me. All I needed was the courage to walk into it.

WITH ONE BEER down and another in my hand, I followed my mother up to my transitionary room. My dad still had no idea I was home, but all the dishes had been dried and put away.

Why I needed a guide, I did not know. I'd stayed in this house multiple times with Matt and Jimmy for the holidays, and we'd always slept in my old room. This was the first time I'd been given guidance. It made me suspicious.

We tread up the worn russet-brown carpet that had long since put up the white flag. My mother had started painting the wall beside me a turd brown, only she hadn't finished, possibly hoping my dad would get the ladder and finish it up. The project cars out front apparently hadn't made an impression on her. The wall looked like a crap-striped zebra, white stripes between the brown, but nobody seemed to notice or care.

Speaking of noticing or caring, the cool painting I'd given them three years ago sat in the little alcove that overlooked the living room, resting on the ground against the scuff-marked wall.

Happy anniversary, indeed.

"Mom, I know where the bedroom is," I said as we passed the hall closet that still didn't have doors thirty years after my dad had designed and built the house.

"Yes, I know, but I made a new quilt and want to make sure it's okay," she said.

"It'll be fine, Ma, I swear—" I fell mute as we reached the room's open doorway. A stiff-looking turquoise and brown quilt rested on the double bed in the midst of a sea of books. "That's…lovely. What's the story with all these books?"

"You think so?" She beamed, heading into the room and pulling up the corner of the quilt. It moved like thin plywood. "I took up quilting. That sewing room is the only place I can get out of the heat!"

I glanced at the open windows, letting in the chill fall air. "Oh yeah?"

"Yes! Your father is so fat, you'd think he'd be insulated enough, but still the house is a furnace." She huffed. "I found some patterns for quilts at the fabric store. I made them extra warm."

I paused for a moment, contemplating the irony of that, but decided to press her about the state of the room instead. "What happened in here?" I asked. "What's that?"

In addition to the books that had been stacked horizontally on every surface and heaped around the bed, a random pile of fur sat in the corner.

"Oh, that. Well, your dad shot an elk last year, but it wasn't big enough to warrant stuffing the head, so he took the skin. It struck me—what was that Native American tribe that scalped people?" I stared at her, struck mute. "All the white men at the time acted so superior about that, didn't they? How barbarian to scalp a kill, they said. And look at this! He cuts off heads and hangs them on the wall, and when that isn't glorious enough, he scalps their bodies. Who's the barbarian now?"

My mom pursed her lips and turned down the bed.

"That's…" Best to ignore. Except… "Why is it in the corner? In a pile?"

"He wants to hang it somewhere."

"But…isn't Chris's old room for all Dad's junk?"

I wasn't the only one who'd bounced back here—my brother Chris had come to stay with them a few years ago after a tough breakup. The state of the place had not only driven him out of the house, but out of the state, as well. He was now on the East Coast, happy to be on his own in a clutter-free zone.

"That's the man cave. He's got so much junk in there, he worried the elk scalp would get lost," my mother replied.

I didn't bother to tell her that scalps were on heads and pelts were on bodies. I didn't think she'd care either way.

"Hmm. Do you need closet space? Because…" She pushed open the dirt-brown closet doors, revealing her clothes and shoes.

I'd never really noticed how many different shades of brown existed in this house. It was like they'd chosen a color palette with various shades of poop.

Sweat prickled my brow. The urge to flee was strong. "Why do you use this closet? Why not your closet?"

"There's a bunch of old clothes I don't wear in my closet." She pushed a few things over, sparing a couple feet of hanging room. "There. That should do you. You mostly wear sweats anyway, right? You don't need to put those in here. They can stay in your suitcase."

I didn't ask what had happened to my old dresser. It wasn't here, at any rate.

"Right. Fine," I said, suddenly exhausted.

"Need another beer?"

"Yes. Keep 'em coming. Morning, noon, and night. Just keep 'em coming."

CHAPTER 2

T HE NEXT MORNING, I blinked up at Brad Pitt with his long hair and little smirk. Some of his chest peeked out of his open shirt. *Legends of the Fall* was scrawled across the bottom of the poster.

My mother slept in this room more often than not because of my dad's snoring, yet she'd never taken down the hot guy poster from yesteryear? Brad Pitt wasn't even that hot, anymore. Sure, he was still technically a looker, but he'd crapped on my girl Jennifer, and he'd gotten all scruffy with Angelina, and then he'd pressured her to marry him, only to get a divorce and contact Jennifer again…

I mean, the guy was a dung-dance of dependency. It needed to be said.

He didn't deserve a place on my ceiling. That was a girl's crush. A girl who hadn't yet played the game and lost—and then glugged all the wine, flipped the table over, and slurred obscenities on her way out of there.

I was older now. Wiser. I was done getting side-tracked by a pretty face. Looks tarnished.

Brad had to go.

I flung the covers away, stood on the mattress, and tore from the edge of the poster. Brad's face split in two. The tape stuck fast.

"Freakin'—" I grabbed the other side and did the same thing. Little blotches of paper stayed put in all of the corners. Brad's eyeball waved at me from the small surviving portion of the poster. "Ugh. Get. Lost. Brad!" I caught the last shred, tore that, and frowned up at the specks still holding strong.

What had I used to pin him up, infinity glue?

Wadding up the poster, I contemplated jumping to the floor like I would've done the last time I'd lived here. Of course, back then I'd had eighteen-year-old knees and half the weight. If I jumped right now, my knees would probably buckle and dump me on my face.

I gingerly lowered to sitting before placing my feet on the faded brown carpet and pushing up to standing.

My phone chimed as I made my way downstairs. Matt, wondering about the closing papers on our old house.

"Yeah, I made it just fine, thanks. Doing great, couldn't be better," I grumbled, finding my mother at the sink again.

On the weekends she usually made a large breakfast,

but it was only Tuesday, which meant she'd placed a cereal box, milk, and a bowl out on the table for my father. Given the bowl was empty but used, I suspected he'd finished up and would soon be heading to work. Or out to tinker with his project cars.

But as I stood at the entrance to the kitchen, the toilet flushed in the downstairs bathroom. Clearly the old man was still here.

I turned toward the bathroom, intending to use it next, when the door opened and too much skin stepped out.

"What the—" I covered my eyes and jerked my head away.

"Ladies do not swear," my father said in disapproval even though I hadn't gotten to the swear word.

"Fathers do not wander around the house without clothes on when their grown daughters are home, Dad! What are you doing?"

My mother turned from the sink, only then turning off her music. "What's the matter—oh for the love of… Pete, *put some clothes on!*" She sighed and shook her head in commiseration with me. "Two months ago, he just up and decided that clothes in the morning were causing him anxiety."

"I didn't say they were causing me anxiety! I said they cut off the morning circulation to my begonias, and that caused me to feel a little tight in my chest, that's all. Not enough circulation."

"Anxiety," my mom said, clearly annoyed.

"Not anxiety," my dad replied, clearly just as annoyed.

"Awesome, great, sound logic—can you put some clothes on now? And use a towel on the dining room chair, please? I don't want to sit on the same seat as your exposed...begonias," I said.

"Jacinta Evens, when you speak to someone, you look them in the eye," my father scolded.

"Pete, you have your testicles out. Of *course* the girl is going to look away!" My mother turned around, muttering, "I don't blame her, quite frankly. You need to go to the doctor. I know those things sag, but it looks like you have a medical condition."

"I can't do this. I can't..." I took two deep breaths, ignoring my parents' continued bickering, and followed the wall to the bathroom. I didn't want to risk looking around. There were many things a person would rather die without seeing, and the sagging bare backside of one's father was at the top of the list.

The small downstairs bathroom stopped me short. An enormous, obviously fake tree stood in the corner. Its bright, unrealistically green leaves stretched out over the counter toward the sink and reached above the toilet. The toilet seat had been left up, showing the disgusting underbelly of both the seat, with its many dark cracks, and the pee-sprinkled edge of the bowl. A large digital painting with a jumping dolphin took up more of the wall than was artistically pleasing, not to mention those pictures hadn't been in vogue since the early nineties. It was clear my dad had been offered some freebies.

My dad never passed up freebies.

I had to kick the seat down so as not to touch stale pee, ignore the plastic leaves poking me in the side of my face, and speed up this soul-searching process. I needed a new place and a new job, fast!

"HOW'S IT GOING?" my oldest and best friend Diana asked later that day with a sympathetic smile. Her wire-rimmed glasses had a smudge on the side that she didn't seem to notice. She cupped her hands around her steaming mug. It was September, yes, but it was also California. She was the only person I knew who drank hot coffee no matter the weather or time of day. She was a true fanatic.

A few people dotted the seats in the independent coffee shop, all hipsters with weird hair, a lot of piercings, and surprisingly hushed tones. They were young and looked ridiculous, but at least they were respectful.

"Good, mostly," I said, dragging the pad of my finger down my sweating glass of iced tea. "It was time, with Matt. I've been a drone for too long, you know that. Jimmy is off to college, so it's about time for me to be...well, *me* again. I don't even know who *me* is, anymore, but it's about time I found out."

She nodded, her eyes crinkling a little at the corners. "I totally agree. You'd shut off for a while there. You can finally turn back on again and *live* for once. Make mistakes. Bang a few younger guys." Her smile turned devilish. "Live a little! Actually, live a *lot*. I want stories."

I gave her a sarcastic huff. She was happily married to her college sweetheart, but she would say anything to make me feel better. She wanted me to be happy. Always had. When everyone else was preaching about the sanctity of marriage and *how could he?*, she was asking if I remembered when I'd stopped smiling. She was the best friend a girl could have.

"I'm not looking for more stories. I'm looking for..." I paused, thinking about it. "I'm looking for adventure, I think. It feels like time is running out. It feels like I need to get my real life started, the sooner the better. Guys can wait."

She bobbed her head, then took a sip of her coffee. "Definitely. But honestly, what I was really asking was...how's it going with the parents?"

"Ugh!" I dropped my head, reminded of the morning. I'd gone on a walk to clear my head, and the instant I'd returned, my mom had asked why I'd taken down the poster on the ceiling. She'd wanted to know where she could get another of those "very pretty young men." "At some point without my knowledge, she grabbed the cute outfit I'd worn yesterday and washed it. Except she didn't care enough about the deed to see if it could be dried. She just went ahead and threw it in the dryer."

"Oh no," Diana said, her eyes twinkling with delight. She had always loved visiting my parents' house and hearing crazy stories about them. Having normal parents with a normal house, she couldn't relate.

"My cashmere sweater is two sizes too small, and the silk shirt is ruined."

"No!"

I told her about my dad's new addition to his morning routine.

"*No!*" She fell against the table in a fit of giggles. "What the hell?"

"I do not know." I shook my head, wishing I could find it funny. "I really do not. But I can't stay there. I can't. It's too much. All my mom does is wash dishes and read, and she stacks the books a mile high in my room. If there's an earthquake, I'll be crushed. Fire? Forget it. I'm toast. The whole place would be ablaze by the time I even opened my eyes. No wonder my brother only stayed for a couple months."

She couldn't contain the belly laughter. Or maybe she wasn't trying.

"You clearly don't see how dire this is," I said.

"I'm sorry, I'm sorry." She fought her smile. A fight she lost. "Sorry! But listen to this. My aunt called yesterday, asking if I knew anyone who would be a good fit for the caretaker role of Ivy House. What a coincidence, right? You'd be perfect for it. You wouldn't need to stay with your parents, you'd have a job, and you'd get to go back to that nightmare house that you loved so much. I told her I'd ask you." Her eyes twinkled. "Just think, no morning begonias."

Memories came trickling back. I'd gone on a lot of vacations with her family. She was an only child and I loved to travel, so she got a playmate and I got to see new places. Win-win.

"That place in that small town near the Sierras? What were we...like, ten, right?" I asked.

"Yeah. The big old house in that tiny town." She clucked her tongue. "What is the name of that town? I always forget. I think I block it out. It's an Irish name. Murphys or O'Connors or Bollocks or... That big old house with all those rooms and that creepy gardener we thought was a vampire?" She shivered. "I hated that place. I still don't understand why you liked it so much. You didn't want to leave, remember?"

A mental image of the guy popped into my head. Pasty white, yellowed teeth, long face, loose jowls—

A sense of euphoria came over me out of nowhere, followed by a strange sense of urgency.

"Yeah," I said, feeling a creeping smile curve my lips. More images came through, somewhat hazed with age. Big rooms with old-fashioned furniture, dark wallpaper, and a foreboding feeling that wasn't exactly unpleasant. A strange trap door that led outside, only it was three floors up without a ladder. The attic floor had been covered with random silver gardening spikes we weren't allowed to play with and a strange old-fashioned mechanical bow and arrow. I didn't have many memories still clunking around my head from thirty years ago, but that house was hard to forget. "That place scared the hell out of you. You're such a scaredy-cat."

"Scaredy-cat? That house was creepy as hell. You're just nuts."

"Well yes…" I laughed at her, my mood lightened.

"I have no idea why my parents even took us there. What kind of vacation is that?"

My grin widened, remembering the secret passage-ways we'd found. It had been so incredibly cool to wander into the hidden places, exploring the house from within its very veins. One spot still throbbed in my memory, a room in subterranean depths.

Blue light from a suspended lantern painted the rough rock walls. Below the lantern stood what looked like a gothic pedestal filled with beautiful crystals, beckoning me closer. My mind had raced, my imagination active, thinking that patch of crystals acted like the organ that kept the house running. That the light glowing within the iron frame of the lantern magically lit all the passageway corridors. That the crystals had whispered to me—*wait, Jacinta, you're not ready. It isn't time. Try again later.*

I shook my head, those brief snippets of time jumbling up, crusty with age. I'd had many adventures in my youth, remembering tree houses in gnarled old trees, or trekking through the creek behind my elementary school, but that house had been a favorite. Nothing else could compare to that creepy factor, to the point that, as I thought back on it, I wondered how much I was dreaming up and how much had been real.

"We didn't stay in that house long," I said, sipping my drink.

I hadn't wanted to leave, I remembered that. Unlike Diana, I hadn't wanted to part with the strange old place.

Then again, I was a great lover of Halloween and Diana was more of a Christmas person. Scary movies didn't scare me. I could watch *The Gremlins* or *The Exorcist* without batting an eye. New horror flicks? I condescendingly judged the effects and the often-shoddy work of the director.

"She wants a caretaker, like…a house sitter?" I asked. "Or like…someone who is going to continually clean it from top to bottom? Because I remember all the spider webs. That place is huge. That would be a nightmare to look after."

"Firstly, we were ten, so things appeared bigger to us than they actually were. That's just logic."

I rolled my eyes at her.

"Second, it would be just you living there and maybe a butler. How much mess could you make?"

"Wait, wait, wait." I held up my hand. "What's this about a butler?"

"Oh yeah. Great Uncle Earl. He's been old as long as I've been alive, but he hasn't kicked the bucket yet. He stays there. He was let go from his position in England because he was creeping out the kids, so my aunt lets him stay at the estate. It's an old family joke, the fact that he's still alive. Everyone says he's afraid he'll die if he ever retires." She must've seen my look of confused horror because she waved her hand in the air, wiping the thoughts away. "Who cares about him? He's clean. He wouldn't have made it all those years as a butler otherwise. And maybe he'll wait on you, who knows? That would be cool, right? Either way, at least he won't be walking around naked."

"I don't know. I kinda want to live alone for once. I've never actually had my own place."

"Jessie, come on, I'm not saying live there forever. Good lord, no. Being raised here and then moving to Los Angeles—you'd go crazy downgrading to a tiny town like...O'Kieff? Was that the name? Hoolahans? Still, the place is available if you want to get away from your parents and figure things out. You could even make a little money. Think of it as a begonia-free transition."

Trading up one crazy living situation for another didn't sound all that great, especially since I'd have to leave Diana to do it. But not having to look for a job right away...

I sighed and took a sip of my iced tea. It was probably best to just stick it out with my parents. The stress of being there would push me to figure things out pronto. If I put my mind to it, I knew I could do it.

Something niggled at the edge of my thoughts, though. A pulsing. A...beckoning.

My heart sped up and a light sweat coated my brow.

The words fell from my mouth before I'd known I was going to say them.

"Sure, why not. When can I start?"

CHAPTER 3

S AYING GOODBYE TO my parents had been easy. My dad complimented me on my quick ability to find a new job, and though my mom hugged me and said she was sad I couldn't stay longer, I had a sneaking suspicion she was happy to get the spare bed back—a place she could retreat to when my dad was snoring.

I nearly changed my mind about this venture when I rolled through the tiny town of O'Briens, named after the founders, a couple of Irish guys who'd come over the Sierra Nevada mountains and settled in to mine for gold. Since then, wineries had sprung up like a plague, their tasting rooms dotting the itty-bitty downtown strip like chicken pox.

The wine I did not mind. At all. I was rather excited about it, to be honest.

It was the size of the town that concerned me. Or, more accurately, the *lack* thereof.

I grew up in a city of over a hundred thousand people. Then I moved to L.A., getting into the millions. I'd never lived in a place where I could drunkenly stagger from one end of the downtown strip to the other. And given the number of adorable boutique wineries, I'd absolutely do that in this town. I'd do it, and then all three thousand residents would soon know about it. It'd probably be printed in the town paper. With pictures. I'd never been great at following convention, even back when I was trying. Maybe *especially* when I was trying. It had annoyed Matt to no end.

The windy road the GPS told me to follow veered off from the downtown strip and cut through the trees, gaining a tiny bit of altitude. Dainty little houses pushed back from the road, with large porches, white pillars, and well-kept gardens. Newish cars parked in driveways, their surfaces glittering in the golden afternoon sun.

At the end of the street with no outlet rose a monstrosity of a house.

My eyes widened and I slowed before I reached it, needing to take a moment before I pulled into the driveway.

Despite the sunny day and bright, electric blue sky, it seemed like there was a black cloud looming over the three-story structure. The gothic-style building rose to a point at the center, and a little glowing attic window could be seen at the top. Dark shadows draped over the front from some unseen source. The large windows curved elegantly at the top. The decorative shutters, curtains, and trim were all black.

At least it's better than turd brown.

Now that I was here, more distant memories came flooding back. The dark rooms, the ominous feeling, the creepy exterior, and the strange feeling of belonging.

Strange, indeed. On first inspection, this place, so different than everything else on this street, was anything but welcoming. It exuded an undeniable *get lost* vibe, from its positioning at the dead end, pushed well back from the road, to its dark and foreboding colors. It crouched like some gigantic beast, a warning written into its wood frame. A chill given out to every visitor who might pass.

Except, even as I sat there, looking up at it, something flowered within me. My heart beat solid thumps, pushing warmth through my body. Pushing a feeling of home, of safety, of belonging. Something about this house tugged at me. Begged me to come closer and rest my weary head within its walls.

I released a breath I hadn't realized I'd been holding. "I've cracked, that's all there is to it. Living with my parents—even for just a couple days—has finally driven me insane."

Still, there was plenty of oddity to go around, from

the way that attic light was emitting a glow despite the bright afternoon sunshine—*magic*—to that strange shadow from nowhere—*dark magic*—to the lovely grass—*diligent gardener.*

My imagination was still active and this beast would feed right into it. I almost felt like a teenager again.

"This is an honest to god mansion," I said into the heavy hush as I pulled into the driveway. "Things looked bigger to ten-year-olds, my butt. This is just plain *big*!"

What was it about middle age and muttering to oneself? Was that a mom thing, or an age thing? I didn't know, but it had become a me thing, and if I didn't watch it, I'd embarrass myself with the super-old-yet-never-seemed-to-die Great Uncle Earl.

I stepped out of the car slowly and a tingle of excitement worked through my body. A smile played with my lips, I could feel it. Something about this move felt right. The house was big, weird, and creepy, but it was exactly what I needed right now.

Struggling to contain a manic grin that would probably scare people, I stepped up to the door and found myself staring at a large gargoyle knocker. It looked silently at me with its strange brass eyes and a mouth full of metal.

"It better not talk," I muttered, remembering the

movie *Labyrinth* from my childhood.

But what would I do if it did?

The manic grin spread wider.

Forget scaring people, someone would probably call the cops on the deranged middle-aged lady loitering on private property.

Diana had instructed me to knock first. If no one answered, I had to report to the first house on the left to get the key.

With a quick glance behind me at the quiet street, making sure no one was gawking, I wrapped my fingers around the cool ring of metal and *thumped* the knocker three times. The sound reverberated through the house, bouncing along the floors and up to the various levels. I could feel it, like a tangible thing. My imagination was already in overdrive.

I took a deep breath as adrenaline coursed through me.

"You *rang*."

"Oh!" I jumped and spun around, clutching my purse to my chest like some old biddy at an unexpected peep show.

A tall, gangly man with more wrinkles than hair stood in front of me, his eyes a deep midnight, his scowl possibly etched into his face from years of use, and his height topping mine by at least a foot, putting him somewhere in between six and seven feet tall. A moth-bitten suit clung to his bony shoulders and a tattered cape dusted the back of his thighs, fluttering in a breeze I couldn't feel.

I didn't know where he'd come from, but he'd snuck up behind me silently.

"Ha-ha," I laughed warily. "Good one. From the Addams Family, right? Lurch?"

I pointed at him for no reason, kind of just needing something to do with my hands. His stare was unnerving.

Silence stretched between us. I lifted my eyebrows, hoping he'd pick up the conversational baton and run with it. When he didn't, I cleared my throat.

"I'm Jess. Jacinta." I shrugged. "Jessie. Usually."

"Are you usually the one person or do you switch between all three?" the ancient butler said with no hint of humor.

I smiled unconvincingly and half-chuckled anyway. The guy was weird.

"So...I'm the new caretaker," I said, trying not to sound awkward. And failing miserably. "Are you Great Uncle Earl?"

"I am not your great uncle anything, but my name is Earl, yes. You may call me Tom."

"Tom," I said, searching his face for a joke. If it was

there, it was hidden behind the scowl.

"Mr. Tom," he said.

I was pretty sure my eyebrows had gotten lost in my hairline. "Mr. Tom." I squinted at him. "Are you kidding, or... I can't tell if you're kidding."

"I am a butler. I never kid."

"Right. Of course."

"Mr. Tom."

"Yes. Right. Mr. Tom, then." I cleared my throat for the second time. "Mr. Tom, should I just..." I jerked my head at the door.

He stared at me. He didn't even blink.

"Should I just...go in?" I jerked my head again, pointing at the door for emphasis this time.

"To whom am I speaking?" he asked.

Oh good, his memory didn't work. We'd get along just fine. We could have the same conversation for days and be none the wiser.

"Jessie," I answered, now pointing at my chest.

"Jessie, you need to report to Ms. Murphy's house. She's a God-awful old woman from a dreary land, but she is the holder of The Key. Visiting her cannot be helped, I'm afraid. Don't ask me to go with you, I simply cannot stomach it."

"Oh. Sure. Ms. Murphy—"

"Yes, Ms. Murphy's house. She is just..." He turned

in a crisp movement that spoke of agelessness and pointed at the first house on the left. This was the neighbor I'd been told to visit if no one answered the door at Ivy House.

"Great." I glanced at the car, debating, then shifted my gaze to the deserted street. "What's the crime rate around here? Probably pretty quiet, huh?"

"Only if we're not raided. Or hunted. The un-crowned alpha has been all the protection we need, though I fear we are adrift. Someday he won't be enough, and then where will we be? Dead, that's where. Dismembered, flayed, burned alive, what have you."

Was it just me, or was this guy completely bananas?

"Okay. I'll just take my purse with me." I edged around him.

"We are only safe because no one is interested in our lowly residents. But mark my words..." He let the silence stretch as his crisp gaze beat into me. I inched backward, wearing a polite smile usually reserved for the drug-addled homeless asking weird questions in the check-out line at the grocery store. "You will not want to take the sandwich. You might take the tea—she'll force it on you—but refrain from the sandwich. It'll keep you there all day."

I stopped dead for a moment, really unclear on what was happening right now. How could I possibly share a roof with this nutter? He'd be unpredictable at best and might end up burying me in the yard at worst.

This might've been a terrible, awful idea. Worse than staying with my parents.

CHAPTER 4

I MADE MY way up to the stoop of the neighbor's door. Two rocking chairs sat on the porch—one heavily used with a neat pile of rocks beside it, the other brand new in appearance.

The polished door knocker on this door was a lovely horse head with a bump on the forehead, like a budding unicorn or something. I used the doorbell instead. Pounding a door knocker seemed more intrusive, somehow. It reminded me of the way police entered a crack house. Not that I would really know.

"I'm comin', I'm comin'." The voice was muffled through the door.

I stepped back, giving the owner some space.

The door swung open and a pleasing floral aroma wafted out. An older woman stood in the doorframe, her hair short and white, her back slightly hunched, and her pale blue eyes lined with crow's feet. Her thin lips curled up at the corners, as though she were smiling about a secret, and her lily-white skin looked baby soft.

"Hi—"

"What in the holy bejesus are you at?" Ms. Murphy demanded, her voice scratchy and coarse and not at all in keeping with her dew-drop appearance.

My eyebrows got lost in my hair line again, trying to decipher the thick Irish brogue.

"What, are ye peddling somethin'?" the woman said into the silence. "Well, sure, you better come in and have some tae."

"Oh, uh…" I felt the pull of her expectations but didn't bite. Just needed that key. I'd had tea on the way up and really needed to pee, but it seemed rude to ask to use the bathroom when my new residence was right next door. "I'm the new caretaker. Earl—uh, Mr. Tom sent me."

"Mr. Tom, me arse." She pushed out onto the porch, reached down, scooped up a rock, and rushed to the side of the railing closest to the mansion. She cocked her arm, ready to throw.

Mr. Tom still stood where I'd left him, facing us.

"Ye eld bugger, ya!" Ms. Murphy yelled. "Could ye not have let her in yerself? Yer as *useless…*" She let fly, the rock slicing through the air as though thrown by a prized quarterback.

Mr. Tom took one step back. The rock landed precisely where he'd been standing—the distance incredible, the aim unbelievable, Mr. Tom's nonchalance about having an old woman throw a rock at him disconcerting. This sort of thing clearly went on all the time.

"It is your job, after all," Mr. Tom said, and though he was across the street and up the walk, I still somehow heard him.

So did she.

"It's my job *da feck*," Ms. Murphy said. Or so I thought. I couldn't quite make out the last couple of words. "Well, now I've got her. And I'll be tellin' her all about the real goings on over there. Just you wait, ye gobshite." She turned and stomped into her house. "Well?" She turned back. "Will ye have a cuppa tae? Ye will, ye will. Come on. I'll put the kettle on."

Her expectations won out. Hard to say no to a retreating backside.

The spacious inside was wholesome and homey, with pictures of green fields laden with cows on walls, little knickknacks on shelves, and a frightening number of slightly off doilies. They looked to have been handmade by someone who both didn't know how to crochet and couldn't see very well.

"Now," Ms. Murphy said in a singsong kind of voice, pointing at the small round table in the kitchen before heading to a bright red electric kettle sitting on the counter. "So you're goin' ta take the post, then?"

"The caretaker job," I said lamely, still unpacking what she'd said. "I have the caretaker job. Just for a while."

"Well. Ol' Edgar will be excited for that. He hates Earl, so he does. Absolutely can't stand the man. I think he does, at any rate. I can't listen to him for long. That Edgar would rot the ears off ye, so he would. Sure, you're half deaf just standing near 'em, that's how bad he is. Pure thick-headed, too. Mean as a badger when he wants ta be. Ah well…" She pulled down a little milk jug and put a slosh of milk into it, then proceeded to grab a silver teapot and drop one tea bag inside. Waste not, want not, I supposed. She stopped in her preparations and turned back. "Will ye have a sandwich, ye will?"

"Oh no, thanks. No, that's okay," I said, remembering the warning and trying to ignore my aching stomach.

"As sure, go on."

I smiled politely. "That's okay, honest. I'm fine, I just—"

"Go on. You will. Just a wee bite…"

I put up my hand and forced a polite laugh. "No, it's okay. Thank you for asking."

"Go *on*."

"No, it's—"

"*Go on.*"

"No, I—"

"As sure, you might as well." She headed to the fridge.

My stomach growled and the old woman must've heard it because she nodded.

"Sorry, I didn't get your name…" I asked, slinging my purse around my knee.

"Niamh."

I leaned forward. "Neve?"

"N-i-a-m-h," she spelled. "Niamh."

"Ne-ahve."

"Close enough." She'd taken various items out of the fridge and started assembling sandwiches. When the electric kettle clicked off, Niamh poured the hot water into the metal teapot and dropped the lid. She carried everything to the table as I half rose.

"Can I help with anything?" I asked.

"No, no, not at'all. Sit, sit." She pushed the plate of four sandwiches my way, all of them consisting of bread, ham, cheese, and a smear of butter. They hadn't even been cut in half.

Once the tea had been poured, and doctored with milk and a little sugar, Niamh finally shifted her focus back to me.

"So. Ye've come to watch the house, have ye? Why

is that, now?"

"I heard there was an opening and decided I might like…" My words died within Niamh's shaking head. "What's the matter?"

"There's no point making up stories. What's the real reason?" Niamh asked.

The wind went out of my sails and I sighed as I picked up a sandwich. "I got a divorce and couldn't stomach living with my parents for more than a couple of days. In a nutshell. I remembered this house from my childhood, and when my friend mentioned her aunt needed a caretaker, *voilà*. Here I am, ready for a new experience and maybe a little adventure."

"A little adventure, is it? Hmm. You are in charge of your own fate, I suppose."

"Aren't we all?"

"Of course we're not, what are ye on about?" She huffed. "Some people are like tumbleweeds—go where the wind shoves them. Not me, I've always gone my own way. Until I got here. Now I do absolutely *nah-thin'*. I hang around all day. Have a wee drinkie at night. It suits me right down to the ground for now. Couldn't be happier."

"That's good. Nice area, huh?"

"Pure dumpster fire, this place."

I smiled at the joke, then realized it wasn't a joke

and looked down at my dry sandwich.

"Not just anyone can be a caretaker in that old place, ye know," Niamh said. "Takes a special person."

"Oh yeah? How come?"

"The house is prickly. Those who serve it are prickly."

Clearly she didn't like Mr. Tom any more than he liked her.

"It's just for a while, until I get my bearings," I assured her. "I let Diana know to tell her aunt."

"Yes, yes, I heard. But Diana doesn't fully understand the forces at work here. She's that tumbleweed I was on about. Blithely rolling along. You're different, you are. You're fighting against the current now. It's time."

The small hairs stood up on the back of my neck and along my arms. I swallowed down my bite and took a deep breath, not sure why.

"The house welcomed you last time you were there, isn't that right?" she asked me, and it felt like a hush blanketed our conversation.

My eyebrows drifted upward of their own accord.

"Diana's aunt thought Diana might grow accustomed to that house, but no such luck, no. Too timid, if you ask me. Clever, but no real…" She fisted her hand. "Independence of thought. Diana is happy to follow the pack, like I said. She's not cut out to lead."

The conversation had lost me. I nodded noncommittally and hurried up with the sandwich.

Niamh took a sip of her tea. "Peggy doesn't have any children, you know. That's Diana's auntie. The house didn't choose her, either. Soul crushing, that. The house always goes to a female heir, and it should've been Peggy. Didn't fit in around here as well as she'd hoped. Almost a plain Jane. She took it hard. Still, a few million in the bank isn't so bad, is it? She married well and made sure he died off quickly." Niamh pursed her lips. "She's got a nice little life now. Money might not buy happiness, but it sure helps with an escape route."

I stared mutely for a moment, once again struggling to unpack all the crazy that was being thrown at me. Was being bananas a requirement to living around here?

"I thought... But..." I regrouped and started again. "Peggy does own the house, right? She just also lives in Europe?"

"Yes, she does. She does own the property, yes. And all the surrounding wood. Wants nothing to do with it."

"Oh, I see."

"No, you don't."

And that was my cue.

"Okay, well." I took a sip of my tea to wash down

the last of the sandwich, stood, and gave her a pleasant smile. "Thank you for the tea and sandwich. If you wouldn't mind getting me the key, I'll go get familiar with the house."

Niamh watched me stand, her eyes calculating. My smile faltered. My eagerness to check out the house, and get the hell out of this one, was whittling away at my patience.

Finally, she climbed to her feet, leaning heavily on the table to do so. "Sure, yeah, o'course. Let me just go grab it. Wait a minute there, you." Her body crackled as she finished straightening up, but her walk didn't seem impeded by old bones.

I wished I could glide half so well. Or was as trim.

Time to get serious about losing weight, toning up, and claiming my body back. If this woman could do it, clearly it wasn't an age thing. It was a motivation thing. Well, color me motivated.

"Here."

I jumped and spun for the second time that day. How did these people manage to sneak up on me so easily? Was there something in the water?

Niamh held out a manila envelope. "There's a few bits and bobs in there for you. If I were you, I'd let the house grow on you first before ye go hokin' through everything. That is…if it *does* grow on you. It's fickle, as

I said, and some things you won't want to find right away."

That thrill of excitement arrested me again. I could not imagine what things I would not want to find. For so long, life had been on autopilot—wake up, be domestic, go to sleep. Those chains had finally been broken. Although the unexpected could be found behind every door at my parents' house, it wasn't exactly exciting—more like quietly horrifying. I had a feeling it would be different at Ivy House. There, the horrifying things would at least be loud.

I took the envelope, feeling the weight of the key inside.

"And don't let that Earl give you any grief, either, the silly el' sod. He hasn't had a master in so long, he's grown fat and lazy. It's about time he earned his keep."

If Earl lost any more weight, he'd float away.

I paused for a moment, remembering something earlier in the conversation. "You knew I was here before, when I was a kid. Why—how is that?"

A little smile crawled across her lips. "I've lived here a long time. A lot of the town has. We've seen the grape-bearing weeds grow up around us, the town change from honest folks to handsy tourists. I remember wondering if Peggy had been right about Diana, only to see her and her parents legging it out of the house three days after arriving. Three of you were running. One was being dragged. You. That's why you stuck in my head. I hadn't noticed you before that."

Memories drifted in as Niamh led me to the door and gently shoved me out. I did remember being dragged, but that was by Diana. I couldn't recall her parents being in much of a hurry. They were upset that Diana was upset, sure enough, but not because of the house.

Right?

"I'm headed to the pub at eight. Meet me out front if ye want to go. I can introduce you to the locals," Niamh said as I crossed the street.

I gave her a noncommittal wave before meeting Earl—Mr. Tom—on the stoop, exactly where I'd left him. The rock Niamh had thrown had rolled up against his polished black boot. He must have stood there, unmoving, for at least an hour.

"Did you get the key?" he asked, eyeing the envelope.

"Yes. Thank you."

He didn't move out of the way. "Are you sure? If she didn't approve of you, you would not have left with the key."

"Yeah, it's…" I shook the envelope. "It's in here."

"Are you sure?"

After giving him my best mom look, which promised someone was going to get paddled if this kept up, I opened the flap on the envelope and extracted a huge, mottled iron key that appeared to have come right out of the Iron Age. Liquid pooled in my bladder as I held it up for inspection. The seal was about to break. Stupid postpartum pee issues.

"I'll just…" I squeezed things up tight, much too old to do the pee-pee dance. "I need to use the restroom, so I'll just go ahead and let myself in."

I didn't make it a question in case he threw something else weird at me.

The key slid into the lock, and something clicked. Not the metal tumbler turning over, but something inside of me. A door opening. A light coming on.

This felt *right* in a way nothing had in a long, long time. Like it was meant to be. Like my strife had not been in vain, at any point, and the next chapter of my life was, indeed, about to start. I couldn't wait.

Except first I had to pee.

"Where's the restroom?" I asked, my nose curling slightly as a side effect of the effort of squeezing all my lower lady muscles.

"Just off to the right, turn left, and straight back," Mr. Tom said, his words coming out slower than they really needed to.

"Great, thanks."

"I will wait right here—"

My feet sank into a cushy rug with a dizzying checkered pattern in orange and rust. I passed a beautiful curving stairwell, the steps lined with the same carpet, barely glanced at a wall of paintings, crossed under an arched doorway, and quickly veered right.

The restroom waited where he'd said it would, with a high wooden door in a lovely white frame. I barreled through the opening, whipped around and slammed the door shut without meaning to. I tore at my jeans with harried fingers, and made it just in time.

"Oh mama, that feels good," I murmured, looking over the large bathroom outfitted with brass and porcelain and oil paintings. What a fine place. Even the bathroom was gorgeous.

The verdict was in—I was excited to have taken this position. Diana thought I was nuts for thinking so, but this was cool. This old house was cool.

If only the neighbor and inhabitants weren't so weird.

"And who the hell is Edgar?"

CHAPTER 5

NIAMH ROCKED HER chair in the silence of the coming night, picking up scents as they wafted by. Every so often, she slowly turned her head until she was looking at the large house at the top of the street.

Edgar stood by the bushes near the porch, waiting. Gloating.

She had come back.

After all this time, after establishing a different life for herself, she'd freed herself up somehow, walked away, and come back.

Edgar had always said she would. He'd read something in her.

When she and young Miss Havercamp—Mrs. Drury now—had found the heart of the house, he'd watched them from the shadows. He'd instantly known the truth. Miss Havercamp wasn't the heir. It was Jacinta.

Niamh hadn't been convinced. People changed, especially Janes—non-magical women—Jessie's age. They were shaped by society. Softened. Had their boldness smoothed out. Niamh had doubted, all those years ago, that Jessie would still be worthy by the time she was twenty. Certainly by middle age.

But lookey, lookey. That old vampire might've been right. It wasn't set in stone yet, of course. The house still needed to assess the new charge. Still needed to see if she was the right fit. But it was a promising start that the house knew just when to prompt Earl to contact Peggy. There was a connection there that wasn't usual.

Niamh had to own, though, that if Jessie was the right fit…well, that would certainly blow her mind. It would be a lot for a Jane to come to grips with at her age. Of course, it wasn't that Jacinta was old. Niamh herself was pushing four-hundred. Earl might as well just roll over and die. Edgar was as old as dirt. Literally. He was so old he didn't even function right. The vampire had turned from a hunter into a gatherer. His clan had shrugged and waved goodbye.

Age wouldn't matter when the magic was once again unleashed from the heart of Ivy House. Everyone who tended the house, who protected it, would get a dose of power. Of strength.

Of youth.

No, Jessie's age didn't matter one lick, but the fact that she'd been blind to the supernatural for forty years would definitely be a problem. Niamh wondered how she'd react to the truth. If she'd believe it if it loomed large enough in front of her face.

Humans were notorious for turning a blind eye to things that didn't fit their world view. Every so often they got privy to magical people, and then there were mass killing sprees, taking out magicals and non-magicals alike, but that only happened once in a great while. Most of the time, humans were shockingly good at convincing themselves the world around them was as mundane as they were, and that was that. Nothing to see here, folks.

Niamh rocked slowly, feeling the age in her joints. The tightness in her back.

Her four-hundredth birthday had been a tough one. Over the hill and past her prime. *Well* past her prime. Old even by the reckoning of her species. Past her child-bearing years, past ripping off heads and sticking them on spikes—hell, she was even past a good old-fashioned village raiding party.

Not that she couldn't muster up the energy if she *really* wanted to, but she didn't. Battle was just too much work. Too much running around. Fairly stupid when you thought about it. If there was a problem, talking it out and reaching a compromise got things done much faster and with a lot less funeral flowers. Those things were expensive.

She sighed, taking in the peaceful street. The pleasant night and soft green grass.

She half hoped Ivy House didn't wake up at all. That it would keep its magic to itself, mostly dormant under that creepy old mausoleum. Because if it did pass its magic along to Jessie, it would draw all manner of masters, packs, clans, and mages. Poor O'Briens would be overrun. And every single one of those incoming strangers would compete for Jessie's blessing and support. Wanting to choose which throne she'd sit on. Trying to plan her life for her.

Niamh grinned. *Fat chance.*

That lady was done with letting other people tell her what to do, Niamh had seen it in her eyes. Seen it in the way she'd ended their conversation abruptly and shown herself out. Seen it in her bearing. Jessie Evens had been through the grinder, and she'd made it out the other side tougher. Stronger. Less likely to deal with anyone's crap. She might need a little convincing of that, but it was there.

Maybe that's why she hadn't made her way back to Ivy House until midlife. Strength and vitality were lost on the young. They simply didn't know what to do with it. They charged through doors and stuck people with knives and chased creatures with silver-tipped arrows, and at the end of it all, they didn't learn a damned thing.

Not one thing.

Give all that strength and vitality to someone with intelligence and experience?

Well. Now you had something.

Maybe fate had unfolded this way for a reason.

Niamh rocked slowly, thinking it all through. If the house unleashed its burden, she and Edgar and even that *eejit* Earl would have to take up their positions as Jessie's protectors. They'd crush skulls and blast...

See, that was the thing. It had been so long, she couldn't even remember all the violence she used to enact. What exactly would she blast once she'd dealt with the skulls? They'd be dead, case closed. Anything more would be overkill. Might as well pop a beer and have a victory chat instead.

What a hassle it all sounded like. The fountain of youth was a great idea and all, but she almost wondered if she'd rather just sit out here, rocking in her chair, and throw rocks at any Dicks and Janes that came to check out the old creepy house. It was a pleasant life. She had great aim.

She checked her watch. Half hour to go. Niamh wondered if Jessie would accept her invitation and head into town.

She hoped not. She'd bet Edgar a blood source that Jessie would stay in tonight, as befit someone her age.

Janes had all these silly preconceived notions about what they could and could not do at various ages. Dress codes, hair styles, what body parts could and could not be shown. If Niamh lost, she'd have to lure a Dick back, and the older she got, it was becoming increasingly harder to find anyone that desperate for a nightcap. The young, stupid ones all thought they'd break her hip.

She also wondered what Austin Steele would think of the new addition to the town. Of all the people in the know, he was the last person who wanted the house's magic delivered to its chosen. The very last.

The question was, if he tried to stop it, how would Niamh and the gang block him?

CHAPTER 6

I SAT IN a lovely velvet antique chair in my new room, the enormous master suite of the house. It had a high ceiling, a large ornate fireplace, and a stately four-poster bed with draping curtains. The table and chairs near the large bay window looked out over the labyrinth hedge maze, created with carefully tended and pruned bushes. Inside, a gorgeous red Persian rug covered part of the polished wood floor.

I was in heaven.

I would have never, in a million years, chosen this room for myself. I was the house's caretaker, not its mistress. I did not belong in this room, no matter how much Mr. Tom—he refused to answer to Earl—insisted otherwise.

He'd led me into the room, paused, and then nodded. "I absolutely agree. Yes, this is the room. Excellent choice."

"What?" I'd said, looking around. "I didn't say anything. I couldn't possibly—"

"There is no use arguing. The tour is over. You're on your own. Good luck. I'll get your things."

I'd stood in his wake, dumbfounded. It was not easy to out-weird me, but this guy was the grand master of batshit crazy. I still didn't have a clue who he'd been talking to. The beasties in his head, perhaps? That didn't bode well for me. Unmarked grave, here I came.

Not to mention my "tour" had consisted of a staircase, and six of the twelve vacant bedrooms. I didn't even know where the kitchen was.

Which, okay yes, was kind of awesome. I got to go exploring by myself. Looking in the nooks and crannies. Peering in cupboards. Hunting based on dusty memories made thirty years ago. If he wasn't around, he couldn't tell me no or warn me away. I was free to investigate my new surroundings without hindrance.

So here I was, in what was clearly Auntie Peggy's bedroom, too afraid to argue with that nutcase Mr. Tom, and secretly delighted he didn't expect me to.

The clock on my phone hit 7:53. I pushed away the dinner tray Mr. Tom had delivered to me earlier, every morsel eaten. The meal had been homemade and delicious, even more so because I hadn't lifted a finger. Matt had always refused to learn to cook, leaving the task solely in my hands. Given that I hated cooking, and really hadn't wanted to do it this evening, I couldn't gush enough over Mr. Tom's thoughtfulness. His oddity had been forgiven for the time being. The unmarked grave forgotten about. Mostly.

"What to do, what to do," I said into the lofty surroundings.

Excitement swirled through my stomach. I felt like royalty. Or a rich person. This was easily the largest room I'd ever slept in.

I ran my thumb across my phone. I'd already FaceTimed with Jimmy so he could see the new digs, and vice versa. Although I'd helped him move into his dorm just a few weeks ago, it already looked like it had been through a tornado. He sounded excited, though—both for himself and for me—which took a weight off.

So now...I could find a home for my stuff, wander around the house, read, or...

I eyed my phone again. It was late to go out. I was usually heading home by eight o'clock. Matt had always liked to be in bed watching Sports Center by nine. Out of habit, I'd kept to our old schedule.

Why had I, though? I didn't go to sleep until after ten if the book I was reading was halfway decent, and sometimes I'd stay up much later if I couldn't put it down. Besides, Niamh was twice my age. If she could head out at eight, why couldn't I? It's not like I was tired...

Okay, yes, I was tired.

But it would probably take me a long time to fall asleep in this creaky old house…

Except I felt comfortable here, more comfortable than I ever had in the house I'd lived in with Matt. I felt…calm. Content. The divorce was final, Jimmy was doing well, the house payments were gone…

I felt liberated! It finally occurred to me that I could do whatever I wanted—even have ice cream for dinner if I wanted.

Screw it, I wanted to go out.

I would go have a drink with the rock-throwing granny across the street. There were worse ways to spend my time. Like hang out with Mr. Tom and probably get told a new name to call him.

When I reached the bottom of the stairs, I looked around for my purse. The antique wood furniture, well-made with exquisite carvings, held all manner of interesting figurines and trinkets, but no purse. The coat rack was empty. The little table by the door had a plate holding the enormous key, but no handbag to put it in.

"Are you going out, ma'am?"

I jumped, spun, and held out a hand like a karate chop. I didn't know karate, but sometimes a good bluff was the ticket.

"Yes," I answered, dropping the hand within his unimpressed stare. "Where's my handbag—oh." I took it from his white gloved hand. For some inexplicable reason, he'd changed from his moth-eaten, tattered suit to a moth-eaten tux. He wasn't much of a sweats guy, it seemed. His cape still hung down his back.

"You're really into super heroes, huh?" I asked, pointing at the cape.

"Super heroes were created by miserable Dicks who can live greatness only through the page. I live it through my life."

Oh super. He was delusional. I'd definitely be buried in the yard before all this was over.

"Okay, well…" I held up my purse for a moment. "Thanks for grabbing my—"

"You'll want a light jacket, ma'am." He left the room.

I waited for a moment, wondering if he planned to grab one. He'd grabbed my purse, after all. But since all my clothes were up in my room, and he wasn't climbing either of the curved stairwells to the landing over the massive archway, it wasn't likely. Besides, we were inland near the Sierras—the temperature didn't drop that much or fast. I'd be fine. The alcohol would keep me warm.

I tucked the key into my purse, frowned at the

weight, and let myself out. Was changing the locks out of the question? I'd have to wear that key in a holster when I went jogging.

"Good evening." A man stood off the side of the porch with clippers in hand. His long face and loose jowls looked familiar.

"You're the gardener, right?" I asked with a smile.

"Edgar, yes." His lips pulled wide, showing yellowed teeth with somewhat long canines. "How nice of you to remember. It has been such a *long* time for you."

By his tone, it sounded like he was commenting on my age. I nearly clapped back with, "For you too, buddy, don't fool yourself."

"It has, yes," I said instead.

"You'll have to come and see the labyrinth," he said, opening the clippers but not leaning toward the perfectly tended hedge. "I've made some additions. You'll be lost for days this time, I swear it."

"Wow, good memory." I remembered when Diana and I had explored it. She'd led the way in the beginning, winding deep into the heart of it. The problem had come when it was time to leave—each path she led us down came to a dead end. We'd been confused. Then scared. We'd worried we'd never find our way out. But then…I just kinda…started walking, I remember. I felt my way, as odd as that sounded, listening to my intuition. We'd eventually made our way out the exit, half a day after walking in the entrance. "How do you even remember that? I didn't until you just brought it up."

He closed the clippers again and winked. "I was waiting to save you girls. It was the shock of my life that you made it out. I knew then that you were destined for great things."

"I was destined for great things because I made it out of a plant maze?" I asked, laughing.

"Yes," he answered, clearly not seeing the humor.

"Oh." I gave him my best please-don't-kill-me-and-bury-me-in-the-maze smile. "Okay, well…see ya."

"Yes."

Niamh sat on her porch, rocking slowly, her pile of rocks at her side. It appeared she hadn't had any more Mr. Tom sightings.

"Hey," I said, coming to a stop in front of her house.

"Well," she drawled back.

I looked down the street, suddenly socially unsure. Then back, wondering if I'd gotten it wrong. "Were you…headed to the pub, or…?"

"Right, yeah." She leaned forward and labored out of her chair. "'Course." She checked her rock pile, glanced down the street, then back at the big house. Her eyes narrowed, but when I looked back, all I saw was Edgar waving.

"Are you ready yet?" she asked, as though I were the one causing the delay.

She was wearing a tighter shirt than the one she'd had on earlier, and I couldn't help but notice her chest. One breast pushed against the fabric, and the other…didn't seem to be there at all.

Before I could pull my gaze away, Niamh said, "Lost it in the war."

"Wh-what's that?" I struggled to say, clearly caught looking. So embarrassing.

"The tit. Lost it in the war."

"Oh…the Vietnam War, you mean?" I'd almost said World War Two.

"What do I look like, a yank? No, the war on breast cancer. Yeah, it won that battle, but I won the war."

"Oh." I was saying 'oh' a lot lately. "Congratulations."

"For what? Getting rid of the tit, or winning the war? Because I'd be just as happy to lop off the other one while I'm at it. They're a waste of space, aren't they, flopping around like they do. Sure what good are they anyway? I don't have an infant to feed—what do I need them for? They're just needless weight, that's what I say."

I nodded because…well, yeah, that was the truth.

"Do you head to the bar every evening?" I asked as

we left the porch and started walking down the street. Although I'd never excelled at small talk, I hated awkward silences even more.

"Eh," she said on a sigh. "Not so much every evenin', no. I shy away on Fridays and Saturdays because of all the Dicks and Janes that fall into da place."

I scrunched my brow. "Dicks... Are there some really rowdy people in this town? Like bikers or something?"

"No—ahhhm." She made a circular motion with her finger. "That's just what I call...ahm...out-of-towners. Tourists."

"Oh right. Because of all the tasting rooms, right? This is a big wine town, I noticed."

"Oh yes, definitely. Harvest season is coming up and there'll be loads of tourists all through here. They'll swarm the place. Miserable bastards..."

She grumbled away until silence fell between us, which became increasingly heavy, gooey, and oppressive.

"And how is the wine?" I asked when I couldn't stand it anymore.

"Strong."

"I meant...like the different kinds?"

"Red, white, that weird halvsie type—all strong."

I'd expected her to walk slow, given her age, but as we continued up the street, I was embarrassed to realize her pace was making me break a sweat.

"Why'd ye leave him then?" she asked, and I half staggered at the unexpected personal question.

"He left me, actually."

"Bastard."

"No, it's good. I was relieved. I didn't want to be the one to initiate the end, but we both knew things had fizzled. Well, fizzled is putting it lightly."

"You're too nice, so ya are. That's yer problem. If you're not happy, figure out why and change it."

"Yes, well, after a certain point, it became easier to stay together than to break up. And also, if I'm being honest—"

"I hope so. Liars just waste my time."

"—I was scared to leave. He made the lion's share of the money and I'd been with him for half my life. It's daunting, going out on your own. Calling it quits on something you thought would be forever. I felt like I was giving up. That maybe I should just keep trying. I don't know. But when he finally ended things, all I felt was relief."

She huffed. "While you were paralyzed with fear, your happiness suffered. That's a call to courage if I ever heard one."

"Well…I don't know about *paralyzed*…"

"You're free now, at any rate. Better late than never. Did that useless gobshite make you dinner at least? Or polish the silver arrowheads? We might need those soon. If we have to take down the uncrowned alpha, we will take down the uncrowned alpha. I do not look forward to it—he is exceptional for his kind—but he does have age working against him. We can manage if we have'ta."

It occurred to me belatedly that she wasn't talking about Matt, and also that she was talking gibberish. Freaking bananas, the whole lot of them, but it struck me that they had a similar vocabulary. Maybe it was something in the wine.

I played it safe. "He made me dinner, yes. It's not really his job, though. He's—"

"It is absol*utely* his job. What else is he good fer? Besides lazing around. No, no, you make him work, so you should. Really give him hell. It's good for him."

As we approached the end of the main drag, she pointed to the right instead of walking straight ahead to a cute little hotel bar I'd seen coming in.

Our destination was a dive bar with a warm orangey glow emanating from the many open windows and two doors. A few motorcycles leaned against their kick-stands out front but most of the parking spots were empty.

"Now," Niamh said in that sing-song voice.

"This is where the locals go?" I asked, following her into the establishment.

A pool table took up the center of the main room, the balls currently in play with two scruffy characters holding cue sticks. The bar lined the far side with a young guy standing behind it and a few guys on the stools pushed up to it, each separated by a seat or two. Down the way there was an open door leading to another room, recessed by a couple of steps. I could see the hint of a pool table beyond it.

Niamh made a bee-line for an empty stool at the end of the bar farthest from the door. I eyed the few tables in the back and down the way before following, claiming the stool between Niamh and a really hairy guy with a pug nose, rosy cheeks, and eyebrows that could really use a trim before they grew legs and crawled off his face.

The young bartender wandered over, visibly swallowing as he did so. "Hello, Missus O'Connor."

"Well, Paul, howr'ya? How's it goin'?" She positioned herself *just so* on the seat.

"Good, tha-thank you." His gaze shifted to me. "Hello."

"Hi," I answered, polite smile in place. He seemed

to relax slightly.

"Do you have a wine list?" I asked.

"Sure." Paul dragged out the word as he turned, looking along the back of the bar, then turned back. "Can I see your I.D.?"

Startled, because it had been quite a while since I'd been carded, I hesitated.

Niamh leaned onto her elbows, eating up a little of the distance between them. "Paul, what age are ye?"

"What?" he asked and his eyes widened, like he'd suddenly found himself looking into the eyes of a predator.

"What age are ye?" she asked again, slower.

"Twenty-three," he answered.

"Twenty-three, what?"

He hesitated for a moment. "Twenty-three, missus."

She nodded once. "And is this woman older than you?" She gestured to me as she said it.

"Yes. Missus!" His face flushed, and I felt mine do the same. "No offense," he said to me.

"And you are old enough to drink, I presume?" she pressed.

"Y-yes, missus." From his tone, it was obvious he knew where this was leading.

My face burned hotter and I reached for my purse. Poor Paul needed a safety line. He clearly didn't have

Mr. Tom's ability to deal with the likes of Niamh. Few people probably did.

"No, no, Paul is right on the cusp of this one." Niamh leaned a little farther over the bar. "I can see it."

"It's just that Austin Steele says that if the person looks under thirty-five, I'm supposed to card. And well…she does, so—"

"It's okay, Paul."

A deep timbre pulled my focus from the buck-toothed kid. A broad-shouldered man with dark brown hair cut close on the sides and longer on top strolled toward us on the business side of the bar. His nondescript, long-sleeved beige shirt did nothing to make him blend in—this was the kind of man who stood out, and the knowing smirk on his handsome face told me he knew it.

"I got it," the man said.

I wanted to stare, because there was a lot of this man to admire, from his confident strut to his raw intensity to his flat stomach and powerful thighs, but I didn't want to get caught staring. He looked about my age, so it wouldn't be creepy or anything (at least not any more so than the usual creepiness of staring at a stranger with one's mouth open), but he probably had a ballooned ego given how hard he clearly worked on his physique, and I didn't want to pump more air into it. I certainly didn't want him to think I was interested—he was out of my league. Hell, he was out of my universe. Guys like him dated models who groomed themselves and wore cute clothes and didn't forget to brush their hair before leaving the house. I didn't have the energy for all that. If I had a bra on, I was betting aces.

I jerked my gaze left in an effort to feign indifference.

Only, now I was looking at the wall.

I pulled it down to the bar in front of me.

Only, the kid had never handed over the wine list, so I was staring at nothing again.

"Yes, sir." Paul said, clearly relieved.

"Niamh, good evening," the man said, stopping in front of us and bracing his hands against the edge of the bar. His muscles flared, straining his lightweight shirt.

My battle to avoid staring wasn't going well, although I was hopefully doing it on the sly.

"Austin Steele, how's things? Are ye well?" Niamh said in a pleasant-enough ramble, her frosty demeanor from a moment ago melting.

"And this is?" Austin asked.

I quickly tore my gaze down to the bar again, only belatedly thinking to whip out my hand and examine my nails. At least it gave me something to look at.

"This is the new caretaker of Ivy House," Niamh

said. "Just moved in today."

Silence met her words for a long moment.

I chanced a glance up to assess the situation.

Cobalt blue eyes beat into me like a tribal drum, his unwavering gaze piercing. The last time I'd looked, his body had been in a jaunty sort of playboy lean, but it was now braced and taut, as though he were ready for action. Thick slabs of muscle flared along his middle. The raw intensity from a moment before seemed incredibly charming compared to his current situation. He looked predatory, almost, and incredibly imposing.

Tingles washed over my scalp and crawled up my spine. This man was dangerous, and not just because of his size. Something lethal and vicious sparkled in his gaze, hidden under his rough and tumble, handsome exterior. An unpredictability that set me on edge.

"How did you get the post?" Austin finally asked.

"She got a divorce, her kid went off to school, and this was better than living with her nudist fat father."

The scary man in front of me suddenly took a backseat to my annoyance with Diana. I turned to Niamh, my face heating up again. "Diana is such a loudmouth!"

A crooked smile worked up her face. "Diana gave the whole scoop to Peggy, who couldn't wait to pass it on. She couldn't stop laughing when she was telling me."

"So she's not a—"

"Jane?" Niamh interrupted Austin. "Oh, she's a Jane, no question—"

"No, I'm not," I said. "I mean, sure, I'll definitely sample the wine, but that's because I like wine. When in Rome, as they say. That doesn't make me a tourist. I came for a job. I'm supposed to maintain that enormous house."

"No idea about this town at all," Niamh went on as though I hadn't spoken. "She needed to get out of her parents' house, and Diana suggested this."

I opened my mouth in defense, then closed it. What did I care what they thought? They could talk all they wanted—it really didn't affect my situation.

"About that wine list?" I said.

"She did have a pleasant experience when she was here last, though. Ten, weren't you, Jessie?" Niamh nudged me.

"Yeah, the house is cool. But the wine list…"

Austin turned and the muscles across his back flared with the movement. Scary or not, he was nice to look at.

He slid a laminated cocktail and wine list in front of me. "Paul, Magners with ice," he barked. Back to talking to Niamh: "Has she explored the house?"

"She just got here this afternoon," Niamh said. "She doesn't know anything about the place."

"And Earl?" Austin asked.

"He just skulks around with his dopey face, he does," Niamh answered. "What a nuisance. No wonder the family he worked for chucked him."

"He's fine," I said, feeling like I had to defend the guy. He'd made me dinner, after all, and brought it to me and everything. It had been incredibly kind of him, even if he was one of the strangest people I'd ever met. "Though what's the deal with that cape? I've never seen someone wear a cape over an old tux. People don't mysteriously go missing around him, do they?"

"It's never mysterious," Niamh answered. "They leave so they don't have to listen to him."

Some things you just couldn't argue with.

"How's this Pinot Noir?" I pointed at a name I didn't recognize. "Is it like a Chianti at all?"

Austin's gaze was still sharp, but for a wonder it softened. His frame followed, the muscles melting back into his shirt. With a sigh he straightened up. "No. It's more like a Merlot. That's your thing? Subtler wines?"

"For reds, yes. I was in Italy for a week and it changed my life. Why punch me in the face with your wine when you can caress me, know what I mean?"

His pupils dilated slightly, and for the briefest of

moments, a look of pure, primal hunger raced across his face. It was gone so fast I wondered if I'd imagined it. My belly fluttered, only this time it wasn't in fear.

I frowned at him, my response to the unexpected sensation.

He frowned back, probably wondering what my problem was.

Social-awkwardness, hard at work.

I dipped my eyes back to the wine list.

"Yes, I do," he said quietly, and turned away.

"Paul, is there a reason you came in tonight?" Niamh called as Austin landed a glass in front of me.

"He just broke up with his girlfriend, give him a break," Austin said to Niamh, a grin tugging at his lips.

"I'd give him a break if he was on the beer, fallin' around the place, legless," she replied. "But when he's workin', he needs to function."

Austin turned with a wine bottle in hand. "You scare him."

The red wine curled around the base of my glass and kept rising.

"Wait, wait." I held out my hands to stop the pour, used to getting a sample taste to see if I would like it. "No, why…"

I sighed as the liquid closed in on the top of the slim glass. There was no room to swirl. I wasn't a connoisseur, but everyone knew you had to swirl red wine so as to look mildly important. Matt had made a big thing out of it.

"Here you go." Austin winked at me.

Paul finally handed over Niamh's drink as I tasted the wine. It was bitter, and the vinegary punch at the end made me scrunch up my nose.

"Ugh." I shivered, my mouth now tasting like garbage.

"That good, huh?" Niamh grinned at me.

"No, thank you." I pushed the glass across the top of the bar. "How about a Coors?"

Austin homed in on the wine. He lifted it to his lips, the top lip a bit thinner but no less shapely than the full bottom lip, and sampled. His brow furrowed. "What's wrong with it?"

I lifted my eyebrows. "You have, like, twenty tasting rooms up and down that main drag. Have you not been in them?"

He looked at me for a silent beat, as though he had a defense at the ready but couldn't use it. "No," he finally said.

I shook my head in disbelief. "It's nothing. Just not my thing. I'll go for a beer, please."

Niamh clasped the edge of the bar with an evil smile. "How will he learn if you don't speak your mind?" she asked me.

Austin's brow pinched. He gestured for me to go on. "What's the problem? Give it to me."

I sighed, realizing they weren't going to let me out of this one.

"Well...honestly, it's not a very good bottle. It's inexpensive, right? Which I'd expect in many dive bars, don't get me wrong. I usually don't order wine in a dive bar. It's just that you're in a wine town, so I figured it would at least be decent. That was my bad. I assumed. Second, it's been open for a long time. It's gone off." I shrugged. "I was hoping to try something from one of the local vineyards. It's okay, though. Coors will be fine."

The guy next to me whistled, his overgrown mustache flaring with the sudden breeze. "And that's why she's divorced," he said.

Austin's shoulders swiveled. His left hand darted out so fast I couldn't even get out a surprised "oh!" His fist smashed into the hairy man's face with such force it knocked the guy off of the stool. His back slammed into the ground, followed by his head. His nose spurted blood instantly.

"Oh my God!" I jerked and turned, pushing into Niamh.

She shoved me back onto my stool, clearly unconcerned.

"What just happened?" I whispered so as not to screech. I'd seen a few fights in my day, but I'd never seen someone punched with such force. "Seriously, what…"

"He disrespected a lady in my bar, and he was served a warning never to do it again," Austin said. "Do you want to try a different wine? I have a more expensive one."

The man got up, cupping his face. With bleary eyes, he gave Austin a somber look. Right before he hurried for the door, he shot me a death stare.

Prickles of unease worked through my body. I'd seen that look before. Although none of this was my fault, I'd just created an enemy. A possibly dangerous enemy in a very small town.

I felt eyes on me from around the room. I shook my head, lowering my heating face. While Austin had probably thought he was being sweet, I wasn't a naïve twenty-something anymore, impressed by his show of masculinity. Violence bred violence. Austin wasn't in any danger—he was clearly the dominant male—but that guy had looked angry enough to go for the weakest link. In this case, me.

Some of the people who'd witnessed the incident probably thought I was at fault. That I'd made Austin react the way he had. The guy with the newly broken nose certainly seemed to think so.

My instinct was to keep quiet. Like every woman I knew, I'd been taught to go with the flow. To suffer in silence. But guys like Austin needed to start thinking about how their actions affected others. Bad guys kept winning because good guys didn't understand they were part of the problem.

So, despite the embarrassment of going against the grain, I spoke my truth.

"I'm really grateful that you tried to defend me," I started. "But that guy is now humiliated. He'll blame it on me, and if he gets drunk enough, I'll be the one he gets his revenge on. You've just created a very danger-ous situation for me. I know you meant well, and I thank you for trying, but often a man doesn't account for how dangerous the fallout can be for the woman. Can you call me a cab? If he's still out there, I don't trust my chances."

My stupid face was red, I could feel the heat, but I met Austin's eyes, anyway. I expected indignation or sullen anger. I wouldn't have blamed him for either. It couldn't be easy to have your world view challenged with information you probably thought came out of nowhere.

But when I met those clear blue eyes, they weren't

brimming with anger, or even narrowed in annoyance. He didn't open his mouth to berate me for my ungratefulness or shrug me off as a hysterical woman who didn't understand the ways of the world. His intelligent gaze silently regarded me.

"Get her better wine," Niamh said, her voice subdued to match the moment.

Austin nodded, the movement so subtle it was almost indistinguishable, and moved away.

"Fair play to ya," Niamh said, nodding. "You're exactly right. Some of these muscle-head nincompoops are no better than oxen. Good for a specific job, then better off put out to pasture, dumb buggers. Put them all in a pen and let them fight amongst themselves, I say. Let Darwin sort it out.

"But I better explain how this town works. This isn't L.A. This is O'Briens, nothing but a speck on the map. The locals here all know each other. We all look after each other. Now, if that man beside you had been a Dick—a...tourist—Austin Steele would've made a very big blunder, yes he would've. But among the locals, if Austin Steele tells someone you are to be respected, then you will be respected. And that hairy sonuvabitch is definitely a local. If he'd shower once in a while, he might get some interest. He needs a pair of scissors and a razor, the dirty bastard.

"Now, of course you wouldn't have known that. That's why I'm tellin' you. Don't you feel bad for speaking up. As I said, you could've been in some trouble if that was a Dick. We get weird ones around these parts, and you're not equipped to deal with it. You don't realize yet that this place is full of opportunities for unmarked graves. That'll come in time. For right now, you've given Austin Steele something to think about. So that was good. Keep that up. I like to see him on his toes. We have too many yes men around here, if you ask me. Spineless, all of 'em. Austin Steele has it too easy. I only play nice because he's the keeper of the alcohol, you know what I mean."

I wanted to ask why Austin held so much clout, whether she'd created any of those unmarked graves, and also why she kept saying his full name, but before I could get any of my questions out, he came back with a bottle of wine.

He lifted the opener, his bicep straining his shirt. As he turned the handle on the cork screw, he shifted his body slightly, giving me a view of his large, flexed shoulder. Another turn of the cork screw, and I got a full display of his popping pecs within his shirt. His cockeyed grin said he knew I was enjoying the show.

I grinned despite myself and then rolled my eyes at his antics. Niamh gave him a confused frown, although

I wasn't sure why.

"You're tough," he said as the cork popped out. His smile dwindled, noticing Niamh. A moment later, before he poured, he leaned toward me, his eyes piercing. "Please know that I would never intentionally put you in harm's way. You will get home safely. I will make sure of it, myself."

I was mesmerized by the fire in his eyes. By the absolute certainty in his tone. I couldn't tear my eyes away.

He nodded then straightened, his message delivered. The show over.

I was still holding my breath. Warmth spread through my middle.

No one had ever made a fuss about my safety before. Not since I was a little girl. Matt had been nice enough through our marriage, but he'd never thought much about my being in danger, not in upper-middle class suburbia.

My heart squished and tears welled up out of nowhere. What must it be like to be taken care of by a man like this?

"And that's why they call him the uncrowned alpha," Niamh murmured, holding up her drink to be refilled. Austin had moved down the bar to help someone. Paul deflated when he realized the job fell to him.

"What does that mean?" I asked, wiping my eyes quickly. I needed to get a hold of myself. An act of kindness shouldn't turn me into a puddle of goo.

"He's like a…" Niamh rattled the ice in her glass. "Mayor. Kinda. Without the votes."

That didn't make any sense, but as Austin neared I let it go. Half the things these people said didn't make any sense.

"So?" he asked as Paul delivered another drink to Niamh. "What's the verdict?"

"It's fine," I managed, reaching for the glass. I sipped it to get him to move away, ready to drink just about anything. But as soon as the flavor hit my tongue, my eyes dipped downward and the world stopped. Spicy, smoky, soft and light, the wine serenaded my taste buds. I closed my eyes, savoring the taste.

"Good?" Austin asked, his voice a deep rumble.

"Very." I took another sip. The second sip was even better than the first. "Del*icious.*"

"There." Austin tapped the bar and gave Niamh a smug look. "See? I can impress a connoisseur. It just takes the best, most expensive bottle from my personal collection to do it." He winked at me and moved down the bar.

"Oh no, that's—" But he was already too far away.

"He shouldn't have done that," I said.

"'Course he should have. You were dead right—what's he doin' servin' flat, cheap wine in a place like this?"

"Not flat—red wine usually doesn't have bubbles. It—"

"Whatever. The point is, all he has to do is walk down the street and get the good stuff. His pride is gettin' in the way of good business. But here now, you've humbled him. He's learned he has to get on the mark."

"It's his bar, he can—"

"Ma'am."

"Heh!" I spun around and nearly fell completely off the stool.

Mr. Tom stood behind me. "You forgot your sweater." He held out my favorite gray sweater.

"Did you…" I took it slowly. "Did you root through my luggage to find this?"

"Of course not, ma'am. I do not *root through* anything."

"Then why were you sacked from the other place?" Niamh asked faux-pleasantly.

He ignored her. "I put all your clothes away except this. I figured you'd want to wear it home."

I squinted at the sweater, looking at it as if I were

investigating some great mystery and the clues were woven into the fabric. "Did you know this was my favorite, or was that a lucky guess?"

"Of course I knew, ma'am. As a butler, I am—"

"Lucky guess," Niamh said. "It's probably the only mildly fashionable item you own."

I opened my mouth to deliver a rebuttal, but there was no denying she was correct. "Thanks," I said, taking the sweater. "But you didn't have to come all the way down here..."

"When ma'am cannot wait to receive an item, of course I must follow her to her destination, or how will she get it?" He straightened his arms at his sides and bowed.

I couldn't tell if that was a nice gesture, or severe disapproval. Probably both.

"Well, thanks." I tied it around my waist.

"Don't thank him, he's the help." Niamh shot Mr. Tom a fiery stare.

"I'm the help, too, let it go," I murmured at her.

"It is perfectly fine," Mr. Tom told me. "She is acting out because she feels helpless without her rocks. Should I prepare a snack for when you get home?"

My grin was for his dig at Niamh and my misty eyes were ridiculous. What was going on? I hadn't properly cried in years. I'd just sorta numbed up at a certain point with Matt, tired of the constant disappointment and the feeling of being overwhelmed. I'd shut off.

I knew it was good that feeling was rushing back in—that I was accessing the full range of emotions again—but this was taking things too far. Why not stick with laughter? Why did I have to go whole hog and start crying in public? Talk about embarrassing first impressions.

"No, I'll manage," I said, blinking profusely.

"Yes, ma'am. I will go shopping tomorrow for all the items you require." He slid a *look* at Niamh. "I wouldn't want to force you to beg for dry sandwiches and the tedious company that goes with it."

"Because you think she wants to hang around you, you prune-faced trollop?" Niamh clapped back.

"Better than a saggy old hag that—"

"Enough," Austin said, and I shivered at the power and authority in his voice. The other two closed their mouths. Their glares still said plenty, though.

"When should I come to collect you, ma'am," Mr. Tom asked.

"I'm fine, Mr. Tom, really. And you don't have to call me ma'am. I'm the hired help, just like you."

"As you wish, madam, but I insist on collecting you. The streets are not safe for the master of—"

"Are you deaf, *Mr. Tom*?" Niamh cut in. "She said

she was the caretaker. Just a regular Jane, like everyone else. She'll be good."

"Seriously, you guys, I'm not a tourist. I *work* here, now. If that's not the definition of a budding local, I don't know what is," I said in annoyance.

"Be that as it may—"

"I'll take her home," Austin said, his hands braced against the bar again.

Mr. Tom's eyes widened marginally and I wondered if he planned to argue. If it was Niamh he certainly would have. Finally, he bowed again.

"I'll see you at Ivy House, madam." Mr. Tom turned on his heel and glided out the door.

"I don't see how madam is different than ma'am, but sure," I murmured.

"It isn't, that thick-headed muppet." Niamh took a long gulp of her drink.

"Mr. Tom?" Austin asked, his shoulders and pecs bulging. He was showing off again.

"Should I call in the camera crew?" I asked him, unable to help my laugh. I dramatically turned to look at the door. "Are they outside? I can go grab them."

His eyes sparkled and a grin crept up his face.

Niamh tilted her head at him, her eyes squinted, as though she couldn't believe what she was seeing. "Don't mind him, he's just looking to get laid." She held up her glass for another. The woman could drink. "Every chick in this bar is looking. Always are." She arched an eyebrow at him. "Though he doesn't usually put on a show…"

She let the sentence linger. Austin wrestled with a smile. His muscles relaxed, though his light shirt left little to the imagination.

"All he has to do is scoop one up when he's ready," she said, glancing around. Her voice reduced to a mutter. "Sure wish it were that easy for me. I might have ta club someone over the head at the end of the night to drag him home."

I froze with my eyebrows up, eyes wide, and a giddy smile pulled down at the corners. It was my *did she just say what I think she said???* look.

I let the laughter bubble out. "Get it, *gurl.*" I put up a fist for a bump.

She frowned at my hand. "What?"

"She's sexually dangerous, not hip to the lingo," Austin said, grinning again, and pushed away from the bar. "And it seems not *every* woman is looking."

"Are you talking about her?" I hooked a thumb at Niamh. "Because I definitely looked. I thought it was ridiculous, but I looked."

His grin finally turned up into a full-fledged smile, his eyes glittering like a disco ball. It boosted his handsomeness ten-fold. The guy was incredibly hot.

"Touché," he said, not at all phased by my comment, and moved down the bar.

Niamh leaned toward me and murmured, "You didn't think it was at all ridiculous, sure you didn't."

"I was too busy drooling to think much of anything."

She huffed out a soft laugh and straightened up. "I do appreciate the view. He'd be too energetic for me, but I do appreciate the view. Now, tell me, how much do you remember of your first trip to Ivy House?"

CHAPTER 7

AFTER TALKING ABOUT all the things I remembered from my first time to Ivy House, Niamh proved to be most excellent at small talk, something that had been sorely lacking on our trip to the bar. She chatted about all things and nothing, her colorful takes on events and her brash descriptions making me laugh more often than not, even when she wasn't trying. People came by to greet her throughout the night, met me, stared blankly for a moment, and moved on. I wasn't the most popular new addition.

"How long do I have to be here for them to stop thinking of me as a Jane?" I finally asked as the fifth person in a row left without even offering an excuse. They'd all essentially pivoted away the second they learned who I was and why I was here.

"Just hang around for a while. These people don't like change." Niamh finished off her…well, I'd lost count. She'd drunk me under the table and then some. Hell, she'd probably drunk the whole bar under the table. Combined. "They've been here for ages and things have mostly stayed the same. Now they have to fit a new face into their list of friendlies. Given most of them are block-headed dopes, this might take a while. Be patient."

"Patience is one virtue I was never blessed with."

"Then you'd better invest in mass quantities of alcohol and a good party trick."

I laughed and the wine buzzed within my head pleasantly, most of the bottle gone. I swayed on the stool. Then swayed back.

Austin's voice boomed out over the bar. "Last call!"

"Oh thank God." I leaned heavily against the edge. "I can't take much more."

"You need to work on your tolerance. You're pitiful," Niamh said, reaching over me for the wine bottle.

"No, no!" I held up my hand. "No, no. I'm good. I'm done. I have to get home at some point."

"Ah *go on*. Sure look, you're almost there. Just a wee drop left. Go on, might as well." She upended the remainder of the bottle into my glass.

I'd tried to go home three times by this point. Each time the window had eluded me, mostly because Niamh kept refilling my glass before I could get my bill. I was beginning to realize that if I wanted to make a clean getaway, I needed to move much faster.

I closed an eye to look at the empty bottle. It was not the same bottle of wine I had started with, although it had luckily been halfway empty by the time it was put in front of me. It could've even been the bottle I had poo-poo'ed earlier. The good news was, I no longer tasted it. Bad news was, cheap wine gave fierce headaches, and tomorrow would be no fun.

"I thought I was good at this. I've had a lot of practice." I blew out a breath, and if that breath had been directed at a candle, the flames would've burned the whole place down.

"Not enough practice," Niamh said as people drifted or staggered out of the bar.

"I need to go." I took a sip of the wine, swayed, caught myself. I ran the back of my hand across my mouth.

"Finish up. Time to get out," Austin said, his deep voice filling up all available space.

A moment later, I heard, "You ready to go?"

I jumped and turned at the same time. How had he gotten behind me?

That's when I noticed the mostly empty bar. Only a few stragglers were left, finishing their last drops. Time had slipped away from me. Paul was rinsing beer mats.

"I'm good. Honest." I pinched the stem of the glass, intending to push it away. Miraculously, it ended up against my lips. I finished the sip-turned-gulp I did not need. "I'll do it."

"Do what? Get lost or fall on your face?" he asked with a wry grin.

"I *never* fall on my face. On my butt, yes. My side, sure. Down some steps and onto my back? That has happened, yes. But never on my face. I"—I raised my finger—"am a professional."

"Go home, Bridie, you're drunk," Niamh said.

"Yes, I am and it's your fault." I directed my point at her. "What's your story, Bridie, you going home?" If I didn't pee now, I'd have to use the bushes later. In this state, I'd probably fall on my back and pee all over my shoes.

"There's...ah..." Austin scratched his nose, and I could tell he was trying to hide a smile. "There's a bathroom just down the stairs, there."

I had a feeling I'd said that last bit out loud.

"You did," he said. "And that bit, too. I don't think your verbal filter is working."

"I do know where the bathroom is, good sir, I thank you. We are well acquainted, John and I." I gestured like he was a knight and I was a lady. Half of that was probably correct. "But you do not need to walk me home. Thank you, it's very gent-le-man-ly—*phew*, that was a long one—but I am well versed in navi... in getting home." All that almost sounded like English. I was doing just fine. "Also, I need to pay my bill."

"Your tab is covered, and you do need an escort."

"Nia-vvvve will watch me. She is a record holder for rock throwing, I am nearly positive."

I slid off the bar stool, hit the floor wrong, and pitched forward. I adjusted my weight, because this was not my first rodeo, and would've swayed to a stop if a strong hand hadn't wrapped around my upper arm.

"Unhand me, you fiend," I mumbled, wondering which movie that was from. Or if it was from a movie at all. I suspected it was, if only because I felt certain a sword would have completed the scene.

"Sounds like it probably is," Austin said, standing close. "Normal people don't talk like that. Or use swords."

"Dang it." I clicked my teeth shut and curled my lips together. I didn't need any more words slipping out.

"Go ahead and take her." Niamh waved me away. "I need to grab a…guy for…something."

"She is my hero," I said, pointing toward the bathroom. "Just need to…"

Austin released me, but from the way he held his body—ready to lunge into action at any moment—he was clearly wondering if I'd pitch forward onto my face.

"I'm good, I'm good." I held up my hands then

grabbed my purse. "I'm a forty-year-old woman. I know how to handle a buzz."

"You're a forty-year-old woman drinking with Niamh. You're a long way past buzzed." Austin laughed, his smile infectious. It really brought out the best in his already perfect features. "You need to learn a better exit plan."

"Don't I know it," I said, bouncing off a wall, stumbling down the stairs, and finally finding my way into the ladies' room. "Why would Mr. Tom warn me about the sandwiches, but not the alcohol? That seems a grave oversight on his part."

A younger woman gave me a dirty look as I emerged from the stall. I wasn't sure why but I also did not care.

"Livin' the dream. Haters gonna hate," I said as she slipped out of the way. "Ballas gonna..." I shrugged, turning on the tap. "Spend money or somethin', I don't know."

She huffed and left the bathroom. In the silence of her wake, I paused and the world floated around me in an alcoholic haze. I had my purse but not my sweater. Given I was mostly numb from the vat of wine I'd consumed, I was pretty sure it would take a blizzard for me to feel the cold. I could just slip out the back exit near the second pool table, away from prying eyes.

"Wait...here it is." I found my sweater around my waist. "Miracle."

Sneaky as I could be, I slipped out of the bathroom, only I wasn't fast enough to avoid catching my toe between the swinging door and the frame. I struggled my way out, pausing just out of sight of the bar. Across the way, on the other side of the second pool table, gaped the exit.

I'd walked through some bad neighborhoods in my day, protected by nothing but a Swiss Army Knife, resting bitch face, and a no-nonsense attitude. No one ever bothered me.

Maybe it was because I looked homeless. Whatever the case, this was a tiny, dead town, even with Broken Nose Harry. I didn't need to embarrass myself by engaging in small talk with a very attractive sober man. I'd likely do or say something stupid, and it would result in never being able to show my face in this bar again. Best not to chance it.

CHAPTER 8

"WHAT'S SHE DOING?" Austin asked Niamh, hearing every word Jessie was muttering to herself beyond the wall, just out of sight. She clearly didn't know she wasn't out of hearing range for someone like him.

"Sounds like she's trying to sneak out." Niamh rattled her ice cubes around her glass. "Any chance for another—"

"No," he said, seeing an elbow poke out and then get pulled back in. It was like she was playing a game of drunk hokey-pokey, a thought that almost tugged another smile out of him. "Has she explored the house yet?"

"Now, that information might cost another—"

"No," he told Niamh again.

She sighed. "She just got there today, like I said, and she only remembers the broad strokes from when she was last there. She's startin' from scratch."

"But you think she'll find it?"

"She found it when she was ten before life trampled the imagination out of her, like. Her life experience will work against her, so it will. She will believe what she sees, most likely, and keep her eyes closed to the magic. That might prove to be enough of a barrier to keep her out."

"And if it doesn't?"

"Then the house will judge. It will be beyond you."

He gritted his teeth. "Instruct Earl to give her no help. He should stand in her way, if need be."

"All due respect, Austin Steele, but that house is out of your jurisdiction. It was here before this town, and will be here long after. It does not answer to you, and neither do those who protect it."

Austin pinned the older woman with his stare, feeling the primal fire build within him. His power expanded, consuming him, easily topping the power radiating from her aged frame.

"I am not young, Mr. Steele," she said in a deathly quiet voice. "Few of the original protectors have been. And yet, the house still stands. There is always someone to welcome in the new chosen. If you pit yourself against us, you will find yourself in a different sort of hell than you were expecting."

Austin's gut flipped. His resolve hardened. "I will not see my town turned upside down."

"You will not have a choice."

"I will if that girl fails."

A sly smile pulled at the woman's baby-soft skin. "She is no girl. She comes to us in the prime of her life, with all the illusions and naiveties of youth stripped away. She is intelligent, independent, and confident in her skin. The only way to derail her is to kill her, mark my words. And if you do that, all that you've worked for will be stripped away. She's protected as a Jane. She is protected by that house. She is protected by us. In this, Austin Steele, you'll need to find another avenue. Brawn won't work. Neither will swinging your pecker around. You will either need to join us and protect her, keeping her on the right path, or step aside."

He leaned in, almost losing control of his fire. "I will not join in the ruin of this town. You're mad, old woman."

"Then help steer her, *child*. Think with your head for once. Flex that muscle between your ears. She will need guidance. Put down your fear, and help minimize the effects of another chosen."

He turned away, anger and frustration raging through him. He'd put his blood, sweat, and tears into sanctifying this town as an independent entity. He'd battled more alphas than he could count, keeping them away from his territory. He'd taken out clans sent for him, withstood higher-level magic, and taken away the sly knives of assassins hired to put him in the earth. And he'd done it all to protect the people of O'Briens.

But if that house chose someone new, everything would change. The new chosen would have the power to tear down the borders he'd struggled to maintain, leaving them vulnerable to magical folk on a mission. Those wishing to align themselves with the new master of Ivy House were likely to trample peaceful residents in the wrong place at the wrong time. Battles would kill innocents in the crossfire.

He'd promised to protect these people, and no big city Jane was going to stop him.

✧   ✧   ✧

NIAMH WATCHED AUSTIN Steele strut out the nearest exit, going after the hilarious, headstrong Jane who would do nicely. She wasn't, in a million years, someone Niamh would've picked for the job. Not in a million. She was…ordinary. Average. Just a normal Jane in middle life.

But therein lay her magic, which was the very reason Niamh was not in charge of choosing for the house.

When Jessie's life had fallen apart, she hadn't crawled under a rock in a puddle of tears. She'd risen up, grabbed life by the balls, and said, "Screw this. I'll find something better."

She'd finally punched fear in the teeth, taken a random job in a secluded town, and marched on in with her head held high.

Looks were deceiving, because that wasn't ordinary. It was *extra*ordinary.

She had fire, that one. She'd come out with a perfect stranger on her first night in town, challenging her comfort zone. She'd stood up to the biggest, baddest alpha shifter these parts had ever seen. And she'd ended the night by sneaking out to drunkenly stumble home by herself, refusing to rely on anyone else to see her to safety.

Niamh chuckled. Tonight had been a hoot.

Jessie had not kept up with Niamh, drink for drink—thankfully, or she would've died of alcohol poisoning—but she hadn't folded in the towel, either. She'd taken it at her own pace.

Yeah, Jessie would do nicely. All she had to do was find the heart of the house again. Without help. And then the house would make its choice.

A couple of young guys sat in the corner, sucking up the last of their way-too-strong drinks. Paul slowly finished up his duties before moving around the bar to put up the chairs. He knew why Niamh was lingering behind.

"Hundred bucks in it if you want to help," she told him as he passed. "All you gotta do is help carry him."

Paul's eyes tightened.

"Two hundred."

"Austin Steele doesn't want people poaching from his bar," Paul said.

"I'm not poaching. I'm going to see if anyone wants a ride. If one of 'em takes me up on it, then I'll go home with him. What I do with him at home, like hand him over to a very thirsty vampire who I have lost a bet to, is no one's business."

"Then what do you need me for?"

"You have a car, don't you?"

"Yes…?"

"Yes? You're not sure?"

"Yes. I do."

"Yes, you do, what?"

The kid started visibly shaking. He'd run away from his wolf pack when he was just shy of fifteen. He'd been the orphaned runt. The weakest link. He'd been starved, tortured, picked on, and belittled. Running had taken great courage, because if he hadn't reached the town limits before his pursuers—if he hadn't reached Austin Steele—they would've made his life so much worse. Death would've been a blessing for the poor kid.

But he had reached the town limits. And when his

wolf alpha, who'd thought he was the toughest, strongest thing on four legs, ran up against Austin Steele, the old fool had turned tail and ran for the first time in his life. He'd swaggered over, and he'd scampered back, limping and baying and missing an ear and an eye.

No one took down Austin Steele.

Niamh had designated herself as the bad cop to Austin's good-guy hero, and she tried to push the kid's buttons any way she could. One day she knew he would push back. Or throw something at her head. Or mutter a nasty name. *Anything.* Niamh had seen late bloomers before, and this kid was definitely a late bloomer. All he needed was a little confidence. Until then, she kept him so focused on her he forgot to be scared of anyone else. When he wasn't scared, he didn't get picked on. Simple.

"Yes, I do, missus," Paul replied. "But I thought you said you were going to see if the guy wanted a ride?"

"I am. Different sort of ride, Paul. Keep up. You're old enough to understand the birds and the bees."

His face reddened. Definitely a late bloomer.

Paul was silent for a long time, going about his business. Niamh eyed the guys in the corner, making sure they wouldn't try to get away. But no, they were nursing their drinks, waiting to be kicked out.

"I don't understand something, missus," Paul said as he made his way back around the bar and took her glass. He emptied the remainder of the ice down the sink.

"What's that, Paul?" she asked, slowly getting up.

"Austin Steele said he won't protect that house. That he'll have nothing to do with it. Even that he'll try to stop the house from choosing someone."

"Heard all that, did ye? Good at eavesdroppin', then?"

"Well, if the house wants to choose Jessie, and he's off getting her home safely—protecting her—doesn't that count as working for the house?"

Niamh laughed. "You're sharp, kid. Yes, it does. It absolutely does. But he needs to put in a lot more service than one measly walk home."

"How much more? Missus."

"That I don't know. It usually depends on how much a person's heart is in it. If he's protecting her to get rewards, then he will be passed up. If he is doing it because he genuinely wants to see her safe, then it will take very little for the house to recognize his service and repay him in kind."

"But doesn't that mean he'll be trapped in the magic too?"

Niamh couldn't help grinning at that. The boy was surprisingly astute when he wanted to be.

"Yes it does, Paul. It certainly does."

CHAPTER 9

THE COOL MOUNTAIN breeze washed over me as I slipped out of the bar, accidentally hitting the door frame as I did so. I bounced off, stabilized, and turned the wrong way.

"Oops," I whispered, pointing at a guy down the way who'd noticed me. He was out there smoking, but he turned toward me a little as if to say something. I gave him a thumbs up. Then about-faced. It was always good to distract people when you were doing something stupid.

Headed the right way, I pulled out my phone and tapped into the GPS app. There were, like, three turns, but just in case, I wanted a little backup. I didn't want Jeeves to come looking for me.

"Trying to ditch me?"

"Hah!" I kicked out on reflex, missed, shoved a solid wall of muscle, went nowhere, then kicked again, clipping a shin. Somewhere in there, I'd dropped my phone.

"It's me, it's Austin." He danced away, agile for a guy so big. Or maybe just sober.

Hands out, adrenaline pumping the alcohol through my bloodstream a little faster, I lumbered after my phone like Frankenstein's monster. It slid to a stop in the dirt beside a spiky weed with a yellow flower.

"I know," I said. I checked my phone screen. Solid as a rock.

"Then why'd you kick me?"

"You surprised me. Like Chuck Norris."

"What?" he said, walking in the gutter, giving me plenty of space. I needed it. The sidewalk wasn't wide enough for my "straight" line.

"Chuck Norris destroyed the periodic table," I replied.

"Huh?"

"He only recognizes the element of surprise."

Light from a streetlight showered down on Austin's face, showing a confused, cockeyed grin. "Did you hit your head on a rock while you were sneaking out?"

"No. I got caught in the door, though. Does that count?"

"Yes."

Turn right in—

I silenced my phone but didn't turn the GPS off. I shot Austin a narrow-eyed glare he probably couldn't see—a silent warning not to lead me astray. It was out there, now. It hung between us in the air.

"Got it," he said.

"Dang it. I hate when I say my thoughts out loud. This was why Matt always bitched when I drank."

"Who's Matt? The ex?"

"Yeah. Dumped me."

"I'm sorry," he murmured.

"Because I got dumped, or because I ended up as a caretaker for a big old creepy house?"

He paused for a moment. "Both. You think it's creepy?"

"Of course I think it's creepy. Don't you?"

"Yes. So…" He stepped up on the curb.

I bumped into him on accident. "You're in my space," I said, weaving in the other direction.

"Sorry." He stepped back down. "So you have no idea about that house?"

"No idea about what?" I stopped and faced him. Swayed forward. Swayed back. "Are there *ghosts*?"

I could just see his bewildered expression in the moonlight. "I…don't honestly know. I've never heard…"

I waved the thought away. "I don't believe in ghosts, but I would've looked for them if there had been reports."

"No, I don't think there are ghosts. Listen…it's a dangerous house. You probably shouldn't…go off the beaten track in it. Just stick to cleaning and you'll probably be—"

"I know all about the dangers." I stopped for a moment, needing a deep breath to calm my stomach. Lots of wine. I'd probably need to eat when I got home to keep everything down.

"You okay?" Austin asked.

"Yup!" I started walking again, nearing the main drag. "When I was ten, I found a trap door that dumps people out of the third floor. Diana nearly wet herself."

"Right, exactly. There's a lot of those…elements."

"Hey!" said a disembodied voice.

I glanced blearily to the right, squinting to see three guys sauntering down the sidewalk in a sort of zigzag. The streetlights, much more plentiful on this street, highlighted their jeering faces.

Younger guys, on the sauce, not ready to go home and looking for some sport.

I doubted they'd bother an older lady on her own—boring! A few words, a joke about MILFs, and that would be that. But Austin was big, he was also middle-aged, and he was with said "older" lady. To a young moron who hadn't been raised right, that would look like good sport. Bait the old dude trying to protect his lady, make a fool of him. Half the trouble of parenting had been making sure my kid didn't grow up to be like these jerks.

"Young people should have an off switch until they can prove they have something to give back to society," I said. I grabbed his arm, my hand finding purchase on one of the muscle groups. "Come on. Just walk. Those idiots won't run to catch up."

"How do you know?" he said, his focus on the guys razor sharp.

"Because I'm a woman, and I've had to assess danger since before I got boobs. It's better to avoid confrontation, trust me."

"Not if you want them to think twice about their behavior the next time." He slowed.

"Yeah, you!" one of the guys hollered, his smile widening. His flat-top haircut was ridiculous.

"Hey!" another barked, clearly not smart enough to think of anything else. They laughed like simpletons.

Austin paused, chest turned toward me, face pointed their way.

I stepped closer and faced him, adrenaline surging through me, knowing this was the way to that confrontation I wanted to avoid. "Look bro, you have a solid punch. You're strong, you're capable, I hear you roar. But you're one, they are three, and I'm a chick. Don't even get me started on the testosterone difference between men their age and yours, or our relative speeds. Look, let's just go. They're drunk. I'm drunk. We're all drunk."

He angled his face down to me. "I hear you. Not just what you are saying, but I hear your fear. I remember what you said in the bar. Nothing will happen to you. Nothing. Not now or in the future. You can trust me, Jacinta. I know exactly what I am capable of. No more, no less."

"Trying to get a little action, Grandpa?" one of the guys said, a hop in their collective steps as they got closer. One guy had lost his smile. That was the mean one. He was the one to worry about.

"Fine." I dug around in my purse aggressively.

"What are you doing?" Austin asked, still looking down on me almost intimately. He was baiting those guys, which really annoyed me.

"I am not baiting them," he said, and clearly my filter was still broken. "I am using my proximity and body language to show them you are under my protection."

I lifted my eyebrows, dropped my mouth open, and opened my free hand wide. The other held the Swiss Army Knife I'd just dug out of my purse.

"What's that body language say?" I asked as the guys drew nearer.

"You are flabbergasted with me, think I'm talking nonsense, think I'm taking an unnecessary risk, and are prepared to stab a bitch."

This time I just stared.

"And now you're incredibly surprised and impressed that I read that right," he said, the guys nearly upon us now. Jostling one another. Working on their collective courage and bad decision-making.

"I don't know about *incredibly*," I murmured, pulling up the larger of the knives and stepping behind him. If he wanted to cause the problem, he could take the brunt of the attack.

"Fine night, isn't it?" the tallest of the guys said, taking the lead, his hair flopping over an eye.

"Kids at home?" Flat-top said with a toothy grin. "Finally getting some?"

"Getting some in the middle of the sidewalk? Kid, we're forty. We don't have to bang in the back seat of cars anymore. We can do it in a house," I said, the world still floating. I had zero inhibitions and a knife in my hand. This would go how it would go.

"What?" someone said.

"Listen, guys, this is a quiet town." Austin put up his hands like he was surrendering. "People are sleeping. Yelling at strangers down the street is not how we do things here. Let's tone it down, okay?"

"That's not how you *do things here*?" the mean one said, edging forward, violence written clearly on his face. He didn't care that Austin was a foot taller or much, much wider. He was fueled by testosterone and stupid, a lethal combination.

"I call Flat-top." I loosened my knees and shifted from left to right, ready for action. Alcohol was a strong deterrent against fear. "My dad has a nice little spot in my old room where I can store Flat-top's scalp. My mom won't mind. She deals with all kinds of weird things. She won't rat me out, either."

"Dude, what the hell?" one of them said.

"Are they Dicks?" I asked. "Because Niamh said we could just throw them in an unmarked grave, no questions asked. I believe her, too. That big old house has lots of woods. We can probably hide them any-where and no one would be the wiser. I don't see any cameras, there's no one on the street, and there is zero motive. No one would be able to trace them back to us. You know, if this altercation goes pear-shaped."

Silence greeted me. Austin's hands were still raised, his body loose as a goose. Nonetheless, I knew he was ready for action. That guy could sucker punch at the drop of a hat.

"Hello?" I asked, slowly peering around Austin's big back.

The three guys stood there, their lips and eyes tight and their expressions suddenly unsure.

"What's the status on this?" I asked, and swayed into Austin's back. "Hah!" I reached around him and slashed with my knife, just in case they got the idea that my drunkenness meant I wasn't primed and ready.

"Dude, what... No." Flat-top shook his head and put up his hands, not unlike Austin. "Screw this, bro. That chick is...weird."

"You all are insane, brother," tall guy said, giving Austin a look that said he was crazy. It was a cover for insecurity, but I'd take it.

I felt Austin's body shake a little under my lean, like he was laughing. I could probably straighten up, but worried I'd stagger back in the other direction. The lean would have to do for now.

Mean Guy stared at Austin, his face flat, a sparkle of *unhinged* in his eyes. He wanted to try his hand at a bigger dude.

"Neck to navel," I murmured, my fingers tight on the knife. "A quick slice, neck to navel. Or maybe navel to neck. I'm not sure what would be best. It's fine, though. I'll aim for the soft bits and just *rip* to the side. That oughta do the trick."

"Bro, come on," Flat-top said, walking backward toward the hotel. "That bitch is crazy. Let's go!"

"I'm crazy?" I asked. "You started it! You started it, and I plan on finishing it. That's just responsible fighting. That's what a mother does, finishes things. Then tidies up. Trash can, unmarked grave, whatever. Garbage goes where I put it, and that's that."

Mean guy squinted at Austin, glanced at me peeking out from behind him, then blew out his breath and backed up slowly. "Until next time," he said with a smirk.

"If only I had a throwing knife, I would stick it right in your smug little back, you…" I gritted my teeth. "Screw him, let's go."

I pushed off Austin, and just as I expected, I staggered backward and almost fell. A strong arm wrapped around my back, keeping me upright.

"I'd be home right now if you'd just listened to me," I said, my eyes drooping. I leaned against his side. "A little nap would be nice."

"Where, in a bush?"

"Sure. A bush, a gutter—I'm in no position to judge."

Another arm, this one down low. The world spun, and then he was cradling me in his arms, my head on his shoulder. So close, so hard, and not nearly as comfortable as a pillow.

"I'm either going to pass out or throw up," I said,

my head lolling into his hot neck.

"Thanks for saving me back there," he said, his deep timber rumbling through his chest.

I was too tired to huff out a laugh. Or maybe too drunk. "Oh." I pulled my head up and held up the knife. "I need to put this away before I forget I'm holding it and drop it."

Stopping, he adjusted his hold so I was balanced in just one of his massive arms, proving that he was much stronger than he looked, and he looked super strong. Moving slowly, methodically, as if he weren't balancing my weight in one arm, he tucked the knife into my purse and looped the strap over his arm before resuming the two-arm hold.

"Are you magic?" I asked, surprised and very close to passing out. "Because *what*?"

"What?" he asked, no strain evident in his voice.

"I feel light."

"You are light."

"Lies." I rested my head back on the worst pillow in the history of pillows. It could've been a rock for all the give it had. "I didn't save you, those guys scampered off. Wait—is this you looking for gratitude or an apology or something? Because as I said, those guys scampered off."

"They scampered off because you are as fierce as

you are crazy."

"Hey, I'm drunk and I have the laws of defense on my side. Screw them."

His chuckle took nothing away from his sleek, graceful movements as he carried me to Ivy House. "Exactly. You made that easy and—"

"Madam."

"Hah!" I kicked the air and swung my fist around. Mr. Tom leaned back and my hand sailed through nothingness, right by his head. "Damn it, Mr. Tom. Like...why? Why do you always sneak up on me?" I clutched my chest, then my stomach. It flipped menacingly. "Down."

"What?" Austin asked.

"Down!" I struggled out of his arms, pushed Mr. Tom out of the way, stopped, turned, kicked him, and then staggered toward the bushes. "Go away. Everyone go away. Things might escalate from here."

"Who did this?" Mr. Tom asked Austin.

"*I* did this," I said, taking deep breaths. Holding my unsettled stomach. "But *why* didn't you warn me about the alcohol? Don't eat the sandwiches, but *what about the alcohol*?"

"She's fine. I've got her," Austin said.

"No." I looked around, seeing Ivy House just down the road. I was almost home. Tonight I would probably get intimate with the toilets. "Just go away. All of you. I'm fine. Honest. Super good. Definitely awesome." I did not feel awesome.

"Leave," Austin said, the command in his tone sending a shock through my body.

My stomach rolled. I groaned. "Why?" I asked no one in particular. "Why didn't I leave the first couple times I said I should go? *Why?*"

"But Austin Steele, she's my charge. I will—"

"Go!" he barked.

I sat down on the grass of someone else's property. I crawled to the side so I was in the weeds and off their lawn. "I'm too old for this."

"It's my fault." Austin knelt beside me. "You're right. If I'd let things be, you'd be home by now, throwing up in peace."

"This is true."

"But I'm selfishly glad I kept you out. I've never had that much fun in an almost altercation in my life. You single-handedly scared those boys crazy. I've never had that effect."

"Bully for you. Did Mr. Tom leave?"

"Yes."

I shook my head. "Why do people always use your whole name?"

He sighed and looked up at the sky. He sat down

next to me. "It's a show of respect. I don't expect you to understand this, but they aren't my pack so they can't technically call me alpha. But they respect me as such, and thus they use my whole name."

"You're right, I do not understand that. I am not going to call you by your full name, I'll tell you that right now. The lot of you are crazy. I'm not climbing aboard that train."

"And yet, you just debated on the merits of slitting a perfect stranger from neck to navel versus navel to neck, and decided on stabbing and ripping any way you chose."

"Yeah. That's just logic. Besides, we were in a battle."

"Ah."

"I guess I shouldn't lie down right here and go to sleep."

"No."

"Niamh can really drink. I mean…she's twice my age. I didn't realize what I was getting into." I took a deep breath and swayed. I felt his hand steadying me.

"Not many do."

"Alpha. Why would someone call you alpha? What kind of an ego trip is that? And why would someone throw rocks at their neighbor? Why would someone create a labyrinth in the back of a house to trap kids? I don't understand this place."

"It defies logic."

He had that exactly right. It defied logic. But then, it was a small town. Clearly small towns had their own brand of weirdness. A big town would probably ring Austin's bell. A person didn't stop to confront someone in a bad part of a big town. That was a way to get you shot.

"Tomorrow is day one on the job, and I'll be hungover," I muttered.

His sigh was soft. "What will you do first?"

"Yell at Mr. Tom for no reason, probably." I tried to lie down. His hand stopped my backward motion. I pushed against it. It was like pushing against concrete. I thought of some choice words I wanted to call him.

"Why do you call Earl Mr. Tom?"

I tossed up my hands. "I do not know. For some reason, he told me his name was Tom. Then he said to call him Mr. Tom."

"And you did?"

"He pretends like he doesn't hear me if I use Earl. It's the only way to talk to him."

Austin helped me up, smiling. "You know, you're in a bubble of weirdness. We're not all that strange."

"Says the guy who speaks in animal behaviors."

That wiped the smile off of his face. "What do you

mean?"

"What do I mean?" I started walking and veered into a leafy bush. I slapped at it and veered back out. "All that body posturing stuff. Normal guys don't think like that."

"And yet, those guys understood my meaning."

"How do you know?"

"I could tell. Guys are different from girls. We're from Mars. You're from Venus."

"That is such bullcrap. I'm an Aries. I *am* Mars. Guys can suck it, number one. Number two, women understand guys a hundred percent more than they understand us. Do you know why that is?"

"We're sensible?"

I stared at him. Then accidentally swayed and rammed my forehead into him. Pushing back, I shook it off and said, "Really? Sensible? You idiots just about rumbled for no reason a moment ago. You're all—I have a penis *weee.*" I waved my hands around. "No, it's because you don't listen to women. You pretend women are these mysterious creatures. And sure, when you don't give a crap about something, it does remain a mystery. But it wouldn't be so hard if you'd put half the effort into learning about us as we put into trying to learn about you. It's *your* negligence that creates the problems."

"That right?"

"And another thing." I put up my finger. Then punched him in the chest for good measure. The alcohol had turned me unnecessarily violent. It was like I was a kid again, playing WrestleMania with my brother on the living room floor.

Except that punching Austin hurt me and not him.

I massaged my hand, ignoring his grin. "What do you think it does to future men when you teach boys that being weak is being a pussy? Pussy meaning female, obviously. Or yelling at men who are doing poorly that they're being girls? Or ladies? Had enough, *ladies*?" I squinted one eye at him. It was all my brain could muster for a glare. "Men are teaching boys that they are equivalent to ladies, to girls, when they're at their worst. At their absolute weakest. And you wonder why we're from different planets? You wonder why men so often disrespect women?" I patted my purse. "Neck to navel."

I'd thought he would laugh at the joke I'd thrown in at the end to lighten things up, but he didn't. Instead, he stared at me silently in the darkness. The small hairs rose on my arms again. Goosebumps erupted on my flesh.

"I hear you," he said softly. "I never put stock in any of that—the taunting about being ladies—but I didn't see the bigger picture, either. Just like earlier tonight—

no one has ever spelled out the dangers women face when a man asserts himself as I did. That blindsided me. So much of tonight has blindsided me. In my life, when it comes to this, I feel like I've been…blindfolded in a way. Not blind, because if I would've looked, I would've seen, but…" He shook his head. "I'm gob-smacked. Thank you. I'll be more conscious of this going forward."

I reached out and placed my hand on his arm, just to make sure he was real. To make sure I was still awake.

He wasn't acting like any of the men I knew. Certainly not like my ex or his friends. I'd attempted to talk to Matt about the dangers women faced, and he'd blown me off. That wasn't his reality, and therefore my fear wasn't justified. The minute, day-to-day suffering women faced for being women wasn't real.

Austin was ten times as strong as Matt had ever been. Bigger, broader, more masculine. He was the quintessential tough guy. And yet…he was all ears. More than that, he was thanking me for enlightening him. And he meant it.

I need to hang out with better men.

Tears filled my eyes. "You're a good man, Charlie Brown. Even if you do randomly flex for no reason."

His smile was soft. He gently removed my hand.

"How about getting you home?"

"Okay, but before we get there, let's steal all of Niamh's rocks. She'll be so mad."

CHAPTER 10

M Y HEAD THROBBED before I even opened my eyes. My mouth felt like a cesspool.

Light sprinkled across my face and a shape loomed over me.

Mr. Tom stood beside my bedside, looking down on me. I hurt too much to show surprise.

"Why are you standing over me like a serial killer?" I asked with a hoarse voice.

"Would madam like some breakfast? Or a rag to wipe off the chocolate smeared across her cheek?"

I let my eyes drift closed and palmed my aching forehead. Then I let myself moan, long and loud.

"Coffee and aspirin, then. Shall I bring it up?" he asked, his face way too close even though it was still many feet away and safely out of my personal space bubble.

"Sure, if you don't mind."

He nodded, straightened, and stepped back. "I took the liberty of laundering the clothes you littered across the floor and re-homing the collection of rocks you had stuffed in your pockets."

Oh God, I'd stolen Niamh's rocks.

Well, technically, Austin and I had stolen Niamh's rocks. My pockets hadn't been large enough to fit the whole collection, so I'd started unceremoniously shoving them into *his* pockets, making him an accessory to the theft.

"Probably best not to mention that to anyone else," I told Mr. Tom. "Maybe just…keep it between us, if you wouldn't mind."

"Of course, madam. Whoever has lost their rocks will never hear a peep out of me."

"What time is it?"

"Ten o'clock, madam."

"Ten? Crap." I struggled to sit up, hurting too much to worry about my tight tank top and lack of a bra. If Mr. Tom cared, he shouldn't have let himself into my room without an invite. "I have to get moving."

"Not at all, madam. I have not been up long, myself. People in this community keep slightly different hours than Dicks and Janes. They stay up to embrace the magic of the night and sleep through the uneventful day."

It was a great excuse, I'd say that much.

"I'll let you get up and showered. The coffee will be

waiting for you."

"Thank you." He'd need to cut out this waiting on me stuff, lest I get used to it and not want to leave when Diana's auntie came home, but today wouldn't be the day.

I waited until he left before trudging to the bathroom. The shower helped somewhat, though it was clear the day would completely suck. There was no getting around that.

A cup of coffee, glass of water, and bottle of aspirin sat on a highly polished silver tray, arranged *just so* on the little table by the large bay window. A single white rose leaned from its porcelain vase, removed a little from the tray but clearly fresh, with a little dew still on the petals.

I smiled through the pain and glanced out the sunny window, looking at the expansive gardens below, stretching to either side with paths and benches weaving through them. Beyond the gardens loomed the large plant labyrinth that should've been so weird but somehow fit this place. Before I could feel too contented, I caught sight of Edgar walking across the grass, dragging a half-naked body behind him.

I flinched, bumped the table, knocked over the vase, and overturned the chair as I bounced to my feet.

"What in the—"

He was using the man's socked ankle as a means to pull his body through the carefully tended grass. The man's skinny jeans hugged his thin thighs, keeping in place despite the way he was being dragged along the ground. No shirt adorned the man's upper body and a dribble of blood ran down his neck and onto his pale chest. His arms flared out to the sides and his head bobbed against the lumps on the ground.

"Oh my God," I said, breathless, running around the table to the door. I stopped, quickly grabbed a couple of the aspirin with shaking hands, and tried to gulp them down with coffee. After burning my tongue, I swallowed them with the water instead. Priorities.

The next moment, I was running down the stairs with my phone clutched in my hand, my heart in my throat, and my fluffy white robe dancing around my calves.

"What is the matter, madam?" Mr. Tom said as I took the last couple steps to the foyer.

"Edgar is dragging a dead body." I couldn't believe what I was even saying. "I need to get a picture for evidence. Call the cops!"

"Oh no, I'm sure there is some logical explanation for this."

I ripped open the door. "Call the cops!"

"Wait, madam—"

I ran across the front lawn and around the side of the house, confronted with a tall wooden fence with a large metal handle. I charged through, realizing too late that the gate led to a path of tan-colored rock dotted with little cement squares.

"Ow," I said, the sharp points of the decorative rocks jabbing into my bare feet. "Ow. Dang it. Ow!"

"Madam, where are your slippers? I left them just below the robe." Mr. Tom kept tight to my heels. It was probably good in case Edgar lashed out.

"Should've brought a weapon," I said, half limping and half jumping to each little cement square.

Edgar reached the edge of the grass, coming my way. I hurried to intercept.

"I've caught you." I pointed and shouted before unlocking my phone. "I've caught you red-handed. I'm calling the cops."

Edgar halted his advance. He dropped the leg and raised his hands like he was being robbed, his nails much too long and quite yellow. "What's happening?"

"What's happening?" I repeated in disbelief, balanced on one of the cement squares, my feet and head both pounding with pain. I tapped into the camera. "*That's* happening." I pointed at the man laying haphazardly at Edgar's feet. "Get my back, Mr. Tom, in case he charges."

"His charging days are long over, madam," Mr. Tom replied. "He's more inclined to hobble. At best he might haltingly shamble. He really isn't what he used to be."

Edgar looked down at the man he'd been dragging. "No, no, he won't run. He'll be out for another few hours, at least."

"I meant *you*. You charging is what I'm worried..." I tapped into the phone app and hit nine before Edgar's words filtered in. I lowered the phone marginally. "Another few hours?"

"Oh yes, he's just stunned." Edgar smiled at me reassuringly, his yellow teeth stained with wine, probably similar to mine, making his canines seem disproportionately long. "He had too much fun."

"It's the drag of shame, isn't that right, Edgar?" Mr. Tom said.

Edgar's brow furrowed. His arms were still raised.

"Rather than the *walk* of shame, it's the *drag* of shame, get it?" Mr. Tom prompted. "Because you're dragging him? After a night of partying?"

"It's not funny if you have to explain it," I murmured, peering at the man. "But...he's got blood on him. And he's not moving. You're *dragging* him, for criminy sakes."

"Oh, the blood." Edgar looked down on the man

again. "Yes. That. That's because…" He paused. "He…hurt himself."

"Did he fall down the stairs or something?" Mr. Tom asked.

"Yes!" Edgar pointed at Mr. Tom. "Yes, exactly. He hurt himself falling down the stairs. Dicks tend to be clumsy. I was just walking him to get a…"

"Band-Aid," Mr. Tom said.

"Yes! Exactly. A Band-Aid. So there, you see? All is normal."

"We are—*ow!*—a long way—*oh*—from normal!" I gritted my teeth over the last couple of feet of rock, my phone held out like a shield, and sighed when I got to the grass. "Get back!" I shifted my phone up, pointing it at him like a gun. It had many uses, all of the current ones imaginary. Thankfully, Edgar complied easily, his hands still raised as if he were the innocent victim of a hold up.

I placed two fingers on the neck of the half-naked man, his skin clammy and chilled. A pulse throbbed back, strong and sure.

"What's going on here?"

Relief washed over me. I turned in my crouch to find Niamh near the opened gate, her hands on her hips and her one breast hanging low in her loose shirt.

Before I could tattle on Edgar, she continued, "Edgar, what are you doing with my date? And for the love of the gods, what happened to my rocks?"

"Your date?" I asked.

"Your rocks?" Edgar asked.

"Trespasser," Mr. Tom shouted.

"Yes. Your date." Edgar reached down and picked up the man's ankle again. "I was just bringing him—"

"Getting a Band-Aid," Mr. Tom said, repeating the ludicrous story.

"Yes, yes." Edgar blinked like all this was starting to be too much. I was in the exact same boat. "I was just walking him to get a Band-Aid because he...he fell down the stairs. And started bleeding. But then I was going to return him to you. Since...he's your date."

"Who took the rocks?" Mr. Tom nodded at me, like I should play along.

"Your date?" I asked again, standing slowly. "From last night? He's..." I looked down at the twenty-some-odd kid, remembering the two younger guys sitting in the corner of the bar. They'd seemed somewhat lacking in both looks and brains, judging on a few snippets of conversation I'd overheard, and I could imagine they'd be desperate. Alcohol would probably have softened Niamh's intense scowl. As far as the extreme age gap...well, who was I to judge? If a woman wanted to experience a younger buck, no matter how ridiculous, who was I to say boo? I didn't like being judged, and so I wouldn't judge anyone else. Of course, that explained nothing else about our current situation.

"A little green?" Niamh finished for me. "True, but they have more stamina. Harder—"

"Good lord, woman," Mr. Tom said, aghast.

Her eyebrows shot up. "Secret is out, old bones. And when I say bones, I really mean—"

"No." I held up my hand. "No, never mind. But…why is he here, being dragged across the grass by Edgar?"

"He said he was handy, so I sent him over to Edgar's to fix the…thing while I cooked breakfast for the poor wee lad. But it's time he headed home, Edgar. Quit monopolizing his time." She stomped forward, peering hard at the decorative rocks under her rain boots as she went.

I wasn't going to ask about her choice of shoes on a sunny morning. It was just one odd detail too many.

"This doesn't sound right," I said as Niamh grabbed the man's ankle out of Edgar's hand. "Why would he go to Edgar's with his shirt off?"

"Oh no. I removed that because of the bite—the blood! When he hurt himself. On the stairs."

I stared at Edgar helplessly. Niamh dragged the guy toward the rocks.

"At least pick him up. He'll get all scratched up," I said listlessly.

"It's his penance for all the crap he was talkin'," Niamh said, not heeding my words. "An absolute wanker."

So it *was* one of those guys from the corner. That part of the story checked out, at least. I'd left her with them last night.

I tried to glimpse his neck, but she was hightailing it. Mr. Tom had grabbed the guy's arms and his back was barely skimming the ground. Before I could get a good look, they were heading through the gate and I was left barefoot in the grass, worried about hurting my feet on the way back.

"Hurt his neck falling down the stairs... We should call the ambulance," I realized belatedly, palming my still throbbing head. And they certainly shouldn't have moved him. I would have said as much earlier, but I wasn't thinking clearly.

"Oh no, he's fine. It was just three steps," Edgar said. "He's okay. When he wakes up in a couple of hours, he'll be tired, maybe a little hungover, but nothing serious."

He said it with absolute confidence, like this wasn't the first time he'd removed a man's shirt and dragged him out of the yard by the ankle after he fell down three steps and somehow started bleeding from the neck.

"I can't." I shook my head, utterly defeated. "I can't with any of this."

"Totally understandable. I get what you mean," Edgar said, walking with me across the rocks.

"I don't think you do."

"No, I don't, but I wanted to provide a united front."

My phone vibrated. A text message from an unknown number: *Did you survive?*

"I know you took them," Niamh yelled at Mr. Tom at the edge of the front yard. The poor young guy lay at her feet, arms and legs splayed. "Just admit it. You didn't want to look bad getting hit by a rock, so you scattered them to the four winds."

"I did not scatter anything. You're clearly senile. You probably came home last night and threw them at the neighbors' houses."

"I've only done that *one time* and it was after they tried to throw me a surprise welcome party. That was justified. You took them!"

I sighed, knowing I had to come clean. Mr. Tom shouldn't have to take the heat.

Before I started forward, I sent a quick text: *Who is this?*

"Niamh, stop arguing and look after that kid, will

you?" I said.

She and Mr. Tom cut off their bickering for long enough to give me a blank look.

"The Dick at your feet." I pointed to help them along, absolutely flabbergasted. They really didn't put much stock in tourists. This was starting to get ridiculous. "Get him home. Or at least to a bed. And call a doctor or something. Take care of the poor guy. And as for your rocks—"

"No. She cannot have ours," Mr. Tom said, crossing his arms. "She has lost her rocks. That is her problem. Your stiff little boy wonder here probably scattered them for fun," he told her. "Young people do those kinds of things. Regardless, it is not our problem. Now, *get off my lawn.*"

"It's not your lawn." Niamh harrumphed as she bent and grabbed the guy's ankle. She hesitated for a moment. "Well?"

Mr. Tom grunted in annoyance, and then they worked together to carry him across the street and into Niamh's house.

I was even more confused than the moment before. Than I'd been all day yesterday. These people were all nuts. All of them. And I was getting a little crazier each moment I spent with them.

Text message: *It's Austin. You programmed your num-*

ber in my phone last night for an alibi re: stones.

"And the plot thickens," Edgar said softly.

I jerked my phone away from his prying eyes, not having realized he'd snuck up right behind me.

"That's not what it seems," I said quickly.

"It seems like Austin Steele is giving you permission to use only his first name. He must think very highly of you. Or perhaps he realizes your potential and wants to create an alliance early. Don't worry, I skimmed over the reference to Niamh's stones."

"Alliance for what? Horseshoes?" I turned toward the house. I still didn't know what was going on, but they seemed to have it handled. Best I didn't know any more details in case I had to go on the witness stand at some point. "He said people call him by his full name because of respect. I still don't get that. He's a bartender. It's not like he's a sheriff or anything."

"Yes. I can see the confusion, being that it is not customary. But we're an eccentric town. It works for us."

"Uh-huh."

I shook my fuzzy, pounding head. The aspirin either still hadn't kicked in or wasn't going to. I was betting on the latter. I'd overdone it last night. *Way* overdone it. And given hangovers were *so much* worse as I got older, I didn't think bouncing back was in the cards. I'd have to suffer through.

But I couldn't handle any more weird. No more. I had to push the brakes.

"Great. Awesome. Fabulous." I walked past him.

I texted Austin: *I hurt so bad it's not funny. Mr. Tom "re-homed" the rocks and is taking the heat for it. Feel bad a little.*

Austin texted back: *Don't feel bad. It'll give him a little excitement in his life. I'll sprinkle the rocks you forced on me throughout town so Niamh can find them again. It'll give her something to do.*

I almost told him about what I'd seen this morning—and the others' bizarre behavior—but I couldn't bring myself to do it. If he didn't find it strange, I wasn't sure what I would do with myself. I wanted to fit in here, and to do that it was clear I couldn't be a Dick or Jane. So for now, I was just going to quietly go about my life and try to figure things out.

I'd also stay away from older people. No drags of shame for me, thank you very much. I'd been in a lot of embarrassing situations over the years, but that would easily ice the cake.

I let myself back in my room and gulped down the lukewarm coffee. Time to get ready and explore the house. I wanted to see what secrets it held.

CHAPTER 11

I STOOD IN the middle of a foyer with gloves, a duster, and a carpenter's belt containing Clorox spray, various other cleaning agents, and a bunch of rags. I'd intended to take the house by storm, starting with dust and cobwebs. I remembered those being the worst when I was here last.

Only, I'd already made my way through half of the first floor, and I hadn't seen any of my eight-legged nemeses. I stood in the foyer now, examining the various surfaces for anything that might need cleaning. Not a single cobweb stretched across the high corners of the ceiling or up in the skylight.

As far as dust, a yellow rubber glove test across the entryway tables had come away clean.

Which was great. I was not complaining. Mr. Tom had clearly been looking after the place, or had hired someone else to do it. Upkeep would be easy.

But instead of moving on like I'd planned, I stood transfixed. I hadn't noticed at first, but the high wooden archway in the first floor landing hosted some intricate carvings. Scrolls and artistic designs caught and trapped the eye. Little faces popped out here and there. A horse's head seemed to neigh from one corner, while a goblin-looking thing, with long claws and pointed fangs, sneered from another.

Everywhere I looked, a new image manifested, creating an exquisite sort of tapestry. Part of me wanted to pull up a chair and stare at it.

"MADAM!"

I crinkled my brow, coming out of my appreciative daze. "Mr. Tom, why are you yelling?" I said in my "patient" mom voice. That voice delivered all kinds of warnings, hinting the patience was just a façade.

"I apologize, madam. I knocked on the wall, called you a couple times—you didn't seem to hear me."

"A good ol' tap on the arm wouldn't go amiss." I tore my gaze away from the images, which almost looked like they were turning and twisting within the frame. Flying through the air, or galloping through the fields. It sort of reminded me of those posters of computer-generated patterns back in the day—when you looked *through* them, an image popped up. Except this was carved wood.

"*Madam!*"

"Oh my God, Mr. Tom, what do you need?" I

turned to him slowly.

He flinched and took two steps back. My expression clearly wasn't advertising the patience I'd tried for.

"Pardon me, madam—"

"Please stop calling me madam."

"Yes, miss"—I sighed—"I went and got this for you."

He held out a travel mug with the lid closed.

"Oh, thank you, but I'm okay. I've had four cups of coffee. I'm buzzing on caffeine just fine. I should probably stop. But thanks for thinking of me."

"It's not coffee, miss." He hesitantly took a step forward, his hand outstretched. "It's to help chase away the hangover. I have a friend that specializes in…draughts."

"Draughts?"

"Modern-day elixirs. Not at all like the witch brews in storybooks. That's…false, those stories. Very unpredictable. This is…medicinal. From…doctors. Doctors without…licenses."

"Are you trying to say herbalists? Like Chinese medicine?"

Relief crossed his face. "Yes, of course. Yes, herbalists. That's it, exactly. We have a few in town. One creates potions—I mean…elixirs that work. One is a useless Jane who is living a lie. Like those storybook writers that go on about superheroes."

I eyed his ratty cape, attached to a freshly pressed black suit that made him look less bony, somehow. "Right."

"It'll help." He stretched his arm toward me but didn't take another step.

Amazing. My son had gotten to a point where he'd started ignoring my mom voice. Also my mom look. Also the classic mom-ready-to-charge-at-him-with-a-paddle-and-get-him-to-see-sense voice/look combo.

That had driven me crazy, because while I wasn't above a swat on the butt, at some point you had to refrain. Like when they were fifteen and in public. Teenagers were the absolute worst. It was like an alien had come to earth one day, picked up my loving boy, and replaced him with a stinky, hairy mutant. Someone should've warned me.

"Miss—"

"Yes, yes, okay." I took the travel mug, pulled off the lid, and looked down at the green liquid. "Is this wheatgrass or whatever that is?"

"I couldn't say, miss."

"Are you trying to kill me, Mr. Tom?"

"No, miss. And you can just call me Tom. I think you've earned it."

He wasn't helping me put the brakes on weird. He really wasn't.

I remembered the body Edgar had dragged across the grass. The kid hadn't been dead, sure, but I did not want that to be me. Those rocks had felt bad enough on my feet. "You take a sip, then." I handed it back.

He took a sip and grimaced before reaching it toward me again. "It doesn't taste good, but it'll do the trick. She is really very good."

I resumed care of the travel mug and turned to look at the scene carved into the landing as I took my first sip. The bitter taste made my face screw up and my stomach swim, but I finished it before handing it back. Time would tell if I'd chugged poison. Given the way I was already feeling, the end might be welcome.

"What room will you move on to next?" he asked, stepping back.

I shook my head, pulling my gaze away again. I couldn't just stand in the foyer and stare at the carvings all day. I had to get moving.

"I've been right. I might as well head left."

Each room was lovelier than the last. The furniture was just as I remembered it from my first visit, stately and homey at the same time. Given no one had been around to use it, the thirty years that had passed hadn't aged it. I trailed fingers across smooth wood arms or tops, felt the crushed velvet of seats, fluffed already fluffy pillows on couches.

Oil paintings stared down at me, men and women from centuries ago, transporting me to a different time. Wallpaper covered some walls, the style incorporating raised elements that gave it texture. Everything in Ivy House was different, unique, but somehow it blended together perfectly.

In the last room on the ground floor, I just stood in the middle of the gorgeous burgundy rug, surrounded by wooden chairs in a ring, and stared out the window at the labyrinth beyond the garden. I felt peaceful in a way I could only remember feeling when I had held my son, rocking him back and forth, comforted by my overwhelming love and his baby-soft skin. This house felt like home. It felt like I wanted to stay. Maybe forever.

"Do you know if this house is for sale?" I asked Mr. Tom, staring at me from the doorway.

I didn't even know how I knew he was there, staring at me silently like a creeper, since the doorway was behind me. I just…did. He was intruding upon my chi. The chi of this room. He didn't belong.

Yet.

I shook the weird thought away, feeling a little strange, and turned to find him exactly where I'd sensed he'd be. One foot in the room. The other out. Looking at me like I'd sprouted a third eye.

"The house is passed. It is not sold." He entwined his fingers.

"Auntie Peggy has no kids, though, and she never comes here. Surely she'd entertain an offer? How much is real estate in this neck of the woods?"

"Ivy House is owned by the person most fit to own it. Everyone else is just a steward."

I sighed. "Did you take a class on being unhelpful or something? It feels like we're having two different conversations."

"I did not, and we are."

"You could probably teach a class like that, though," I muttered, turning away so I couldn't directly see him. It was probably for the best I didn't get my hopes up, anyway. This house was enormous, the grounds even more so, and I didn't even know how much of the woods she owned. Not to mention the place came with a gardener. I couldn't exactly pay Edgar without having a job myself. It was a foolish pipe dream. I just needed to be happy in the moment and carry on.

"Are you interested in a little lunch, miss?" Mr. Tom asked. "Or a snack? Dinner isn't far off, but it isn't for another couple of hours."

I ran my hand across the top of a chair and then skimmed it over the bookshelf against the far wall. I'd long since taken off my gloves. I hadn't found a speck of dirt.

"You've done a good cleaning job," I told him. "It must've taken you a while."

"The time flew, I assure you. There is nothing quite as sad as a neglected home."

I shooed him in front of me. "Have you done the whole house?"

"Not the whole house. I do not know of all the…little nooks and crannies."

"Like the trap doors and secret passageways and stuff?" I followed him to the glistening kitchen.

"Correct. I have found but two."

"Really?" I sat at the little table in the enormous kitchen, following his gesture. "How long have you been here?"

"Fifteen years, now."

"I think I only found two when I was here. That's probably all there is, then."

"Probably."

His answer rang false, like a parent agreeing with a chatty child just to make them stop asking questions.

I leaned my face against my hand, belatedly realizing two things. The first was that I felt great. Just like new. Maybe better than new! My back, which sometimes ached for no apparent reason, felt perfectly fine. Not even a dull ache when I'd bent to sit. That was nice.

And my joints hadn't protested once since I'd downed the green drink, even though I'd been picking things up and checking things out. This was all in addition to my headache having completely cleared up. My stomach was just fine. I would have noticed sooner if I hadn't been so entranced with the house.

I mentioned all of this with what I knew was a goofy grin.

"Agnes is about as talented as they come. A late bloomer, as it were, but a great addition to the town. Just don't try the other one. She's a lunatic."

"Right."

The other thing I noticed was that Mr. Tom was busy making me food again, and I didn't feel bad about it. I hadn't even asked what he was putting together. I'd just sat at the table like a child, waiting for what I was given.

What had gotten into me?

"So now that I'm here, I take up the cleaning mantle, then?" I asked, rising. I needed to at least look like I was an active participant.

"No, no." He gestured me back down and stared at me until I complied. Which I did, as though I wasn't really in charge of my limbs. "Other than the issue of scattering rocks and dirty clothes around, I doubt you'll be any hassle—"

"Yeah, look, sorry about the rocks. I get a little mischievous when I've been drinking. I'll tell Niamh—"

"You'll do no such thing. She needs someone around who isn't afraid of her."

"Afraid of Niamh? Is she that persistent with the rock throwing?"

"There is no reason why you have to bother with the mundane work," he said, either not hearing me or simply ignoring me. "You'll have more important things to do."

"Like what? I didn't get a list or anything from Auntie Peggy."

He delivered me a triple layer sandwich with all the fixings and a little salad on the side. I widened my eyes at it. He'd knocked that out incredibly fast.

"Wow, thank you, this looks—"

"We cannot know the tasks until they are assigned," he said, taking a step back. "At this rate, it won't be long."

"Oh. Auntie Peggy sends a list or…"

He walked out of the room without a word.

I stared after him for a moment. Every time I thought I was getting a handle on his idiosyncrasies, he just went and blew my perceptions all to hell.

Without anything to clean, all I really had to do was look around the house. And maybe find more secret passageways.

CHAPTER 12

MR. TOM WAITED on the recently swept front porch of the meanest woman he'd ever met in his life. Feral cats couldn't compete with the bad temper of this woman.

"What do you want?" she said as she opened the door, her features closed down into a scowl.

"Was it some trauma in your past that made you so horribly unlikeable?"

"How about I give you some trauma?"

"Yes, exactly. That's exactly the kind of answer I expected out of you." Mr. Tom sniffed and clasped his hands behind his back so she couldn't misconstrue his body language. Knowing her, it wasn't out of the question that she would suspect an attack from him and return the imagined slight in kind. "I thought you would like to know—it won't be long."

"What won't be long? Your personality change? I see you're already dressing smarter."

"As befits my position, yes. Your powers of observation are remarkable. Well done." He looked toward Ivy House, a shadowed, crouching thing, yearning to reclaim its status in the magical community. Magical kings and queens would come calling to behold its magnificence. To behold the magnificence of its handler. The best and brightest from all around the world would petition to join Jacinta's court. To share in the glow of her magic.

"How do you know?" Niamh asked in a low, thick voice. He didn't detect any excitement at all.

"She sees the magic. In every room she's been in, she has seen the magic."

"Which rooms has she been in?"

"Downstairs, only. She is currently eating some lunch."

"Is she looking for it? The heart, I mean."

"Have you drunk away your brain power? She doesn't know about *it*. She is looking for cobwebs and dust."

"Cobwebs and dust?" Niamh crossed her arms. "Why in heaven's gate would she be looking for cobwebs and dust? Are you already trying to shrug off your duties?"

"Because her job title is caretaker, you insufferable woman. She doesn't realize she is at an audition. She thinks she has to clean the house and I let her believe as much today so she'd have a reason to look around. At least *one* of us is aiding the poor girl in her destiny. By the way, how's the search for your rocks going? Any leads?"

Niamh chewed on her lip for a moment, studying his face. "You want her to find the heart, you do?"

He paused for a moment. That question sounded like a trap. The woman could be cunning when she set her mind to it. Was she trying to get rid of him in the final hour?

He narrowed his eyes. "Don't you?"

She sighed, and looked at the house again. "Ah sure, I don't know. It's a nice, quiet little life here. Austin Steele has things…peaceful. I wouldn't mind just finishing out my days like this."

Mr. Tom was struck mute for a moment. Of all the things he'd expected her to say, that was certainly not one of them.

"But shifters have a mostly human life span," he said, now wondering if she wanted to step down. She was crotchety and stubborn and a real pill, but those very qualities made her Ivy House's greatest asset. He'd realized early on that she was integral in keeping the riffraff away, and so he'd put his dislike aside for the betterment of all. Sometimes it was not easy, but he had managed. It was why, he suspected, the house had accepted him as its protector after he'd moved on from his last butler job. "He's already forty-two. In another ten years, he might not be able to protect this territory. Strength fades, as does power, even for him."

She sucked her teeth.

"Stop that, it's disgusting," he said, unable to help it. "When Austin Steele can't protect this town, someone else will come through and try to claim it. That could be anyone. We might not like the new situation, but we'd be too old to run them out."

"Speak for yourself."

"Do you play hide and seek with your mirrors? You're so old, Father Time pities you. No, the only thing that gives this town a chance to thrive is Ivy House being restored to its former glory. And the only way it—"

"Yes, yes, I know, the girl has to resurrect the house. Don't lecture me as if I were a child."

"She is a woman, not a mere girl, and why shouldn't I treat you like a child? You're acting like a child."

She scoffed at him and turned to go back into her house. "Keep me updated, Mr. *Tom*."

"What do you think I'm"—the door slammed in his face—"doing."

Shaking his head, he noticed three rocks next to her chair. He kicked them with his boot, scattering them across the porch.

"I saw that!" The door swung open.

Mr. Tom took off running, adrenaline making him feel like he was half his age. He heard shoes scuffing wood, Niamh going after the scattered rocks.

"Think you're protected now that there's a possible chosen?" she hollered. A rock pelted him in the center of his back. "Stop messing with—" Another clicked off the cement beside him and bounced away. He zig-zagged to make it harder for her. "—my rocks!" Another smacked him in the leg.

Breathing hard, he stopped on Ivy House's porch and turned back.

Niamh leaned against the railing, her arms stringy and her short hair white. She lifted her hand and showed him a backward peace sign, Europe's equivalent of a middle finger.

Age certainly had a hold of her. She was slow, creaky, and sat more than was probably healthy. She was in the twilight of her years. He understood why she might want to retire from this line of service. He'd had those thoughts, once or twice. But he'd worried lack of purpose would propel him into a decline that would slide into death, and he wasn't ready for the big Good-night.

He hoped Niamh realized she wasn't, either. In her

prime she'd had mighty magic. Battle lords had feared her joining the opposing side. Royalty had invited her to their gilded tables.

Ivy House would restore all that.

He let himself into the house quietly, feeling Jessie off to the right. She'd already been in that room, but she'd missed the secret passageway. Maybe now she was giving it a second chance.

He'd lied. He knew the location of every hidden entrance leading into the veins of the house. Every protector did. Ivy House did not keep secrets from those it trusted. He couldn't tell her about them, though. She'd discovered a few when she was here last, but from what Niamh had said in her phone message, Jessie only remembered two. Which was why he'd only claimed to have knowledge of two. He couldn't help her find the heart again. She had to do that on her own to be worthy of the magic. It was part of the trial.

He drifted to the door, soundless.

"Don't you have something to do?" she said without turning around.

He jumped, just as he had in the council room earlier when she'd stood at the center of the Circle. The thirteenth piece, surrounded by her powerful twelve. Twelve she and the house would choose to serve.

His spot was secured, he knew. Lucky number nine.

Niamh was three, the numbers assigned by the house in order of importance, he guessed. Edgar was twelve, if he made it that long—the old vampire was starting to go fruit loops.

"Sorry, miss."

"Please, just call me Jessie."

"Sorry, master."

She turned back to him, her brown hair up in a ponytail with some frizz around her head. A sprinkle of freckles covered her nose and cheeks, and lines gently creased her forehead. A track suit covered her once athletic frame, currently host to a bit more girth from motherhood or inactivity.

The signs of age didn't diminish the bright intelligence in her sunburst eyes, the hazel flaring between long black lashes. Nor could it diminish the easy confidence in her bearing. Jessie clearly knew who and what she was, and liked herself more for it. She must've been a beauty in her youth, and her loveliness had blossomed with age. She would be a good choice for Ivy House, and for the magical elite.

"Right, okay, miss will be fine, then." She shook her hand in annoyance and touched the mantelpiece against the side wall. Her delicate fingers trailed across the marble in reverence. Her gaze skimmed the faces of masters past. Her eyes lingered on a few of the legends.

He slipped out of the room and headed to the second floor. He needed to make sure it was spick and span so as not to slow her down. Despite Niamh's strange misgivings, the train had left the station.

Now they had but to wait.

CHAPTER 13

I'D ALWAYS HAD a sense for danger, especially if Jimmy was in said danger, and had a knack for knowing when one of my friends was about to call. Those were my only claims to the supernatural, and they were small ones. But something was going on here. Something strange.

The marble was warm beneath my fingertips, as though there were a fire in the hearth. But there wasn't.

The floor felt warm beneath my feet, too, even though I was wearing shoes.

I dropped my hand in front of the blackened insides of the fireplace, letting the weird phantom heat soak into my fingertips.

"Am I cracking up?" I whispered, straightening up again.

I felt a compulsion to make my way to the far side of the room. A decorative cabinet had been pushed up against a corner. Just like in the foyer, the carvings moved and twisted, exposing ornaments hidden within their depths. Faces and figurines. A chariot and a horse. A great oak tree.

Toward the side, the moving shapes and decorations swirled around one central point. Around a circle.

That circle seemed to have a pulse.

Memories surfaced, of the same thing in a different room.

Moving without intending to, I let my finger hover in the air. Slowly, not sure what would happen, if anything, I fit the pad of my finger into a tiny groove I hadn't seen when I'd first inspected this cabinet.

I pushed.

Click.

The side of the cabinet popped open.

I stepped back, surprised. Excited.

I glanced around, but Mr. Tom wasn't behind me this time. I pulled on the cabinet. It swung open on oiled hinges, revealing a small doorway into the darkness beyond.

I fished out my phone, staring into the dark depths, before switching on the phone flashlight and stepping forward.

Which was when the situation caught up to me.

When I was a kid, I would've rushed into that small space without looking back. I would've—and did— check out the bowels of the house with all the wonder of youth. And I'd nearly plummeted from a third-story trap door to my death.

Anything could be in that space. Bats. Poisonous spiders. Rats with huge fangs.

My phone's battery said twenty-one percent and the time read 9:02. It was late, my battery was low, and this probably wasn't a good idea. At least not at the end of the day.

I took a step back. Mr. Tom had said he knew about two passageways—was this one of them?

Curiosity pulled at me like a tow rope attached to a monster truck.

"Could be dangerous in there," I reminded myself, staring into the depths.

A step forward.

Memories flooded me. Giggling. Pushing the button and gesturing for Diana to follow me. Running through the walls and coming out in another place altogether. It struck me that we'd never gotten lost within the walls. I'd never been turned around.

Two more steps.

I angled my flashlight, feeling the walls close in around me. Usually I wasn't good in small spaces, but this was no problem for some reason. It felt safe. Comforting, almost.

"I'm definitely cracking up," I whispered, the sound

of my voice muted within the tight space.

The cabinet stayed open behind me, allowing in some additional light as I worked into the dark depths. When I turned a corner, though, external light was no longer needed.

Soft blue light filtered down from the corners by the ceiling, partially illuminating the tiny passageway, big enough for one and a half of me, or just one Austin. It provided enough light to see, although not so much that it blinded me to the surrounding darkness. It must've been recessed lighting of some sort. I shut off my phone light and noticed that no cobwebs stretched across the walls. Nothing skittered around my feet. It was just as clean as the rest of the house.

A little square room opened up off the passageway, which continued onward. On one side of the space sat a bench big enough for two skinny people. On the other side was an alcove with a picture frame at eye height and a little metal orb embedded within it.

Naturally, I stepped up to look through it. The orb was some sort of glass, and through it I got a fish-eye view of the space on the other side. Mr. Tom stood stock still in the middle of the small sitting room, one I had wandered through earlier. It had held little fascination for me compared with the rest of what I'd seen. He stared off at nothing.

"Yes, yes, quite," he said.

I jerked back from the orb. Then pushed in closer again, because what in the holy hand grenades? Who was he talking to?

His hands were at his sides, so no phone, and there was no one else in the room. This wasn't even a good talking-to-yourself mumble. The words had been crisp and clear, even from this side of the hidey-hole.

Mr. Tom was the last person I wanted to spy on.

Quietly, because if I could hear him so clearly, I assumed he could also hear me, I returned to the passageway and continued to explore. Another small room, this one looking into the laundry room. Moving through the house, I found the kitchen, the drawing room, and worked all the way around to the front sitting room across the foyer from where I'd started.

The fish-eye lens showed Mr. Tom's back as he stared out the window.

"Yes, yes," he said. "Quite."

"What a weirdo," I whispered, barely loud enough to hear myself. He didn't turn around.

The small hallway through the walls kept going, and so did I, feeling a little like a rat running through a maze. Another corner led to a small stairwell. At the top, I noticed a latch in the floor, and a coil of rope next to it. An escape hatch, probably.

I stepped well over it so as not to fall through.

On the other side was a viewing orb, this one without a frame. The ceiling was low enough that I had to hunch a little. When I looked through the lens, I saw Mr. Tom standing at the front door, opening it. I hadn't heard the door knocker or a door bell.

"Hello, Austin Steele," Mr. Tom said, and a little flutter rolled through my belly. I wondered how big of an ass I'd made of myself last night. He'd texted this morning, so he couldn't be too mad about anything. He'd made a joke about the rocks. And I hadn't made a pass at him, so that was good.

Still, I'd been drunk and he'd been sober. I was sure I had plenty to be embarrassed about.

"I'm here to see how Jessie is getting on," Austin said.

"Ah. Yes. That unbearable woman across the street filled me in. You hope Miss Jessie doesn't acclimate to the house, is that correct?"

I lowered my brow, anger coursing through me. He hoped I failed? Why in the world would he hope that?

"Correct," Austin said. "I think you know why."

"Because you enjoy being the master and chief of the town, and don't want to step aside for someone more powerful."

Austin shifted his weight, either angry or uncomfortable. "It's not about power. You know as well as I do that this house calls to the wrong sort of people. This town doesn't need that sort, plain and simple. It'd be better if—"

Irritated and a little hurt, I moved away from the orb. The sound cut off as I did so. There had to be some acoustic trick to that, or maybe these viewing areas made use of modern surveillance technology. Whatever the reason, I didn't need to hear any more.

A sick weight had settled in the pit of my stomach. I felt disillusioned. I'd thought I'd become a better judge of character over the years, but I'd clearly read Austin wrong. He'd acted like he cared about my opinion, my perspective—hell, he'd gone out of his way to make sure I got home okay. All of that, and he was actively rooting for me to fail. Was this some messed up *keep your friends close and your enemies closer* situation?

And why would he see me as a threat, anyway?

I huffed out a breath, hitting a T-intersection, and straightened all the way up as the ceiling rose higher. I chose right randomly, checked out a bedroom, felt creepy, and checked out the next.

This wasn't right. These passageways shouldn't be looking into bedrooms.

Dread filled me at the realization that this loop likely led to my bedroom, and Mr. Tom had access to it.

The third orb I came to had a handle just below it. I grabbed the handle, turned and pulled. Nothing happened. I pulled again, giving it a few little yanks. I pushed out a little on one of those yanks, which made me realize I'd been trying to open the door the wrong way.

"Dummy," I muttered, pushing the large door open.

No, not a door. The back of a closet.

No shoes lined the shelves and no clothes hung on the hangers. I left the passageway open behind me, intending to return as soon as I got my bearings, and pushed out through the closet door.

A murky room greeted me, the hall light spilling in through the open door. Bright moonlight streamed in through the windows, the full moon a few days away.

A shape loomed in front of me. "Good evening, miss."

I froze. My heart thumped wildly.

Mr. Tom stood in the center of the space, his hands at his sides, facing me.

Why the hell was he in this room at the same time I emerged from the secret passageway? How'd he even get here so fast from downstairs?

Sweat broke out on my brow. "Is this where you kill me and bury me in the yard?" I asked through a suddenly hoarse throat.

"Good heavens, no. What would be the point in that?" He walked away from me (*thank God*) but stopped near the door.

I took a step back. He was graceful, but how fast could he move? Could I get into the passageway and out of the house before he could catch me?

The light flicked on, showering the room.

A new dread overcame me. One I doubted I'd ever be able to shake as long as I lived.

CHAPTER 14

"**W**HAT IS THIS hell?" I asked through suddenly numb lips.

Eyes. Eyes everywhere. Painted eyes or marble eyes, some eyes uncannily tracking my movement. They stared at me from atop their human caricature bodies.

Mr. Tom spread his hands. "I present the doll room."

I could actually feel the look of horror on my face.

Dolls sat on little chairs, their chubby plastic faces turned a tiny bit to imitate life. Others stood gathered in the corner, little girls with porcelain smiles, wrapped in their frilly dresses.

I gulped, trying to make sense of this horrific scene. "Bu-but why are there doll heads stacked on that shelf?"

"Ah yes. That is in case any of the doll heads need to be replaced. There are bins of arms and legs, as well."

I didn't look where he gestured. I didn't want to add to this nightmare. "That one looks like it has two black eyes," I said, pointing, "like it got beat up. Why not replace that head?"

"That's the style of the doll. She has those lovely red-haired pigtails and quite the mean temper. She's a tough one. The gingers always are."

My gaze skittered over the little bodies covering every available surface and spewing onto the floor. "Okay, but that one has black lips, stitched Xs for eyes, and black hair with gray streaks. That isn't right."

"That's the Halloween doll."

"You have a man doll with big teeth and a huge crazy smile. What the hell, Mr. Tom? That is going too far."

"Please, call me Tom. And I don't see the big deal. They're just dolls."

"Until they come alive and toddle after you, sure." Unease slithered along my skin.

Some people hated clowns. Some mimes.

Me? I hated dolls.

It wasn't right that they were of a size and shape of babies, *almost* lifelike, but inanimate. It confused the mind. So did the ones with the little girl faces and adult dresses. It felt like they were staring at me accusingly. I couldn't find the words to express how disturbing I found the Halloween doll that looked like a dead kid, or that horrible man face that didn't belong anywhere.

My brain recoiled. Created nightmares upon

nightmares. Imagined all of these nearly lifelike creatures coming after me, one halting step at a time. One jarring movement after another.

"No." I shook my head, stepping backward. "Nope. All this has to go."

Mr. Tom's confusion was evident. "I don't understand."

"That makes you suspect." I stabbed my finger at him. "*Suspect.* And you better not be peeking in my room!"

I pushed past Mr. Tom into the hall. No way was I exploring more dark places right now. Rats and spiders were one thing—I'd deal with those. Dolls, though? No. Count me out.

"I would never." Mr. Tom was quickly on my heels. "If you could, you would see that certain rooms are blacked out. Those are the rooms with the master in them."

"I'm not the master of this place, so I don't see how that is relevant." I turned and jammed my finger through the air once more. "Go close and lock that room. I'm going running."

My crazy stare brooked no argument. He about-faced immediately.

"Close the secret passageway, too. I don't want those things running through the walls of the house."

"They don't come alive unless the house does," Mr. Tom yelled back. "And then they are a wonderful army. No one ever expects them."

"I've landed in hell." I charged into my room, slamming the door behind me, and rushed into my closet. Nothing called to me like it had on the first floor.

"Oh my God, can you even hear yourself, Jacinta?" I huddled in the corner of the closet and quickly changed into running clothes.

I wasn't even huddling because I cared if he saw my nudity. This drooping, disheveled body hadn't been the same since having a kid. Sometimes it didn't even feel like mine, anymore. I couldn't care less who hazarded a gawk at it.

No, I was huddling because I worried I'd get stuck halfway into my sports bra and he'd see the struggle.

"Young dudes being dragged across the lawn, hot middle-aged men talking about being town alpha, the weirdest butler in the history of people, and now a room full of militarized dolls? What kind of Hades's honky-tonk had I landed in? And here I am, in the middle of it all, looking around the closet for moving wooden carvings? This is bad. I've slid past a midlife crisis—I'm on a crash course toward insanity."

It didn't help that I was full-on talking to myself.

I slipped into my trainers and exited the closet.

Mr. Tom waited for me by the bedroom door with his hands out in front of him. On his palms sat an 80's style sweatband with a green stripe running through it and two matching wrist bands.

"Nope." I pushed past him.

"Well at least take some water with you. Here." He hurried down the hall.

I didn't wait, instead heading to the stairs.

Mr. Tom met me there, carrying a small backpack with a water tube extending out of the top.

"It was only used once. I decided running wasn't for me. It's in great condition." He got to the bottom of the stairs, his cape fluttering, and held it out. I heard water sloshing within its depths. "It's important to stay hydrated."

"It was only used once...but did you change out the water?"

He paused in his urgency. His eyes dipped to the backpack.

"Or wash the water tube?"

A relieved smile crossed his face. "Don't worry about that. I don't backwash. And water doesn't go bad." He extended the backpack a little farther.

There were no words.

"Wait! Do you want me to come with you?" he called after me.

I walked down the stairs and into the cooling night. Although I wouldn't go running in certain L.A. neighborhoods at night, I wasn't too worried about O'Briens. Even still, there was Broken Nose Harry and the normal safety concerns of being a woman out at night. I'd only keep one earphone in so I could hear if someone ran up behind me…

I stalled on the walkway, realizing I'd forgotten my earphones in the mad dash out the door. I did have my phone, at least, having managed to slip it into my sweats when huddle-changing in the closet. At least I could call for help or use GPS if needed.

I noticed movement from Niamh's darkened porch. She stood as I neared.

"What are ye at?" she asked, a rock in her hand and only two next to her chair leg. She was apparently selective in her weapons. "Goin' for a jog?"

"Yup. Need a little air."

"Here. I'll come. Wait there."

Why did everyone want to escort me everywhere?

As soon as she'd disappeared inside, I took off. I needed alone time, and I felt like pushing myself. It was mean to say but running was a different beast than walking fast. I didn't want to be held up and Niamh didn't look so spry.

It only took until the end of the street for me to realize I *did* want to be held up. By a hammock.

My knee twinged in pain, my lungs burned, and everything ached. Running with music was so much better because I could get lost in the rhythm and lyrics and forget the pain. Forget some of the pain, anyway. Without it, I had nothing to focus on besides each jarring step. Each tree slowly passing. My ragged breath.

Feet thudded behind me rhythmically. Someone faster than me was rushing at me.

My heart stuttered and my adrenaline spiked. Self-defense lessons I'd taken in my twenties cycled through my head. I looked over my shoulder, playing it cool.

Niamh was on my tail, wearing an 80's sweatband nearly identical to the one Mr. Tom had offered, a wrist band set and tiny running shorts showing off wiry, bleach-white muscles that nearly glowed in the street-lights.

I slowed to speak, or at least grunt, but she put up a hand in a wave and passed me by. "Meet ya at the pub after. First round is on me."

I gulped air in her wake, watching her form practically zoom up the street and around the corner. The woman was trucking it! What an ego crusher.

Legs wobbly, I carried on. If she could do it, I could do it. Eventually. One day.

A HALF HOUR that felt like years later, I finished a large circle, landing me at the opposite end of the downtown strip from home. Deciding it was time to cool down before I fell down, I slowed to a walk.

All in all, besides the fact that a woman twice my age had mopped the floor with me, it had been a decent first run. Everything hurt and I probably looked like Quasimodo, but at least I'd gotten out and done something. Which didn't mean I was about to join Niamh for a drink.

The downtown strip, all few blocks of it, was mostly quiet. Loud laughter came from the hotel down the way, with soft orange light spilling onto the wide sidewalk from the open door. Someone—a woman it looked like—stepped out of a little cottage a block down, probably some sort of business rather than a dwelling, and locked up.

I straightened up, still panting, sweat dripping down my face, and marshaled on. Darkened or covered windows dotted the way. Doors were closed. It wasn't that late, but most of the businesses had already shut down for the night.

A squeal erupted from the hotel. I peered in the open door as I passed. A few younger people sat at the far end of the bar, the women scantily dressed and the guys in variations of the same outfit: a blue-collared shirt and artfully distressed jeans.

My gaze lingered on the bare midriff of one of the women. What I wouldn't give to have my four pack back. If I had one, I'd show it off, too. No jiggling when this forty-year-old moved, no-siree. I'd want to put it out there as proof.

I gritted my teeth. I *would* put it out there as proof. Why else was I running? Soon I'd get my diet under control—no more binging cookies right before bed— and then I'd be a rock star. I could do this!

Okay, not *as many* cookies before bed. A lady had to live.

A loner sat in the middle of the bar and the bored bartender stared at his phone, leaning near the cash register. Didn't seem like much of an exciting place unless you brought your own friends. Not like Austin Steele's place, with people playing pool and most of the clientele chatting and exchanging greetings.

The memory of what he'd said swam through my memory. My gut twisted.

Maybe he was right. I clearly didn't fit in here. Yes, that was starting to look like a compliment, but the betrayal still stung. He'd listened to me. He'd walked me home. Those were things gentlemen did. Things that seemed to be dying off with the younger generation.

But he wasn't a gentleman at all. He thought I was

lowering the status of his crazy community.

I walked on, approaching the edge of the strip.

What was Austin's game, anyway? Why help me out if he wanted me to fail?

And what was the deal with the name Steele? Really, *Steele*? He probably came up with that name himself. A silver fox rebranding his middle age—"I can still hang with the young bucks, because I'm made of steel!"

Well, I didn't need to rebrand myself to know I was awesome. I might be in the middle of a full-blown identity crisis, with a mom bod and no craps left to give, but I could still run circles around my twenty-year-old self.

Okay, not *run* per se. The only thing that bitch couldn't beat me to was an ice cream truck.

But I'd think circles around her! I had money matters on lock. I knew how to juggle running a household, managing bills, working, taking classes at the city college, and raising a human being. At twenty, I could barely keep myself alive.

I had become fiercer, too. Being a mom really taught you the meaning of self-sacrifice and absolute courage. I would run into fire for my son. I'd step in front of a bullet. I'd throw myself at any danger, no matter how terrifying, just to see him to safety. And I'd do it all without blinking.

The courage of a mother could not be measured. We toiled in the background, day in and day out, without thanks, so our children could become their best selves. We sacrificed ourselves for our loved ones, and we did it silently. Gladly. Full of love.

I blew out a frustrated breath. What kind of bad sort of person was Austin calling me, anyway?

You know what? I didn't even care. I liked that house. It spoke to me. It felt like home. So what if the neighbor was violent and drank like a sailor. And so what if the gardener liked to fool unsuspecting children with his well-tended shrubbery. And who cared if the butler thought he was a super hero and didn't really understand personal space—they all had big hearts. They'd welcomed me. That said something about their character. If the only problem was some muscle-bound guy who'd never grown out of his hotness, so be it. I didn't need friends like that, anyway. He would not find a way to push me out of that house. It was my home now, and I protected my home.

Except for the doll room. That still had to go. That was too far.

I nodded to myself, approaching the intersection that would bring me to Austin's bar. Niamh was probably there, a six pack in and not feeling it.

I hesitated on the corner in indecision. It's not like

we'd had plans. Or even that she needed me. Based on what I'd seen last night, she had a history of heading to the pub alone.

Besides, I didn't have any money, and *really* didn't want to drink.

Mind made up, I continued on toward the house. Which was when I noticed a strange sensation burrowing between my shoulder blades, like someone was watching me. Like danger lurked somewhere out there.

This area was host to mountain lions that came down from the hills. Bears, maybe, in search of trash cans. I hoped so, at any rate, because I'd take an animal stalker over a human one any day. Humans could be sick and twisted, and they weren't likely to scare off if you played dead or put your arms wide and said, "Hah!"

Gulping, playing it cool, I glanced right, trying to pierce the darkness with my gaze. Nothing moved but the restless leaves.

Looking straight again, I monitored the other side in my peripheral vision. Still no movement. But I didn't doubt what I felt. A predator awaited me in the shadows, their interest in me keen.

Pressure building in my chest, I slowly increased my speed, half thinking of running back toward Niamh.

Okay, fine. Maybe I was also thinking of heading toward Austin Steele. That guy had made it clear that he didn't tolerate aggression in his bar, and he did not shy away from a fight.

I pulled out my phone, ready to tap the screen.

A shape coalesced a ways in front of me, slinking out from the shadows. Thin but without curves, I pegged it as a man.

A man who'd better watch himself, or he was going to get an aggressive eye-gouge.

Still playing it cool, though my heart felt like it might pound through my chest, I tapped the screen of my phone. Niamh's number, tested last night, was near the top of the list.

"Hello," the man said, strolling forward slowly. A stroll that suggested his interest was me, and maybe also the lovely dark street where a villain could get away with murder if they acted quickly enough.

"Hey," I said, thinking of crossing the street.

I pulled my phone closer to my face, shaking a little with the warning tremors of a potentially bad situation. I tapped Niamh's number and called, no justifiable reason to call the cops since nothing had really happened, but needing backup just in case. If something happened, hopefully she'd call the cops for me. Or call Austin.

"Lovely night," the man said, veering into the center of the sidewalk, blocking my way.

Ten feet to go. If I crossed to the other side of the street, it might motivate him to chase me, but passing him this closely posed its own risks.

"Sure." I opted to cross the street diagonally, walking fast but not running. He was trim and an old lady had passed me earlier, I didn't want him running after me. I doubted I would win that race, and the effort would only tire me out.

"Hello?" I heard, Niamh thankfully answering her phone.

"I wanted to speak with you for a moment," the man said and moved to intercept, his gait long and his speed picking up.

"Jessie?" Niamh said, talking and laughter in the background. She was clearly at the pub.

"Need help," I said into the phone quickly. "Almost home. On our street—"

The phone was ripped out of my hand.

Surprised, terrified, I reacted with my usual linguistics.

"Hah!" I twisted and threw out an arm.

My elbow battered someone in the mouth, cracking his head back. My phone skittered across the ground.

"Help!" I shouted, already running.

My face smacked into solid air. My body *splatted* against…

There was nothing there, I realized as I staggered back, wide-eyed. Nothing was in my way. What had I hit?

Large hands clamped on my upper arms. A backward glance told me it was the man I'd bashed with my elbow, his lip bleeding and a surly expression on his face. This was a second guy, different than the one who'd followed me.

"Help!" I cried, still disoriented but knowing my phone was on. Knowing, if I yelled loud enough, Niamh was liable to hear. "Help! I'm nearly home."

The guy that held me pivoted and stomped on my phone.

"No!" I yelled, balling my fists. "What do you think I am, made of money? Why would you do that? Just freaking turn it off."

"'Bout that home…" The first man stepped in front of me. I hadn't gotten a good look earlier—too intent on getting away to care what he looked like—so I hadn't noticed his weird attire. He had on black gloves, a long black velvet cape, and a tuxedo underneath. Mr. Tom clearly wasn't the only would-be superhero magician.

"Trick or treat," I muttered, my mouth getting away from me.

"What role do you play within that house?" the man asked.

"I'm the new caretaker. I clean the place, that's it. It doesn't belong to me. It's my friend's aunt's. Do you want some tea or something? I'm sure Mr. Tom, the butler, will happily make some for you. My neighbor definitely would. She'd even throw in a sandwich or two coupled with a little abuse about your outfit. Not that anyone would blame—"

"Your friend's aunt's…" His eyes squinted. "You're not of the Havercamps?"

"No! I'm an Evans. Well…legally I'm an Evans. I started out a McMillan. I don't even really have my own last name. It's just given and taken away from me based on which men are in my life—"

"Silence."

I clicked my mouth shut, cutting off the random babbling. Panic fuzzed the edges of my awareness. Deep breaths helped clear my vision a little, but the second man's grip was starting to hurt, digging into my flesh. I still didn't know what they wanted.

"Those who guard it are letting you clean it?" the first man asked.

"That's enough."

I whipped my head around, relief flooding me. Niamh had come. And she'd brought back-up.

CHAPTER 15

AUSTIN STEELE STOOD in the middle of the street, moonlight outlining his powerful body. His strong arms hung loose at his sides and his raw intensity electrified the air. He leaned forward, just a little, balancing on the balls of his feet, obviously ready to charge forward at a moment's notice. He'd come to fight, there was no denying it, and he clearly did not plan to lose.

Relief washed over me. We might've had beef, but damn I was glad to see him.

A little removed from Austin stood Niamh, still decked out in her running sweatbands, and unbelievably holding a beer.

"What is this, a pack?" The first man smiled and took a step toward Austin Steele. The second man jerked me around, making me his shield. "A bit long in tooth, aren't we?"

"I'm not with him, no," Niamh said, motioning to Austin. "I'm with them." She gestured behind us.

Glancing back, I could just see Mr. Tom and Edgar walking down the middle of the street, Mr. Tom's cape billowing out behind him.

The first man laughed. "What a hilarious little town. The four of you geriatrics are its protectors?"

"The *town's* protectors? I wouldn't bother me arse." Niamh laughed, the sound conveying the speaker's idiocy. She immediately became my bestie. "No, we are that lady's protectors." She pointed at me. "The notion of us protecting the town would be nearly as hilarious as your getup. You have an awfully large cape. What are you trying to compensate for, then?"

"So she *does* intend to be the chosen," the man said, a smile curling his lips. "And here I believed that she wasn't Miss Havercamp."

"She isn't Miss Havercamp, no. Fun fact, Miss Havercamp is actually called Mrs. Drury now," Niamh replied. She took a sip of her beer. "Terrible last name, I know. I tried to warn her away from taking it. Diana, I said, it doesn't matter your age, people will still make fun of you for that name."

The man's smile dwindled. The second man lightly shook me for no reason, drawing Austin's attention.

"Then…what is she doing here?" the first man replied. "I received reports that someone new was applying to be Ivy House's chosen."

"She's not applying," Niamh said. "She's stumbling

into the situation without a clue about what awaits her at the other end."

"I can make sure it will be me," the man said, his tone silky.

"I will make sure that it isn't," Austin replied, absolutely no bravado in his promise. It sounded like he was stating a fact, and his confidence made it absolutely believable. His confidence, and the rough viciousness of his voice.

The small hairs rose along my arms and a shiver ran through my body, fear at his savageness...and a little excitement for the same reason.

"Let her go, and get out of town," he said. "She and this place are under my protection."

The man laughed. "Is that right? Your protection?" He turned dramatically and looked behind him, then all around. "Are your faithful subjects hiding in the brush? Or are you as solitary as you seem?" He laughed again. "Felix, bring her—"

"Sorry." Niamh wiped her mouth with the back of her hand. "I should've introduced ya—this is Austin Steele."

A quiver ran through the two men. The smile dripped off of the first man's face and his body froze. The man holding me squeezed harder in reflex. He jerked me around, directing his Jessie-shield at Austin.

"Ah. Austin Steele," the first man said, his voice tight. "Your reputation precedes you, of course. Funny, I'd heard you weren't interested in pressing for more power."

"I'm not. We don't want any trouble."

"You don't want any trouble." The first guy made a small gesture to his pal, and the hands squeezing my arms relaxed and then pulled away. "You don't want any trouble, and you're not strategizing for more power, yet here you are sidling up next to Ivy House. The coincidence is...amazing."

"The coincidence is just that, a coincidence. Ivy House has been without a master for generations. Long before I arrived. This is a sleepy little town, and I plan to keep it that way. You have overstayed your welcome."

The man's gaze zipped to me. I'd been edging away to the good guy side, but I froze in place, like we were in some demented game of red light/green light. His gaze flitted around the others before settling back on Austin. "What a tangled web, indeed. Well, Mr. Steele, if you plan to halt progress, I hope you're prepared to go up against your match."

"And who might that be, *you*?" Austin said, power coiling in his body.

"My employer, actually." A white card magically appeared in the man's gloved hand. He flung it, the rectangle cutting through the darkness and skidding across the road. He turned to me and bowed, his cape swirling around him. "Watch yourself, lady. You wouldn't want to pick the losing side."

He flared his cape and stalked away, melting into the brush and disappearing, his exit as strange as his entrance. His lackey followed suit.

Limbs shaking, heart racing, and phone cracked or worse, I tried to round on the three elderly people and Austin all at once. Their positioning made it impossible, so I aimed my miserable uncertainty at Austin.

"Lucy, you have some s'plaining to do!"

A blur of movement caught my attention in my peripheral vision. A second set of hands clamped down on my arms, fingers long and spindly though strangely strong. A face leaned in toward my neck.

My adrenaline spiked. Fear coursed through me.

A sharp blast of pain dug into my neck, prompting a sort of primal fear I'd never felt before. I was already moving.

I jabbed over my shoulder, catching the perpetrator in the eye. He jerked back and howled, and I realized it was Edgar.

This would not be the night I was buried in the yard.

I shook out of his hands, turning to sprint.

Blackness overcame me before I took a step.

CHAPTER 16

EARL WATCHED, STRUCK mute with surprise, as Edgar jerked away from Jessie, howling. His fingers and fangs came loose from her neck.

Austin Steele was there in an instant. He lifted Edgar with one hand and launched him into the bushes on the side of the street. Jessie was already succumbing to Edgar's bite, stunned and headed for sleep. She fell bonelessly to the ground—or she would have if Austin Steele hadn't swooped down and scooped her up mid-fall, cradling her to his chest gently despite his size and strength.

"My goodness." Earl clapped. "Quite the fast-acting hero. I am impressed."

"Oh sure, yeah, clap after someone else saved your charge, you donkey," Niamh said to Earl. She turned to Edgar, crawling out of the bushes, green shoots sticking out of his clothes. "And what the hell do you think you're doing?"

"I don't know," Edgar answered reflexively, quailing

under everyone's attention. He shrank back into the bushes.

"Why'd you bite her then?" Niamh demanded.

"I don't know," he repeated, eyes wide. The bushes shook around him.

"He's panicking," Earl said, his comforting smile withering in the face of Austin Steele's stare. "He's a vampire—you know how they are. Bite first, ask questions later. I'm sure there is a good reason for all this. Edgar, let's see if you can come up with a better answer, shall we?" Earl said, edging away from Austin Steele. He didn't trust the big alpha when his dander was up, even with Jessie hanging limp in his arms, her head lolling on his shoulder. Maybe *especially* with Jessie hugged possessively in his grasp. Austin Steele's protective instincts made him uncommonly violent, even for a shifter. Earl would just as soon keep his arms attached to his body.

"Well, we can't tell her about the house," Edgar said in a small voice, now completely hidden within the bushes, "and she's going to demand some answers, so...I stunned her to give us time."

"There, you see?" Earl said. "That is a fair point. And Austin Steele was on hand to make sure her head didn't crack against the cement after she poked Edgar's eye out. Collectively, we've done well, I think."

"She had good reflexes, she did," Niamh said, chewing her bottom lip.

"We can visit Agnes and get a draught," Earl said. "I'm sure a memory potion will do nicely for tonight, and then tomorrow she can hopefully find the heart of the house, and—"

"No." Austin Steele's voice sent an uncomfortable shiver racing down Earl's spine. Earl took another couple of steps away. "Tonight was just a sample. A precursor. If the house grants her its magic, we'll see more kidnapping attempts. Stronger magic. There will be no protecting her from it. The whole town will be overrun."

"Sure this place will be overrun eventually, anyway," Niamh said, crossing her arms.

"If she doesn't find the heart, and no heirs come forward, no one will be interested in this town," Austin Steele replied.

"There is always someone interested in this town, Austin Steele. You've sheltered a great many magical folk here, but what happens when ye get too old to keep them? What happens when the next alpha comes looking for a lost pack mate, or simply because he'd like to challenge the legendary Austin Steele? One day, that other alpha will be younger and stronger and more ruthless. He might take your precious townspeople for sport."

His muscles popped along his powerful frame and his jaw clenched. "It is a long way from that day."

Earl involuntarily gulped and thought about joining Edgar in the bushes. Niamh was the only person in this whole town who would even think of butting heads with Austin Steele. She'd always been one joker shy of a full deck, but every so often she went a step further and pulled on the devil's teats. No one in their right mind wanted to be in Austin Steele's way when he lost himself to his beast. The woman was mad. But at least Earl had gotten through to her.

"Not as long as you might think," she said. "Not to magical folk, who live five times your lifespan. Regardless, that day will come. You are a patch on an old pair of jeans. A Band-Aid. Without someone else to take up your mantle—and we both know you are one of a kind in the magical world—this place will be claimed sooner or later. Maybe by the Red Cloaks, trying to"—she made bunny ears with her fingers—"*purify* the magical race in this derelict town you have set up. Everyone else will be banished or worse. Or the fae, seeking to cast out the human and uncooperative magical people, and capture the wine industry profits—"

"I got it, I got it," he said through clenched teeth.

"You are not a long-term solution. You are a short-term solution—"

"I said I got it. What about you? You've told me that you like the slower life. Do you really want to take up the sword again to protect the chosen?"

She shrugged. "I do like retirement, that's true. It's probably easiest for me if someone takes out the girl. Then, in a few years, when you go down in fiery flames—"

"Redundant," Edgar said from the bushes, and then the leaves trembled, as though he hadn't meant to say it and didn't welcome the attention it might bring.

"—I'll be just fine. No one will bother an old Irish woman with one tit and a bad attitude. An illegal one, at that. There are many porches in the world. I can throw rocks at strangers from any one of them. But Edgar there won't fare so well. At his age? He'll be sold to an old rich man for a vampire hunting party. He'll be the hunted, o'course. And Earl there will continue to be useless until he eventually goes insane running around the inside of those walls, spying on dust motes."

"Firstly, I am anything but useless—" Earl said.

"Your old employer would beg to differ."

"—and second, there are no dust motes in that house. I am very exacting in my duties." He finished by mumbling, "And it's Mr. Tom, now. As so dubbed by the future chosen. I always wanted to be called Tom. No last name, either. Just Tom."

"See? He's almost there," Niamh said. "Nearly insane. Just needs a few more years of an empty nest."

"You're under the impression that allowing Jess to find the heart will solve all our problems?" Austin Steele asked, his biceps bulging.

"No," Niamh retorted. "I'm saying she's the only chance this town has of staying this town for the length of her reign."

"She's a Jane," Austin Steele said. "The supernatural is all around her, begging to be noticed, and she hasn't. She'll get that power, not have a clue what to do with it, and be whisked away by the first prince who shows up offering her the world. She'll be gone from this town in a heartbeat, leaving us to fend for ourselves."

"She won't leave that house," Edgar said, rising slightly from the bushes. "She loves it. She's always loved it. And now she has come back to it. She won't leave."

"She has come back out of convenience," Austin Steele said.

"Austin Steele, if I may…" Earl put up his hands to block his view of the alpha's eyes, which contained a vicious sparkle. The words nearly dried up in his throat. "Living with her parents was a matter of convenience. The same cannot be said of coming here, to a strange town, where she has no friends and no safety net. Especially considering the company she is forced to keep."

"You better be talking about yerself," Niamh drawled.

"She came back here because the house was calling her home," he continued. "It was time. She is ready. Today she stood in the foyer, staring at the archway for two solid hours. Lost to it. The house is waking up, and she is bonding with it. Her connection to it is much deeper than what any of us feel, and none of us have left. Neither will she."

"She won't go for some egotistical prince, either," Niamh said and huffed. "She's much too jaded for that. You think she made it out of a battle that raged for half her life only to lose the war at the final stretch? My goodness, no. She isn't looking for a man. If some clown wearing a feather in his tunic struts into town swinging his dangly bits, talking about love too soon and making a show of sweeping her off of her feet, she'll laugh in his face and probably jab him in the eye like she did to that poor fool hiding in the bushes. Though Edgar did deserve it, I can't say that he didn't."

Earl had to agree with her there, much as he hated the practice.

"No, she is perfect for this role," Niamh said. "She's

got fire and wit and she's a load of fun. Most important-ly, she won't be easily swayed from doing what she knows is right. No, I won't walk away from her, and if she wants to stay in that house, then I'll help her do it. She's worth running back into battle for, even if I have to lose the other tit to do it."

"Can you stop saying that word?" Earl asked, pained. "Breast or mammary gland or—"

"You think I'm going to walk around and call it a mammary gland, do you?" Niamh shot back, fire sparking in her eyes. "What am I, a doctor?"

"Better than tit, like some backwoods goblin with a stone for brains," he replied, his voice rising. "Though, I guess, if the shoe fits—"

"Enough," Austin Steele said, his focus acute, pin-pointed on Niamh, thank God. "I have heard what you've said. I will think on it."

"That's all I can ask, Austin Steele," she said, and bent her head, as close to a bow as she'd get without someone breaking her kneecaps. Or so the stories had said.

"In the meantime, how do we handle this?" Austin Steele looked down at Jessie's face.

"We have about an hour before my bite wears thin," Edgar said, still crouched in the bushes, holding his injured eye with a bony hand.

"Maybe it's time we worked her into the supernatural life," Niamh said.

"It's forbidden," Earl replied.

"It's forbidden to disclose the secrets of the house," Edgar said. "But most of the heirs in the past have come to the house knowing about the supernatural. Many of the candidates know what the house's magic will do, just not how to access it. Filling Jessie in about the magical world isn't against the rules. We are allowed to discuss magic with the non-magical when it affects their well-being, their life, or they are poised to become magical. She meets all three criteria."

"Yes, yes, right, right," Earl said, knowing Edgar was right.

"Someone paid attention in magical school." Niamh grinned.

"I didn't go to school," Edgar said. "I was a field hand before I was turned. They wanted to keep us uneducated and illiterate so we couldn't think for ourselves."

"I didn't mean... That's not..." Niamh rubbed her eyes in annoyance. "We've all got problems, man."

"I say we explain all this to her, and see what she says," Earl said. All eyes turned to him, one less than before Jessie had jabbed Edgar. "We explain our way of life. We tell her what's at stake. Then we let her decide."

"She's been a Jane for forty years. Do you honestly think she'll believe us?" Niamh asked.

"Seeing is believing." Austin Steele's tone was resolute. "We'll get her a potion for tonight so she doesn't remember this attack. Tomorrow…I'll see just how far she's willing to let her reality stretch."

"And what about Mr. Magician?" Niamh bent and picked up the white card. Her face paled and she swore under her breath. "His boss is Elliot Graves."

Austin Steele's eyes tightened. Earl suspected the alpha wouldn't admit he was afraid, not even to himself. It didn't matter who came to threaten this place (or Jessie?), Austin Steele would not back down from a challenge. Not ever.

With Jessie in his arms, the alpha turned without a word, heading toward Agnes's house and a forgetting potion.

CHAPTER 17

A S EARLY AFTERNOON set in, I looked across the well-organized attic, with its dressers, trunks, and boxes. All the random silver spikes that had littered the floor in my youth were gone, the floor bare and swept. The medieval arsenal was still around, though. The silver-tipped spears, crossbows, mace, and war hammer had been hung on the wall in neat rows, easy for grabbing. They even had names stenciled above them. "Jake," the battle axe, was in great shape, but "Ron," the bludgeon, had seen some trauma in the past based on the marks scarring its wood.

Mr. Tom had done this, I knew. No one else would skip labeling an item in favor of naming it like a friend. The guy was well and truly cracked.

This morning I'd woken up to him looming over me again, but this time his expression had seemed particularly anxious.

"How'd you sleep, miss?" he'd asked, leaning forward to peer into my eyes.

I'd tried to wave him away, disoriented from waking up, and he'd jerked back with a screech, clapping his hands over his face as if I'd attempted to gouge out his eyes.

Delicate orbs intact, he'd then commenced chattering about the evening, how excellent my running must've been because of how tired I'd been upon returning home. How I'd drowsed through a late supper...

Scrunching my nose, I walked across the attic to the dresser, something that looked like a wooden tool chest.

Truth be told, the second half of running was mostly a blur. I remembered walking past the hotel and looking in, but after that everything was a big black hole until dinner. I'd obviously walked home in some kind of an exhausted daze, but it was hard to forget dinner.

It had been some sort of soup with *way* too many herbs and spices. It had tasted almost medicinal. But it had also cleared away some of the fatigue, and Mr. Tom had been staring at me like he really wanted me to finish it all, so I'd sucked it down. I definitely needed to start cooking for myself.

The small drawer at the top of the dresser contained a collection of pins. Long and thin, short and fat—some were polished to a high shine, and some looked like they had lived in the ground for years. None of them had a loop at the top for thread, so they couldn't be sewing needles, though I had no idea what they might be used for. Darts? Voodoo pins?

"Weird," I said, opening the next drawer. "Ah. Here they are."

The silver garden spikes looked exactly like I remembered. None of them were remotely tarnished. In fact, they reflected more light than should have been possible from the bare bulb above my head and the small round window at the end of the room.

I scratched one, feeling the softness of the metal. Then frowned. They certainly seemed like silver, though why someone would have purchased silver garden spikes, I had no idea. The expense must have been ludicrous. And while Mr. Tom certainly would've done something weird like polish up a bunch of garden spikes, they'd looked just like this—bright and shiny— thirty years ago. At that point, the house had been shut up for a long time. No one would've been polishing them then.

A strange pressure settled over me, interrupting my thoughts. Cocking my head, I tried to analyze the feeling. It felt like a presence had entered my space. Someone I knew, but not overly well. Was I okay with this person being in my house?

I looked around in confusion. What the hell was

going on here?

My house? A presence entering? Either my sixth sense had gone into overdrive in this place or I was cracking up and would end up like Mr. Tom.

Oh God, I hoped I wasn't cracking up. I didn't really want to end up like Mr. Tom. Or any of them, for that matter.

Either way, the pressure increased and tingles worked up my spine. A warning, of sorts. The not-quite-a-stranger was coming. His or her level of welcome was, as of yet, undecided.

I took out a spike on impulse. Just in case I wasn't cracking up, I wanted to be prepared.

Austin's big frame grew in the doorway as he climbed the steps, his expression curious and his eyes wary. Once he filled the frame, he stopped, seeing me. His gaze dipped to the spike in my hand. Fear, rage, and an indescribable emotion sparkled in those cobalt blue eyes.

He tensed, his muscles popping out like a surprise party. His shoulders drew my attention, wide and powerful and nearly spanning the door frame. His stare, vicious and primal, froze my blood. I wasn't usually the type of person who'd freeze in a flight-or-fight moment. Typically, I would run. Or fight.

But I'd never encountered a look like that. A man

like that, oozing ferocious power and strength and sporting a crap-load of working muscle. He'd catch me if I ran, and then he'd snap me in half. He'd pound me into dust.

I could barely swallow from fear.

Without warning, the door swung shut in his face.

I jumped, and the spike in my hand clattered to the floor.

My heart pounded in my ears and I took a deep breath in the ensuing silence. Holy crap, Austin Steele was scary when he wanted to be.

The question was, why had he wanted to be?

Had he wanted to be?

A soft knock sounded at the door.

"Who is it?" I asked lamely.

"It's Austin. Still. Why were you holding a silver spike?"

The breath gushed out of my lungs and I shook my head, wondering at my reaction. Wondering how he'd managed to so thoroughly freak me out when he hadn't even taken a step toward me. Hadn't uttered a word. All he'd done was look at me.

And now he was knocking and politely asking about the psycho holding a polished garden spike in a room displaying weapons marked with friendly names.

Maybe I was the scary one in this equation, not him.

He probably thought I was like the others who lived around this place.

I crossed the distance and opened the door. His eyes still wary, he checked my empty hands for the weapon.

"I was holding it because I was trying to figure out if it was actually silver," I said. Because I didn't really want to look at him, I glanced behind the door and put up a hand, feeling for a breeze. "Why'd that door shut, I wonder?"

"That's not what it looked like you were doing."

When I moved on, he inspected the area around the door as well. Then tested its swinging ability.

"What did it look like?" I picked up the spike, poking it with a fingernail.

"You had warrior eyes."

I crinkled my nose at him. "Warrior eyes?"

He scanned the wall of weapons, his hands clasped behind his back. His mood had shifted. Darkened, like it had fallen down a well, and was now worried about a basket of lotion and a hose. This room was apparently playing hell on his nerves.

"Yes. Warrior eyes. Like you were about to take that spike and charge into battle."

"Ah." I watched his broad back as he worked his way across the wall of friends, as Mr. Tom probably thought of them. "And that made you nervous?"

"Yes, actually. Very."

"Because someone of my age and size and inexperience could take someone like you?"

"Age is only a number, Jess. Don't let it define you. You are only as old as you feel."

"So somedays eighty, and somedays eighteen."

When he glanced back, his smile was faint. "Exactly. Size can be worked around, too. With training, even the smallest of us can be potent warriors."

"Like Jet Li."

"Exactly. Or Cynthia Rothrock, who could probably still ring my bell in her golden years. The point is, our only limitations are those we set for ourselves."

"Ah, but you haven't commented on whether someone like me could take someone like you." I lifted my eyebrows at him, returning the spike to its drawer and opening the drawer under it.

"I didn't want to ruin your day," he replied and laughed. "Listen, I was wondering if you wanted to go wine tasting with me? I need an expert palate."

What he'd said to Mr. Tom yesterday floated into my memory. He wanted me to fail. He wanted to sidetrack me.

My mood fell down the well with his.

"I don't have one of those," I replied, staying civil. "You can just ask the pourers. They are all too happy to talk about their wines. It's their job."

"Yes, but I was…" The words drifted away from him as he got closer, catching sight of the organized daggers in the large middle drawer. Jewels of all colors and sizes adorned the golden hilts. The blades looked like serrated steel or silver.

"This is why I was checking out that spike. I mean…" I picked up one of the weapons that looked like it had a silver blade, perfectly polished. "This really does look like silver."

"May I?" Austin put out his hand, his eyes tight again, as though this were a trust exercise.

"What do you think, I would randomly stab someone just because I have a knife in my hand?" I handed it to him, hilt first. "I live here now, yes, but I'm not unhinged like a couple of the other inhabitants," I picked up another dagger with a darker metal blade. "In fact, I don't even know where Edgar stays. I assume on the grounds somewhere because I have been in, or looked in, every room in this house and he is not in any of them. All but two—Mr. Tom's and mine—are unoccupied."

I pointed at the hand-drawn map I'd put together that morning. "The hidden passageways in this place are legit. I've documented five routes, so far. Don't stay in this house if you want privacy from me, by the way.

Turns out I'm the only one who can see everything. One of the perks of staying in the master suite, according to Mr. Tom. He can't spy on me, but I can spy on him. Must be some crazy kind of facial recognition software built into the security system."

His gaze was hard. "How can you be sure? I mean, doesn't it seem more likely anyone who goes into those passageways can see everything?"

I squinted and nodded at him, my suspicions brought to light. "How *can* I be sure, right? I'd have to trust Mr. Tom, and he is a yes-man. Sure, his squeals seemed genuine after he saw what I'd done to his room…" I scratched the hilt to see if any gold plating would flake off. "I had him watch through the passage-way orb while I messed everything up. He said he couldn't see anything, and he about crapped himself when he entered the room, but still, he named all these weapons and assigned them homes. Who knows with him."

"The arrangement of these weapons is certain-ly…odd." Austin surveyed the wall again. "I can help, if you like?"

"Well, now," I said, turning frosty. "That would mean I'd have to trust you."

"And don't you? Trust me?"

I opened my mouth for another passive-aggressive

comment, hoping I could get my point across without actually having to tell him what I'd overheard—but I stopped myself. Why was I pussy-footing around the issue? I was upset, and I had a right to be upset. He was in the wrong here. If he got upset with my honesty, tough.

"No, I don't," I said. "I was looking through one of the orbs when you affirmed that you wanted me to fail. I heard you say that I was the wrong sort of person to have around these parts."

I held his continually hard gaze even though it felt like my spine was about to break from the pressure.

He sighed, his shoulders bowing a little, and the blistering intensity of his eyes reduced until I finally sighed as well.

He pinched the blade. A sizzle preceded a string of smoke rising from the place he was touching it. "It's real silver." He dropped the dagger into the drawer and showed me the pads of his thumb and finger. Red burns marred his skin, already blistering.

I grimaced and took his wrist, dropping the dagger I held back into the drawer. I shut the drawer with my foot and dragged him toward the door. "Do you have a silver allergy or something? I've never seen anything like that."

"You could say that." He tried to pull his hand back.

"No, no, there's a medicine kit in, like, five places in this house. A little anti-allergen or maybe some aloe will help that."

I got him as far as the bottom of the attic stairs before he slowed us and finally stopped. My tugging now did nothing to budge his feet.

"It's fine," he said, gently extracting his wrist from my hands. "A few minutes and it'll be back to normal."

I scrunched my brow, looking pointedly at his hand. "That burn will go away in five minutes?"

"Yes." He studied me, and something about the scrutiny made my stomach feel fluttery. "Listen, you're right. I did say those things. And I meant them. I hadn't thought things through at the time. I still haven't totally wrapped my mind around it, to be honest."

I took a step back, not having expected him to come clean so quickly. Part of me had wondered if he'd try shifting the blame onto me, something my ex had excelled at. I'd gotten used to the emotional manipulation.

"Oh?" I said to cover my shock.

"But parts of what I said you mistook."

I crossed my arms over my chest and leaned on my right leg, preparing. Here it came.

"I wasn't implying that *you* were the bad sort who'd show up. You're already here. You have shown up. I'm anxious about the people who will follow. And I don't want you to fail. Not at all. If you've found a home here, I want you to thrive in it. That's what this town is all about—second chances. New beginnings. It's why...I have reservations about your role here."

I'd already loosened my arms, reassured by his explanation, and now I wondered if I should tighten them up again. I shook my head in frustration. "I'd love a straight answer."

"I know." He studied me for a moment, and my stomach fluttered again. I wiped at it absently, waiting. "I'm asking if you'll hear me out. Like when you explained your worries regarding your safety the other night, I wonder if you'll give me an opportunity to explain my worries. The worries I have for the whole town."

"Yeah, sure." I spread my arms to get the show on the road.

He hooked a thumb over his shoulder. "I thought we could do it while we do the wine tasting. There's a lot to...unravel. I'll have to give a few confusing explanations."

My guard went up, and I felt my lips curve into a placating though nervous smile. Given what I'd learned of him so far, I didn't think there was any way in hell he'd be interested in me romantically, but just in case, I needed to clear the air.

Besides, even if he was thinking about friendship (which single guys didn't often pursue with single women they didn't also want to bang), alcohol had the habit of changing red lights to green. He was hot, but I was not about to have a one-night stand with one of the pillars of the community. Firstly, wham-bam wasn't usually awesome for the ma'am, and second, I'd only been with one man for the last twenty years and worried I'd embarrass myself. I didn't need to feel self-conscious every time I joined Niamh for a beer.

In theory, all of this would be easy to explain, but some guys didn't take *no* very well. While I didn't think he was one of them, I also didn't know him very well.

"Oh, sorry. I just have so much to do here. And I know you probably didn't mean it like this, but I'm not really dating right now. I just got out of a long marriage, and I'm trying to—"

He put up his hands in surrender. "No, no. Sorry about that. No." His smile was disarming. "I apologize. I wasn't suggesting we go on a date. I've chosen a solitary life. I don't date, either. I would happily explain in a couple chairs overlooking the backyard, but I do actually want some help navigating the tasting rooms. If I went alone, I'd feel like a complete lummox. And a little…" He half shrugged, and it was the first time I'd seen embarrassment in his expression. "You caught me. I wouldn't feel very manly. There. I said it. It's out there. Tasting rooms seem a little frou-frou to me."

"But going with a woman is okay?"

"Going as a bar owner, with a woman who took me to task over the quality of the wine at my bar is okay, yes. Both of those things. Together."

It was my turn to study him, wondering about the alcohol and the whole red light/green light situation.

The humor sparkling in his eyes melted away. "You can trust me, Jacinta. I've been given the okay to be completely honest with you. And I will be. I only ask in return that you trust me as I will be forced to trust you. Be real with me as I will be with you. I want you to succeed in life. I want us *all* to succeed in life. Together. But your position is unique, and I'll explain why that is. I'll explain the things Peggy Havercamp left out."

CHAPTER 18

"**B**UT HOW CAN the house possibly know I'm in the room and it should block the view?" I asked, getting further proof when Austin had stood in the passageway and looked in on me. "Does it use facial recognition? And if so, is it being recorded somewhere? Because I'm so not okay with that." I nearly fell out of Austin's Jeep it was so high off the ground.

He was there in a flash, steadying me. "It's magic."

"Yes, technology tends to be, but I didn't think the house had much technology in it. The kitchen is seriously old school. It's half the reason I keep letting Mr. Tom make me meals."

"Half the reason?"

I grinned, navigating the uneven shoulder. The sidewalk didn't start until the next block, at the edge of the downtown strip. Bright sunlight showered the street, such a different scene than after the sun went down. People strolled along the sidewalk, stepping into shops or wineries. Cars cruised slowly, townspeople heading off to do their shopping.

"It's nice that someone is cooking for me, I admit it. It's like having a wife like I used to be. Except this one is very strange, sometimes creepy, and often pops up where you least expect it."

He laughed, stalling by me, looking down at my Vans. His hand shot out, ready to steady me.

"Good lord, I'm not that clumsy." I laughed.

"Right. Sorry." He took a step away. "I'm used to girls wearing heels. This area can be treacherous."

"You must be a very conscientious date," I said as my toe hit a pivot in the gravel. I made a ladylike sound like, "omph!" and staggered the last couple steps to the paved street.

Austin fastened his hand around my upper arm, probably assuming I'd land on my face.

"I just tripped to make you feel needed," I said, dusting myself off even though I hadn't actually fallen.

"Yes. Thank you for that. And no, I'm not much of a date. At least not as far as relationships go. Just out to have some fun, that's all."

"Have some fun, yeah. I heard that line a few times in college. So how does that work? Are you upfront with everyone, or do you get some action and then ghost them, or…"

His expression turned serious. "The town knows

exactly where I stand. It is no secret. And if I meet someone I don't know, then I am upfront, yes. Though…" His brow pinched.

"They don't believe you," I guessed, crossing the street.

"No, they don't. I've stopped…entertaining those who are new to the town and plan to stay awhile."

"Entertaining, huh? I've met a few players, in my day. They weren't very *entertaining* though, if you know what I mean." I waggled my eyebrows and grinned, razzing him a little.

"I do know what you mean. You aren't very subtle." He held out his hand as we got to the sidewalk, and because I didn't want to tempt fate by refusing the help, I took it.

He helped me onto the curb like a gentleman from a different era. Once I stepped onto it, he turned and stepped closer, bending down a little to catch my eyes. His face was only a foot from mine, his eyes serious and so incredibly blue.

"I am *very* entertaining, I can assure you," he murmured, and I was immersed in his smell, clean cotton and sweet spice. "Multiple times until I am sure she is having a *genuinely* satisfying night. If you know what I mean."

He didn't waggle his eyebrows or grin but spoke

with the utmost sincerity, his intensity vibrating through me. My breath caught and butterflies swarmed my belly. I felt unnerved by his sudden proximity. Electrified by the unexpected heat crackling between us. Terrified by my response.

He straightened up and turned, surveying the street, his message delivered.

I sucked in a breath I hadn't known I'd been holding.

The way he'd said *genuinely* rolled around in my head. The deep rumble of his voice as he'd said it had caressed me in a place that hadn't been caressed in a while. Hadn't been properly caressed in a great long time, actually. But it was the confidence behind that word that was sticking with me.

Many men could be fooled into thinking they got the job done, but from the utter conviction in his tone, I suspected that Austin Steele delivered. He made sure he delivered, even. Just like he'd made sure I got home safely the other night. It was becoming clear that when Austin Steele set out to do something, he did it. End of story.

I let out a long, slow breath, my face as hot as my blood. My whole body humming. *I* wasn't supposed to be the one who flicked the red light to green. I had to watch myself around him.

"What did you mean about you choosing a solitary life?" I asked, not facing him so he didn't see the impact of that little tête-à-tête.

He hooked his thumbs in his jeans pockets. "That's not something that'll make sense yet. Let's wait until we have our talk, then you'll hopefully forget to ask about it."

"I never forget."

"No?"

"Okay, yes. I forget everything. Since having Jimmy—my kid—I cannot keep a thought in my head. It's a problem. It seems like it's even worse in that house. You know, Ivy House without ivy. I just get lost in a carving and lose all track of my thoughts. Or go up to the library—which is unreal awesome, by the way—and forget what I was doing there. That kinda thing."

"Tamara Ivy is the one who built the house. When she was murdered within its walls, she imparted her magic to the house. That magic lives there still, on loan to its master. When its master dies, the magic retreats into the house's walls, waiting for its next master. And the next. And the next. Thus, the house retains the name of its creator. Which winery do you want to start at?"

"First, the nearest winery, obviously. If we don't like it, we don't buy anything. Second, *what*? She was murdered in the house?"

"Yes." He started walking as I wrapped my mind around that.

"Where?"

"I don't know. It was hundreds of years ago. More than a thousand, actually."

"But this town isn't that old."

"It is if you read the right records."

I shook my head, frustrated and already regretting agreeing to this excursion. He hadn't seemed as crazy as the others, and then this came…

I checked my damaged phone, the screen spiderwebbed with cracks. I'd apparently dropped it on my run without realizing it. Niamh had found it on the sidewalk and brought it over this morning. I owed her one. The poor phone hadn't fared very well, but it was still working. Mostly.

"What do you mean, she imparted her magic to the house?" I asked. "Is that your way of saying she haunts Ivy House? Because you said you hadn't heard any rumors about the house being haunted."

He stopped in front of the second winery along our path, having apparently decided to be choosey. "You'll need to forget everything you've ever known for this conversation."

"Pretty hard."

"You'll need to keep an open mind."

"I can do that."

He jerked his head at the tasting room. "The woman who works here knows everything I am about to tell you. That is the only reason I'll be frank with you when she's in earshot."

I felt my eyebrows lowering, suddenly very uncomfortable. Maybe it was because we'd gone from that whole *genuinely* situation to talking about some woman knowing everything, but my mind jumped to places I did not want to go. Sexual places that were sticky and raunchy, and honestly I didn't want to know him well enough to throw open the closet doors and see all his skeletons.

He opened the door to the tasting room and stepped aside. I looked into the cheery interior and thought about running.

"Come on, I won't bite," he said.

Shivers coated my body. The glimmering blue of his eyes and the definition of his muscles made another *genuinely* curl through my mind.

"Sure, yeah, why not," I mumbled, skulking through the door.

A twenty-something girl with dirty blonde, lazy curls falling past her shoulders gave me a professional smile.

"Welcome," she said. Her eyes lit up when Austin walked in behind me. "Austin Steele, hello! Finally got you in for a tasting, huh?"

If he noticed her fawning he didn't show it. His expression was flat, his eyes hard. "I need to talk business. Just the essential information to get us set up will do."

"Yes, sir. Of course." With flustered movements and a flushed face (probably not unlike mine from a moment ago), she busied herself behind the bar. "I'll just open fresh bottles, if you'll give me a moment."

Taking stock of the situation, I lowered an elbow to the counter. On second thought, I could hear about a couple of skeletons if it meant getting preferential treatment. Who was I to say no to fresh bottles and eager staff?

The glasses clinked as she placed them on the counter. "I'm Donna," she said for my benefit. "Should I start from the top of the pouring list?"

I glanced at Austin. He looked at me.

"Well, do you want to try whites?" I asked him.

"I want the experience. You lead."

"Okay, but here's the thing." I took in his robust chest, thick arms, trim but not small hips, and powerful thighs. "You're a big stack of muscle. How long will it take you to feel alcohol? Because I refuse to take part in this if I'm the only ridiculous one. We've already been down that road. It's an embarrassing road."

"You weren't ridiculous, you were hilarious."

I raised my eyebrows, waiting.

His crooked smile made him incredibly handsome. "I can hold out longer than you, but not as long as Niamh."

"Not as long as Niamh could be anything. She's an endless pit."

"I'll keep on your level, how's that?" Austin said, still wrestling with that smile. I wasn't sure why he didn't just let it gleam. He looked better for it and I liked the view. "Somehow. You don't have much tolerance."

Donna poured out a taste for me and a full glass for Austin.

"No tolerance?" I said, aghast. "I drank a bottle and a half of wine the other night."

"Yes."

I lifted my eyebrows at him. He returned the expression.

"Well. I'm not going to try and work on it. You can just forget it," I said, turning fully toward the counter. "That way lies alcoholism."

"Wait…is she a Jane?" Donna asked.

I threw up my hands. "What is with this town? I thought small towns were supposed to be welcoming. I am not a freaking tourist. I'm only in here because Austin asked me to come. That's it. I have a job. Let it *go*, people."

"Jess is the one that just moved into the Ivy House," Austin explained.

Donna gave a long, drawn out, "Oh." Clearly she'd heard of me.

"Jess, a Jane is not a tourist." He paused while I grimaced at the taste of the wine.

"Yikes. This one is…tart," I said. "And not in a good way."

"You might need to let it breathe a little," Donna said, moving that bottle to the side.

"It might be kinder just to let it die," I murmured.

"So that we're on equal footing." Austin downed his glass.

"Good God, man, no! You're not going to enjoy today if you do that."

"I haven't been drunk in…years."

"Fine, but there are better ways to go about it."

"After last night, I need to get drunk."

I tapped an air microphone. "Is this thing on? Bud, I *just* said there were other ways to go about it."

"Maybe after today I'll like wine."

"Oh my God, this was hopeless before it began." I threw up my hands as Donna glided out of the room. "I don't even care, either. Keep charming everyone, brother. I want the preferential treatment, because I'm still going to have fun."

"So. Are you ready?" he asked, his mood sobering.

"For all of this?" I waggled my finger as he reached over the bar and then filled up his glass. "Not really."

"Don't worry about me—"

"Can't help it. Chugging wine is absurd."

Donna glided back in with a tiny smile curling her lips. She clunked down a shot glass and a bottle of Scotch. "Maybe this'll make things a little...less terrible." She then put a row of freshly opened wine bottles on the counter and met Austin's eyes. "From this one..." She moved her finger down the row and stopped on the last. "To this. Let me know if you want anything. If anyone comes in, make them leave until you're ready." She nodded and made her way back out.

"Well, now you'll have to buy something from here," I said. "She's too nice not to. Hopefully the wine gets better."

"Jacinta." His voice sucked all my focus to him. "We use the term Jane for non-magical people. The bar you were in the other night—my bar? Except for a couple of people, everyone there was magical. Niamh is magical. So are Earl and Edgar. So am I. So is Ivy House. Magic is one-hundred-percent real, and almost always kept from those who are not magical."

I couldn't even laugh because of his special ability to make me believe the things that came out of his mouth. In this, just like in most if not all things, he was supremely confident, as though he spoke from a place of authority and experience. What he'd just said, to him, was absolutely real. I could tell that he believed it with every fiber of his being.

I chuckled uncomfortably, because what else could I do? He might not wear a cape, but he was still clearly certifiable.

"You've heard stories about werewolves, right?" he said. "Vampires, mages, druids…"

"Not druids, no. Not sure what those are."

"Fine, whatever. Well, they are all real. Edgar is a vampire. Earl is a gargoyle. Niamh is—"

"No." I held up my hands, shaking my head. "No, you have to stop. You have to. Have you always believed this, or has the town rubbed off on you?"

Austin poured me a taste of the next wine, exactly as much as Donna would have given me. He poured himself a full glass.

"Please don't chug-a-lug that wine," I begged despite the situation. "It really kills the spirit of the thing."

He shook his head, a smile wrestling his lips again. "It's impossible to stay serious with you."

"I was being serious with that request."

He started laughing. "That's what's so funny. Look, you grew up thinking that magic exists only in storybooks." He paused for my reaction. I gave him a blank stare. "Did you ever wonder where the ideas came from?"

"Nope. I always assumed it was drugs and/or alcohol."

"But what if the ideas came from life?"

"Hallucinations, you mean?"

He showed me his fingers, the burns gone. "Normal humans don't heal this quickly."

I grimaced at the taste of the Chardonnay. "This one is a nope. Big nope on this one." I leaned closer to his fingers. No remnants of the burn were left on his thumb and pointer. "Okay, but you said it was an allergy."

"Normal people don't have their skin sizzled away when they touch silver."

"People have sun allergies. That has to be a lot rarer than a silver allergy. What's not normal is this conversation. Look, Austin…what you're saying is not logical. People probably haven't been honest about that with you because of your size and scariness, but I'd be doing you a disservice if I didn't say anything. Now, I should—"

"You're going to have to change," Donna yelled from the back room. "She's been a Jane all her life. It's like imagining the impossible is possible without any proof. She'll have to see it for herself."

"See what?" I asked.

"Donna, you do it," he commanded.

"Donna, do not enable him because of a crush," I called. "Don't try to change men—if they don't do it willingly, it'll never stick."

Donna re-entered the tasting room, stripping off her shirt as she did so.

I paused in confusion, watching her come around the bar and stop in the middle of the space. Her bra followed her shirt onto the floor.

"Nope." I stood. "Strip shows and that God-awful Chardonnay are a nope." Austin put his hand out to stop me. I pushed it to the side. Or tried. It didn't budge. "Get out of the way. I'm done. I'm not here for...whatever this is. I'm going home. Then maybe reconsidering this whole move because O'Briens has gotten to be entirely too much."

"Watch," he said, then squinted and pulled his head away, as though nervous I might jab his eyes.

Why were people in this town so protective of their eyes? Usually people didn't think about that vulnerability. It didn't speak well for my favorite self-defense technique.

I pushed at him again as Donna said, "This isn't a striptease. This is magic. *Look*."

A flash of light and heat drew my attention. Donna, stark naked, mottled and bent and reduced down into a huge, hairy black rat.

"What the f—!"

CHAPTER 19

I BLINKED AT the giant rat for a moment. The rat blinked back up at me. I looked around the room. I looked at my hands.

Then my wine.

"What did you guys put in this wine?"

"It isn't the wine. She's a were-rat. Her parents are both were-wolves, but her mom...had an indiscretion, made evident when Donna first changed. Our animals are passed down directly from our parents. There aren't dominant and recessive options, like normal genes. Shifter children are usually shifters, and they always shift into the same animal as either their mother or father. Upon learning that Donna's mother had cheated, her father divorced her—or the shifter equivalent. He made life difficult for them within the pack. Her mother found a place in another pack, but it was also all wolves, and Donna was the odd one out. She was ridiculed. So much so that she ran away at sixteen...and found this town."

"There is no way being a rat among wolves is less normal than this crazy town," I said, downing the awful Chardonnay in my glass.

"You know what a shifter is," Austin said, and I just wanted him to stop talking. I wanted to wake up from this sudden nightmare. Because I'd tried hallucinogens in high school, and I knew how they worked. If the wine had been drugged, more things would be morphing and changing. I wouldn't feel this horribly sober if I'd just hallucinated a woman turning into a rat. A rat that docilely stood in the center of the wine tasting room, staring intelligently up at me.

I shook my head and turned around. "This isn't possible."

"You learn new things all the time," Austin said. "How is this so different?"

I widened my eyes at him and pretended not to see Donna change back to human out of the corner of my eye. My stomach rolled with the implications.

"This is different," I said, my voice uncontrollably rising. "This is *much* different."

"How?"

"How?" I gestured around me. "*How*?" I pinched the bridge of my nose. "If magic existed in the world—*real* magic, I would know about it. It's that simple. People would know about it. That's not something you can keep a secret."

"Governments keep things secret all the time."

"The government knows about this?" I screeched.

He poured a larger taste of the next wine. I gulped it down. Then coughed and grimaced. "See?" I said hoarsely. "That's why you don't gulp wine. It's gross."

"A very tiny sector of the government knows about it, and they use their influence to make sure everyone else, including the rest of the government, stays unaware. Magical people don't want Dicks and Janes knowing about them, for the most part. Watch the X-Men movies and you'll see why. It's easier just to blend in, and it's surprisingly simple."

My head probably looked like it was on a swivel, moving back and forth and back and forth. "No. Vampires? People sucking blood?"

"The legend had to come from somewhere."

"Yeah, from TB sufferers who turned sallow. Their gums receded, making their teeth look elongated, and they coughed up blood..." All the blood left my face as I remembered Edgar dragging that guy's body across the grass. His red-stained teeth. His long canines. His—

I was running out of the tasting room before I could stop myself, needing to get away from this. Unwilling to believe it.

"Jess. Jessie!" Austin caught up to me and stood in

my way with his arms out, corralling me. "Jess, talk to me."

"I do not want to talk to you. I want to get in my car and go back to L.A. I want to go back to a place where everything makes sense."

"This won't go away—you're too bright and inquisitive for that. If you go back, you'll start noticing all the magical people in that great big place. Those who glide instead of merely walk. Those who move like predators. Those who hunt the night. Now that your eyes have been opened to what is possible, you'll continually notice the proof that it exists. There's no hiding from this, Jacinta. It's all around you. It always has been."

I pounded a fist against his chest, tears in my eyes. I pounded him with the other fist, too, needing a release from this insanity. He didn't move away, but closed his arms around my back, pulling me closer.

"*Shhh,*" he said, trying to rock me. "I know this is a shock, but—"

"But do you?" I struggled to get some space so I could look up into his eyes. "Do you know this is a shock? Did you always believe one thing, only to have someone destroy your reality?"

He shook his head slowly. "I change into an animal—I was clued in pretty early about all this."

"Then don't pretend to have any idea where I'm at

right now. Don't…" I wiped a tear and scowled at someone walking by. They increased their pace. "I'm sorry, I don't mean to take this out on you, but…"

"It's fine. I've dealt with much worse."

I sighed, but I sank into his hug instead of pulling away. He was mostly a stranger, but the solid warmth of his embrace felt like a rock in a turbulent ocean. "This is going to take a minute for me. I mean…" I pushed back again. "This is crazy!"

He nodded and directed me back to the tasting room. "I…can't imagine, but I…am…supportive of imagining."

"You sound like William Shatner." I wiped another tear, laughing, my head spinning. My brain not wanting to handle it. Within the space of a few minutes, another world had been revealed to me, one where fairytales and nightmares were as real as 101kα

"Are there fairies?" I murmured, realizing a young couple had walked into the tasting room when I was in the process of storming out.

"Yes. They are mean little buggers. I avoid them at all costs." Austin strolled up to his place at the bar, his shoulders back and chest puffed out slightly. The magnitude of his presence nearly engulfed the room. It was certainly felt by the twenty-something guy, who rolled his shoulders and sent over an annoyed scowl.

I didn't have the ability to rein in Austin's dominating behavior. And honestly, I didn't want to. I needed some time to process my new reality, and for that, I needed the strangers to skedaddle. I had a feeling he could make that happen.

"Really bro?" the guy said, shifting slightly and giving me a better view of his companion, a petite, cute girl. "Maybe a little room, huh?"

His voice sounded like that of a spoiled rich kid accustomed to getting his way. He could've moved over to accommodate Austin's larger size—our glasses were still in our places, it wasn't like he hadn't known someone might return in—but he instead expected those around him to make his life more comfortable. I'd met a lot of guys like that in L.A. and I wasn't a fan.

Austin glanced over at the kid, and suddenly the mood in the tasting room changed dramatically. The size of the space shrank. His stance, his brawn, and his swagger all screamed *predator.*

The effect nearly took my breath away. It suffocated courage. I knew Austin wouldn't hurt me, yet my whole body vibrated with fear. The energy he radiated felt dangerous. Deadly, even.

I desperately wanted to get out of there.

But *out of there* was a strange world where a woman could change into a rat.

Instead, I put my hand on his arm, needing the solidity of touch (since I didn't have a Xanax).

His large bicep popped under my palm. He wrapped his arm around me and drew me in protectively. Donna, clearly feeling the same pressure I had, remained behind the counter but took a couple of halting steps to the side, behind Austin. She clearly craved the same comfort I did.

The younger guy stiffened. Then his spine gradually bowed.

"Whatever, bro," the guy said. He snatched his phone off the counter. "Service was slow, anyway."

He turned and walked toward the door, leaving the girl behind. She flashed Donna an apologetic glance before following the guy out of the tasting room, only pausing to open the door the guy had let close in her face.

As though pricked with a needle, the pressure in the room instantly dissolved. Austin released his arm from around me and leaned against the counter, all ease and good humor.

"What in the hell," I said, my breath exiting me in a whoosh.

Donna let out a shaky breath as well, smiling through it. "And that is why you could've been alpha of any pack you wanted." She chuckled to herself. "No alpha I've encountered could do that so effectively. You barely needed to posture."

"Ah." I wiped the hair out of my face with a shaking hand. "So this is where your connection to the animal kingdom comes in handy, is it? Scaring douches?"

I belatedly noticed Austin's mood had darkened with Donna's comment. He reached for the scotch. "It is an effective way to scare douches, yes."

"Right. Where were we?" Donna touched two of the bottles.

"At the one that tastes better," I said.

She smiled and picked the second, once again pouring a taste for me and a glass for Austin.

"Okay." I took a very deep breath, remembering what Austin had said about keeping an open mind. Then pulling up the many, *many* books I'd read in the fantasy genre. And the fairytales I knew. And the folklore. Turned out, I had a lot to work with. "Werethings. Shifters. Uncrowned alpha—that makes sense now. Why don't you have a pack, then?" I swirled the wine in the glass. Pushing his scotch aside, he watched what I was doing and then picked up his wine glass and emulated it. For a bar owner, he hadn't bothered to learn much about wine.

"I thought this town was a better use of my talents," he said, and I noticed Donna looking down and tightening her lips. There was clearly more to Austin's story, but based on his quickly deteriorating mood, he wasn't keen on sharing.

"And what talents do you bring?" I asked, tasting my wine...and was immediately distracted. I nodded and looked over at him, motioning for him to taste. After he sipped, I said, "Well? How does it taste?"

He looked at it for a moment, then shrugged. "Like wine."

"Better or worse than what you have in your bar?"

"Better, definitely. Also more expensive."

"People will pay, trust me. They will pay for good wine, especially if they came to this area to wine taste. They'll expect to pay, and they'll expect good wine."

"They'll also be Dicks and Janes and I don't need them in my bar," he replied.

"Magical people don't indulge in wine tasting?" I asked. I pointed at Donna. "They work in tasting rooms. You don't think they like wine?"

He sighed, entirely put out. "Yes, fine, they do visit. And they do drink wine. There, happy? You're right, I'm wrong. That good?"

"It's good to see you smiling for once, alpha," Donna said, eying him hungrily.

"I'm not your alpha."

"Yes, sir." She bit her lip and busied herself behind

229

the counter.

"Not to make light of the smiling thing, because you are much hotter when you smile and you should definitely do it more, as she said, but yes, I am always right, and of course that makes me happy."

He leaned a little heavier on the counter. "In answer to your question, my talents lie in making sure the people of this town stay safe. I don't need a pack for that. I provide a sanctuary for those who don't really fit anywhere else. Yes, the town has some oddity to it, but the people here are just trying to live a quiet life. I am letting them."

"Because magical people...don't like people doing their own thing?" I asked, trying to piece this together.

"Certain magical people can do their own thing, sure. But some don't have the power to do so. Donna was trapped in a pack with a beta—the second in charge—who was giving her unwanted attention. She didn't feel safe and the alpha wasn't handling it because she was different. The beta wouldn't let her leave. I made him see reason."

"You went and got her?"

"No. She made it to my territory and I stood in the beta's way. The beta tried to push the issue, and I gave him a better option."

"What option was that?"

"To leave peacefully," he said, getting another glass of wine.

Donna barked out a laugh, spraying spit everywhere. "Sorry," she said, hurrying to wipe it up.

"What am I missing?" I asked.

Austin swirled his wine.

"It was only peaceful after he ripped the beta's tail off and permanently crippled his hind leg," Donna said. "Which is not easy to do with a shifter. We can heal almost everything."

"Wow. And...you don't get in trouble for that? No one calls the cops?" I asked.

Austin straightened up as though he were stretching his back. Donna, on the brink of answering, tightened her lips instead.

"The magical world is...complicated. The slice of government that keeps knowledge of us secret also makes sure local police don't get involved in certain magical issues. For that, we have territories. Each territory, large and small, is ruled by a magical group, like shifters or a hierarchy of mages. Most of the territories are fair and actually leave most of the law enforcement to the Dicks and Janes. It's easier, cheaper, and let's be honest, the slice of government that is supposed to be working for us is still government—it has its inefficiencies and bureaucracy problems. It has become more effective to let the Dick and Jane laws be our guiding light. But for some things purely magical, like shifters fighting for placement within the pack, for example, the territory leaders govern. And if those leaders are less than savory…well then, things can be dicey for the justice within that territory. It's sad but true."

"So what do you do if a magical situation gets out of hand but the…Dick and Jane government don't step in?" I asked, a memory of a man in a cape feathering my mind. It wasn't Mr. Tom. "Who do you turn to?"

"Here…it's me," Austin said. "Police in this town have very little to do. They usually only deal with Dicks. I take care of the rest. I'd like to think I'm fair and equal."

Donna nodded adamantly. "Fairer than the law, easily. Because the law is upheld by those with prejudices. Austin Steele doesn't give a crap who you are—if you cross the line, you'll have to deal with him." Lust sparked in her eyes. She busied herself with another bottle. "Virtually no one crosses the line anymore."

"No," Austin said, but he didn't say it with pride. It was said in reflection as he strummed the stem of his glass.

"It's cool that people have such faith in you," I said, nudging him with my knuckles.

"And that is my dilemma with you, Jacinta. That is why I wanted you to fail—might still want it." He must've seen something on my face because he held up a hand. "Remember that I don't mean fail at life. At present, I am keeping this town safe. I am enough. But there are people out there who are more powerful than I am. More vicious than I could ever be. For *the moment*, they don't care about this small town. We're nothing to them. If nothing changes, this town will remain safe as long as I'm able to protect it."

"And this is where I come in," I said.

"This is where you come in." He nodded. "I mentioned Tamara Ivy. She was an incredible sorceress. Her magic was exceptional, or so the records indicate. Powerful beyond compare. Robust and diverse. Very few magical people have ever possessed magic such as hers."

"And that's the magic you're saying she put into the house?" I amazed myself that I was only sweating a little bit as I tried to keep up with these completely fanciful ideas. It was easy if you pretended you were talking about a movie you watched, or a book you were reading. I wondered when my grip on reality would wobble.

"Yes. That is the highly sought after magic that was transferred to the house. Only the one selected by the house can wield the magic, but there are powerful people out there with candied words and an affinity for manipulation. They may not be able to wield the magic themselves, but they could wield the magic holder. They can direct the magic, so to speak. Or so rumor has it."

"And you said somehow...the magic leaves the house and...gets into another person? An heir?"

"Yes. Oftentimes the ability to receive the magic travels within the female family line. It usually skips a generation or two. Whoever has the ability to receive the magic becomes the master of Ivy House."

"So Auntie—Peggy Havercamp has the magic?"

"No," he said, pouring himself a full glass from the next bottle and a taste for me. It struck me that we should just head to the bar. This wasn't really a tasting anymore—it was a mind-bender. "She thought she'd get the ability to receive the magic, since an heir hasn't been selected in...three generations, I think. Maybe four, I can't remember. Three hundred years or so, I believe. But the house did not choose her."

I wiped my hand down my face. "So even if a Havercamp girl is born with the ability to get the magic from the house, she still has to be chosen?"

"They're one and the same. Or, at least, they were thought to be. A girl child is born with the ability to receive the magic, and this birthright is usually why the house chooses her. When the house chooses, it imparts the magic."

"Right," I said, drawing the word out. "So Peggy wasn't it. She had a brother, who couldn't be the heir. What about Diana?" My face lost color. "It's Diana, isn't it? She's the one!"

He shook his head, his focus acute. "Diana was taken to the house, I've been told. She thought it was a nightmare, right? The house should feel like home. She isn't the one."

"So then…" I stared at him.

He stared back.

I shook my head.

He nodded.

"Can't be me." I shook my head harder, as if that would be the deciding factor. "Can't be. I have my dad's salty nature and his bubble butt, among other things. I'm definitely his kid—my mom didn't have any indiscretions. I'm not part of the Havercamp family."

"This wouldn't be the first time the house chose someone not of the current family lineage. Usually it chooses someone magical, but…" He shrugged. "Looks like you fit the bill."

CHAPTER 20

AUSTIN'S GUT TWISTED as tears started in Jess's eyes. None of this was fair. She'd left a hard patch in life looking for a fresh start, only to land right back in the stink. His heart went out to her.

He'd thought long and hard about this situation, sleeping very little last night and this morning as he mulled it over. Much of what Niamh had said was right on the money. His head might've said he was better than ever, but his body told a different story. He wasn't as vicious as he'd been, preferring to maim instead of kill, or avoid the fight all together. He wasn't as fast, and while he was every bit as strong or stronger, he didn't bounce back from injuries like he once had. He was sore for days instead of hours.

Age hadn't stolen his vitality, but he wouldn't live forever. Eventually he'd need to pass on this mantle, and he'd find out there was no one to pass it to. No one strong enough, at any rate. Guys like him usually headed up a pack.

That said, he still had a solid ten years and probably a lot more. His kind didn't live as long as Niamh's kind, or Edgar's or Earl's, but he would live longer than a human, and he'd stay fit well into his fifties or sixties. By the time he had to retire, or a stronger enemy tucked him into his grave, most of the people he'd offered to protect would have long since been forgotten by their pursuers. They'd be fine. Safe and obscure.

Unless Ivy House went active again.

"But the house didn't choose me," Jess said, her eyes pleading for the comfort of the life she used to know. That life was gone. This was her new reality—magic. Possibly danger, if last night was any indication.

He took a shot of the scotch. He needed it. The wine wasn't having much of an effect.

"Now we come to what I said about you failing," Austin said. "Ivy House is coming alive with you in it. Mr. Tom—" He grimaced and shook his head. "Now you have me calling him that. *Earl* said you have been increasingly transfixed by the moving carvings. Those carvings don't move for me. The house has already shown you how to access the passageways. I've been in there many times, actively *looking* for the passageways. I even know roughly where one is located. I still couldn't find it. The master bedroom chose you. The orb won't reveal a room you are in. These are all signs."

Jess stared with her mouth hanging open. She was struck mute.

"Now, the house still might not choose you," he said. "I can't say for sure, but it is certainly leaning your way."

"So then...what happens if I get this magic? Why would you want me to fail?"

"If you got that magic, all the seedy characters I mentioned would be drawn to this town. Suddenly O'Briens would be on the map again in the worst way possible. Powerful players in the magical world would want you to rule by their side. They'd want to harness your power for their own gain. They'd want you to have their children—"

She snorted. "They can go screw themselves if they want that. I'm done-skies."

"You're only forty, you—"

She slapped his face, clearly on impulse. He froze, not having expected it. She was a Jane—catching him off guard like that shouldn't have been possible for her.

Donna's eyes widened and a smile blossomed on her face.

"I am so sorry," Jess said immediately. "I didn't mean to do that. But don't you dare jinx me. I've already raised my son. The last thing I need right now is a baby. Nice guy, scary evil magical guy—all nopes."

His posture shifted, mimicking the body language he'd used to send the Dick and Jane couple away. His posturing wiped the smile off of Donna's face. But Jess didn't seem to notice. She was, essentially, calling his bluff.

Which was made evident when she said, "I'm not an animal, and if you hit me, they'll put you in prison. I'll make sure of it."

Donna spit out a laugh. "Sorry," she said, wiping the counter for a second time.

"They will court you," Austin said. He needed her to take this seriously; they all did. "They will try to promise you the world, and they'll have the means to deliver. I will not be able to stop these people from invading this town. I will not be able to protect it from the magical elite, who never take on a situation alone. Even last night—those grunts came in a pair."

Her brow furrowed and her eyes started to blink. She looked down in confusion. That must've been the memories from last night resurfacing. Agnes hadn't wanted to give her the potion, thinking it would endanger her in the long run. He'd taken her point. Jess needed to know what was coming her way, and those kidnappers were a portent of what was in store for her if she was chosen. But Austin and the others had also needed time to explain everything.

The compromise had been a potion that temporarily created forgetfulness. Like temporary amnesia, it would allow the memories to come bursting forth when the event was triggered in her mind.

He'd just triggered it.

"Wait…" She held her head in her hand for a moment. Her wide eyes came back to rest on him, amber wrapped in thick black lashes, incredibly intoxicating.

"About last night…" He explained about the potion and Agnes, whom she seemed to know from Earl.

"So…basically, I'm in danger until I get that magic, because the magic will allow me to protect myself. But if I do get it, I'll endanger the whole town?" she asked, frustration and anger burning hot in her eyes. "That about right?"

"Afraid so," he said, his heart sinking further.

She shook her head, her eyes sparkling with intelligence. "But won't I be able to protect the whole town with that magic? Assuming, of course, it comes with an instruction manual."

"That's what I was wondering, too, if I'm being honest," Donna murmured.

"I don't think you have any idea what kind of offers your new suitors will throw at you. Business deals or marriage proposals, they'll do whatever it takes to get you. While they are trying, they'll declare war on each other—a war that will be unleashed here in town. They'll take out any innocents who get in the way, by accident or on purpose. If you leave, they'll still bombard the house, trying to destroy it so as to destroy you. It'll be mayhem. A war zone. It won't be somewhere decent folk want to live."

A silent beat passed as Jess took that in. She shivered for some reason, a full-body shiver, and then she leaned toward him, her eyes a little crazy.

"First of all, I'm not twenty anymore. I'm not a naive little chick who thinks of nothing but love and marriage and consents to *I do* because she's afraid no one else will want her if she says no. Right now, on the other side of that naive girl, I don't give two craps if no one else wants me. *I* want me, my friends want me, and that's plenty. So those anonymous magical people can shove their marriage proposals up their butts. I've been to that circus and I've seen all the clowns. I'm in no hurry to go back."

"Yes, but—"

"No." She held up her hand and her eyes sparked fire. It felt like she was tugging an invisible wire right down to his groin. It was not a welcome feeling. Not in their situation. "You've had your turn to speak. Now it is my turn."

Donna poured her a little more wine. Although she

wasn't smiling, her posture was jubilant—she was responding to those sparks in Jess's eyes, to her tone and demeanor. The call of the hunt was in this woman, Austin felt it too. He wanted to soak it in. Bring her somewhere secluded so he could explore it further.

Ivy House was interested in Jess for a reason.

"Second," Jess continued, "I chose this place as my home. I haven't lived in that house long, and Mr. Tom is definitely a nutter, but I love it. I'll live there for as long as I can. If this magic is super powerful, as you say—and, for the record, I'm having a hard time believing any of this—then we can work together to keep this town safe. We can keep it small, keep it quaint, and keep it weird. Maybe not *as* weird, but I'm willing to compromise."

"Girl, you are all kinds of awesome." Donna offered Jess a fist bump. "Life goals right here."

Austin didn't know what to say. He couldn't deny Jess had great points. There were holes in his argument, but one thing was obvious. It would be more dangerous for all of them, Jess included, if she hung around *without* claiming the magic.

It struck him that perhaps the old guard was right. Maybe he was wary about losing his place as the biggest, baddest guy in town. Except the new dawn would not belong to some young, upstart alpha, but to a middle-aged woman setting out to conquer the world.

She would do it, too. Austin could see it in her confident bearing and the determined set to her jaw. In the electric sparks lighting up her beautiful amber eyes. She would re-write her story, and this time, she'd get it exactly how she wanted it.

Fuck, but Austin wanted to be there for that. He could not deny it. He wanted to witness the glory of her accomplishments. The pride of a comeback story. And then he'd throw her a sweaty after party, where he would prove his prowess to her in a mess of twisted sheets.

"Donna, get out," he said, his whole body clenching in his effort to cut those thoughts short. Her story was not his. Her journey was not entwined with his. He had to maintain his distance. He'd found his calling. His second chance had already been used up. "Out of earshot."

"Yes, alpha."

"I am not your alpha."

"Yes, Austin Steele."

"I'm not magical. I'll call the cops if you get handsy," Jess said, uncertainty peeking through her determination.

When Donna was gone, he allowed himself to slouch. "You continually make me take a harder look at myself and my surroundings." He blew out a breath and poured himself more Scotch.

"Sorry," she said. "When I came here, I wasn't looking for any of this. I saw this as a rest stop until I could figure out what to do next."

"Instead you got another circus. Look, I'm not going to tell you what to do. I've given you all the information I have. You seem like a smart lady and this is your life. You'll do what you need to. I just ask that you remember the town. The people here are good people. They deserve a fair shake, like you do."

"And you? You don't deserve a fair shake?" she asked.

"I'm not worried about me."

"Maybe you should be." She dropped her hand onto his, her eyes open and supportive. The frost locking up his heart thawed a little.

He pulled his hand away. "And there's one more thing you should know."

"Ugh!" She dropped her head onto her arm, resting on the counter. "No more. *Please* no more."

"No one can help you get that magic from Ivy House. No one can tell you how."

When she looked up, it was in the direction of Ivy House. Her eyes turned distant. Her teeth snagged on her plump lower lip. "I think I know how. It would just be a question of finding my way back there when or if the time comes."

CHAPTER 21

THE WHIRLING OF my mind only slightly dulled by the non-conventional tasting, I emerged from the tasting room back into the glorious sunshine. Colorful crystals pulsed in my memory from when I was a kid, pulling at me. Diana pulling me away.

"Why would it choose me and not Diana?" I asked as Austin stepped up behind me.

His touch on the small of my back was slight and his movements coaxed me forward without words. We sauntered down the street, the world at our beck and call.

Or so it seemed. There was nothing quite like afternoon drinking for a good time.

"I suspect this means the legends about the genetic component to the magic aren't strictly true," Austin said, bumping into me slightly. The scotch or the wine was starting to work. "If they were, a non-magical person from a completely different lineage wouldn't awaken the house." He shook his head at the next tasting room we reached. "I hate that guy's voice. I would sooner eat glass than listen to him drone on about wine."

I laughed as we continued on.

"It seems like the house found something in you that it had been looking for in the Havercamp heirs," he said. "There was a quality in you it craved. So it traded up."

"Lord knows what that quality might be."

He looked down on me as we stopped at the corner, waiting for a few cars to roll past.

"Courage, confidence, a desire for adventure, quick wit, steadfast, trustworthy, loyal… I mean, take your pick."

My face flamed hot. "Boy have I got you fooled."

"Nah. I was just making all that up so you'd feel good about yourself."

"Oh well, thanks a million, man."

He put his hand on the small of my back again as we crossed the street, guiding me. It was almost like he thought I'd randomly decide to go sprinting into oncoming traffic.

Wouldn't have mattered if I did, though. There was no oncoming traffic. The pace in this place was slow and tranquil. No one was in a hurry. Time didn't compress until you felt like you were always in a race.

The difference was welcome. I felt like my shoulders were looser, my blood pressure lower.

"There sure are a lot of tasting rooms for a town this size," I said as we got to the other side of the street. They dotted our path.

"It brings in a lot of tourism. It's good for the town, though the tourists are mostly pompous old fuddy-duddies or obnoxious twenty-somethings. I try to avoid this strip in the tourist season."

"Are we in tourist season? Must be, right, because October is harvest?"

"Correct. Add smart and insightful to that list."

"I hope you're not trying to get me to list your per-sonality wins. I'm still struggling to find any."

"You're intent on boosting my ego, huh?" His crooked grin was back. This guy didn't need my help to bolster his confidence—he knew exactly what he was good at, and based on the way other people in town reacted to him, he was dead right.

We passed a small alleyway with baskets of flowers hanging on the sides of the buildings, no dodgy streams of murky water and not one piece of litter. This defi-nitely wasn't L.A..

Standing against the wall, halfway down the alley, stood Mr. Tom. He wore a trench coat, bowler cap, and a pair of circular Harry Potter glasses. His arms hugged his sides and he stared straight ahead. It appeared he thought himself either disguised or invisible.

I paused, squinting at him. Austin backed up to see what I was doing.

"Good God," he murmured. Rather than confront Mr. Tom, he immediately shifted his gaze away and kept walking.

Big belly laughs wracked my body. I hurried to catch up, grabbing his arm to steady myself. We stopped in front of the tasting room, and I gulped in air—I'd laughed so hard I'd stopped breathing.

"Part of his magic is blending into buildings, especially stone, and certain types of scenery," Austin said, looking the other way. It seemed like he didn't want to catch Mr. Tom sneaking out of the alleyway after us. That just made me laugh harder. "He's clearly lost the knack. Because what is he thinking?"

"With the trench coat·in eighty-degree weather…"

"And the glasses. What's with the glasses?" He ran his fingers through his hair. "He's lost his touch."

I calmed down a little and wiped my eyes. "You said he was a gremlin?"

"Shall we?" Austin opened the door for me. "Gargoyle," he whispered, following me inside.

A couple of groups were tasting wine, one of them much merrier than the other. The latter group listened to the attendant in polite boredom as he described the wine he was about to pour.

I led Austin to the edge of the counter and looked over the list of available wines to taste.

"I cannot see how his kind inspired the stone carvings on gothic structures," I said, leaning against the counter.

"That's because you haven't seen his other form."

"His other form…" I let the words drift away. It was impossible to think Mr. Tom was cool enough to don another form, let alone one as awesome as a gothic-looking gargoyle.

Before I could ask more about it, the tasting room worker bustled up to us, grabbing a couple of wine glasses as he did so. His eyes widened when his gaze landed on Austin. Immediately, his spine bowed.

"Hello, welcome," the man said, in his fifties with a comb over and a previously pleasant disposition. "Are you here to taste?"

Austin looked at me, waiting for me to take the lead again.

"Yes. Do we just go down the list or…do we pick and choose?" I tapped the paper.

The man wet his lips, his eyes flicking to Austin. "Of course, yes, down the list. Right away. Actually…" He held up a finger, his gaze flicking to Austin again. "Let me go ahead and open some different bottles. We have better bottles than… Just hang on, if you would."

He hustled into the back without a word to anyone else.

"Should we be worried that he's acting strangely?" I whispered, watching the pourer disappear. "I'm all for the preferential treatment, but that seemed…suspicious."

"Jesus. Don't look behind you," Austin mumbled.

But of course I couldn't help it.

Mr. Tom stood at the edge of the front window, the collar of his trench coat popped to cover half of his face. His wire-rimmed glasses had been swapped for dark shades.

"Are we in danger?" I asked, tensing.

"Because of Earl?" He shook his head, now clearly incredulous. "No. That's part of his nature. Gargoyles are extremely protective of those in their charge. He has clearly decided *you* are in his charge, and even though I'm all the protection you need, he's providing fairly odd and obvious backup. I think being fired from that butler job addled his brain. I really do. I don't think age can take all the blame for this one. He's gone fruit loops."

"No, not that—" I had to pause as laughter bubbled up through me. "What's the deal with that guy suddenly acting all sketchy and taking off when he's got people to wait on? Is he…a Dick? Is that why Mr. Tom thinks I need backup? Because it seems like you set that guy off."

"Oh that." Austin rested an elbow on the counter, angling toward me. "I make him nervous. He's a Dick, yes, but he feels the alpha in me. He realizes I'm the more dominant male, and it makes him uncomfortable because he's supposed to be the one with authority here and I'm pulling rank."

"But how'd you pull rank?"

"By showing up."

I narrowed my eyes at him. "No wonder you're so strong—you have to carry around that enormous ego."

His lips quirked into a grin and he shrugged. "I'm just telling it like it is."

"If you're so alpha, then why don't you assume the title?"

His smile dripped away. The tasting room attendant hurried in carrying four bottles. He set them all down as Austin straightened up. The rest of the patrons were glancing over impatiently, their glasses empty.

"Why don't you just pour us a glass for now and see to the others," Austin said.

There wasn't a hint of command in his voice. His body was relaxed, his tone easy. Even still, the man nodded as though he'd been barked at. He grabbed a bottle marked reserved and poured us each a glass to sip.

"I'll be right back." He hurried away to attend to the others.

"You need a pack to be the alpha of," he said quietly, and I could hear emotion riding his words.

"How do you get a pack?"

"Take one over by force or find a mate and assemble one."

"Going by everything I've seen and heard, you could do all of the above, including find a mate. You're still hot and guys can produce children until they're seventy—you're all set. So what's the real reason?"

Silence met my question for a good few beats, and I wondered if he would answer this time. Finally, he straightened up and turned to me, his expression uncomfortable. His raw intensity beat a drum inside my chest.

"I don't usually talk about this," he said with resolution, "but given this is a unique situation, and if you invite people into this town I'll have to combat..."

"I mean, it's not like I'm going to send out save the dates or anything. None of this is my idea."

He sighed and moved a little closer, lowering his voice to a deep hum. "I had a mate picked out. A long time ago. She wanted an alpha. She wanted power and strength—a man who threw his weight around and made everyone quail in his presence. She wanted the prestige of being with the man every woman wanted and every man—shifter male, I mean—wanted to be. I was young and stupid and she was older. Not much older, but enough to know my potential. Enough to…steer me in the direction she wanted." He shook his head and took a big sip of his wine. "I was a fool. A dangerous fool. I put a man in the hospital for flirting with her—"

"For flirting with her?"

"She knew how to bring out the qualities of an alpha that are less than savory. When she worked her way through a party, touching men intimately, laughing suggestively…" He gritted his teeth and fire sparked in his eyes. Even after all this time, the memories clearly still got to him. "It set me on edge. My natural posses siveness turned to rage-filled jealousy. I tore men off of her and beat them senseless. I threw them across rooms. I upended tables. Destiny liked to see me fight over her. Defend her honor. And I did. Every time. And every time, I won. Even at twenty, I did not lose, just like my dead-beat father, who'd left us when I was young, may the devil keep his soul."

He rubbed his hand on the back of his neck, struggling with his emotions.

"Just checking in, miss," Mr. Tom said, popping his head through the door, his hat, trench coat, and glasses removed. His expression was wary. He must've seen the change in Austin. "Everything okay? Day going well, I trust? How's the wine? Good enough to attract all these infernal tourists?"

"I'm good, Mr. Tom, thank you."

"Call me Tom, please. I'll be around, should you need me."

"You can head home, Mr.—Tom. I'm fine."

"Yes, miss. And oh, Niamh mentioned that she is anxious to have a drink with you later. She'll be sitting on her usual bar stool like some derelict lush who has nothing left to live for."

"Got it. Thanks."

He nodded, closed the door, reapplied his coat and accessories in full sight of everyone, and resumed his post in the window.

"What would he even do if I did need help?" I asked as I ran my hand down my face. "Niamh at least throws rocks."

"In his prime, he would've transformed into a winged, muscled, foul-mouthed powerhouse capable of mowing down any enemy that dared to threaten you. Age has not been kind to him. When you hang up your gloves to be a butler, or watch an old house, you're in the twilight of your life."

I turned slowly to stare at the old, withered man in the window, his face drawn and his back bowed with age. I could not imagine him doing any of those things. Then again, Donna—fun, lovely Donna—turned into a big rat. What did I know?

"So what happened?" I asked Austin. "Why did you leave your home town?"

"With Destiny on my arm, I became a nightmare. Guys like me—like I was—would normally be subdued by the alpha of the pack. The alpha would force the young shifter to see reason. Force him to submit. But my older brother, the alpha, had inherited my mom's smaller, weaker animal form. He'd also inherited her soft way, her balanced nature. Those were the very things that made him an exceptional alpha. Someone who helped the pack thrive. It was his job to subdue me, and he tried. He did try.

"But at that point, I was ready to take the alpha role for myself. Rise and take what's yours—that's what Destiny always told me. She'd sex me up really good, or tease me, then whisper those words in my ear, over and over. Rise and take what's yours, Austin. It's your natural given right—*take it.*

"My brother—ten years older—had tried to get me to see reason many times, but he'd always done it as family. This time—the last time—he came at me as my alpha, which was his right…" Austin blew out a shaking breath. "I would've killed him. I nearly did kill him. I was"—he put his thumb and finger close together—"*this close* to ending his life. To creating a widow and taking a daddy away from two adorable children."

"What pulled you back?"

"My niece. She wasn't supposed to be in the room when my brother challenged me, but she burst in at the last minute. She was wondering why no one would help her daddy fight off her crazy uncle Auzzie. As I was coming down with the killing strike, she managed to evade all the adults and lay herself over her father, protecting him with her body."

Tears clouded my vision and I held my breath.

"I will never forget, to this day, seeing her wheat-colored hair glistening with her father's blood as she turned up her little cherub face to me in defiance. Her little expression was screwed up in anger and courage. That little girl defied my strength and power to stand up for what was right, something no other adult man or woman would dare to try."

His eyes misted and he bowed his head over his forearms. He took a deep breath.

"I backed off," he continued. "I backpedaled, fell to my knees, and submitted. Destiny called me a coward.

She spat on me. But the image of little Aurora standing up for her daddy..." He shook his head. "What kind of monster had I become?" He huffed. "Scratch that. I knew exactly what kind. I'd become my father. And the realization sickened me. I begged my brother to let me stay so I could learn from him. I told him that when he started to feel I was usurping his authority, I would leave.

"He wouldn't have asked me to go. He thought I was good for the pack. He would have sacrificed everything for his people, including his position. He certainly wouldn't have fought me. I'd only grown stronger and better. Five years later, after he'd taught me everything I needed to know to be a good leader, neither of us could ignore the pack's shifting allegiance. I walked away. I left my family, my friends... It was the hardest decision I've ever had to make, but I do not regret it."

"But why not start up somewhere else?"

"Because I am still that monster I was twenty years ago. I am still filled with raw, uncontrollable rage, I just keep it on a very tight leash. I rule my emotions with my logic, avoid my heart entirely, and only let the beast out when I have no other choice. I do not trust myself to assume control of a pack, because if I should lose myself, no one would be able to tear me down. No one would be able to stop me."

He reached over the bar and grabbed the bottle to refill his glass. He topped up mine, as well, though it was only halfway down.

"And a mate?" I asked.

"I enjoy relations with women, but I do not allow them—or myself—intimacy. I don't let anyone close enough to love."

"Is it because you're afraid you'll club them and drag them back to your cave by their hair?"

He sputtered into his wine and then pulled the glass away. He beat on his chest, coughing. I pounded on his back.

"You belong in that house. You're just as cracked as your butler," he wheezed.

"You were having a touching, tear-soaked moment. I wanted to ruin it for you."

He wiped off his mouth with the back of his hand and laughed. "Thank you, yes. Good looking out. Me man. Me no like emotion."

"That's your caveman voice, I take it?"

"Yup." He quieted. "In answer to your question, no, it isn't the woman I'd club. I am afraid of what I'd do if she flirted or laughed with another man. That possessive quality doesn't just go away. It's in there. That's the only reason Destiny was able to pull it out."

His haunted expression crushed my heart. His worry that he was still off-kilter, that he was untrustworthy in the most basic of ways, threatened to bring tears to my eyes.

"Yeah, but…" I spread my hands, straightening up. "You're not a dingleberry twenty-year-old guy anymore. Those idiots are ruled by their hormones, everyone knows that. Guys your age have actually reached maturity and can therefore be trusted a little more. As long as they're good guys, I mean. And whatever you were like back then, Austin, you are a good guy. Doesn't matter who your dad is. I mean look, my dad is a real asshole sometimes. Who has two thumbs and takes after her father?" I pointed my thumbs at myself. "This girl. But you don't see me crying that I have a short temper and a gift for chasing people away, do you? No, you do not. And do you know why?"

He stared at me with a bewildered expression.

"Because I cry about it alone in a dark closet with wine and chocolate. So…" I smiled at him, hoping I had lightened the mood just a little.

A guy a little down the way looked over, clearly eavesdropping.

Austin turned his body the slightest bit, giving the guy a quick stare. The man started, lowered his brow, hunched, grabbed his wine, said "Dude," and scooched down the bar. In that order.

"Your monster qualities can be helpful, though, you have to own that," I said. "You can clear the room."

"What can I do that a fart can't?"

"Oh my God!" I burst into laughter. "Gross." I smiled and bumped his shoulder with mine. "Just don't be so focused on the bad that you miss the good. You made this town a haven where people who don't belong anywhere else can feel safe. You're providing that safety for them. You had a troubled spot in the past, but you took responsibility for it, and you made yourself better because of it. Now you are in a position of power, and you're using your strengths selflessly. You won't even allow yourself the title of the job you are clearly doing. That's a damn good man in any book you look in…the very *best* guy. So be proud of that. Be proud of who you are, and don't let the past negatively color your future."

His eyes were intent as they beheld me. His gaze drifted down my face before settling on my lips. His intensity whispered across my skin, every bit as raw and dangerous as he'd claimed. I felt helpless within his magnetism. I wanted to reach out and touch the thick cords of muscle running his length. To taste those full lips. To let those large hands explore me while I basked in his safety and protection.

I knew what Destiny from his past must've been thinking. How exciting it would be to have a man who was ferocious and lethal to everyone else melt against you in the small hours of the night. To know your man would keep you in a cocoon of safety, protected from all of life's demons, and would tear down the world to keep you there. Something about that spoke to the parts of me that were distinctly feminine.

But that man was a menace, as Austin had found out the hard way. And even if he wasn't, life with that guy would get dull. You'd have to stand around and wait while he crushed heads, *yet again*. You'd have to keep a stock of Get Well Soon cards and your hand would absolutely ache from writing apology letters. Watching a movie in the theater? Forget it. He'd have the whole place in a riot. He'd be a royal nuisance.

Austin had so much more to give than some numb-skull barbarian. He was funny and witty and so much fun. He was caring and steadfast. Welcoming to strangers. I loved seeing his eyes glitter when he was trying to hold back a smile. Or his focused expression when his mind churned, taking in new information.

"Destiny had half a man," I said, my lips tingling as his intense gaze rooted to them. "Not the bad half or the good half, just half of a man. I think you needed a hard lesson so you could see the darkness that lives within you. And that's okay. We all have demons. It forced you to find the other half of you—the kind, funny, steadfast, selfless half of you that balances out the whole. You are in the role of alpha, even if your situation here is not traditional. You guide people, protect them, and offer them a home. You lend your strength to the weak. You celebrate their wins. And yes, you unleash your monster on those who would hurt the family you've created. But that's a necessary evil, and these people thank you for it because it is necessary for peace. You've struck the perfect blend, I think. In my opinion, you're the best man you could be because of your past, not despite it. And I'm happy to have met you."

In a rush he stepped toward me, wrapping an arm around my waist and grabbing the back of my neck with the other hand. He pulled me closer and pushed his soft lips against mine.

CHAPTER 22

ELECTRICITY AND ADRENALINE ran my length as though I'd grabbed hold of a live wire. Heat pooled in my core, throbbing. Aching.

I opened my mouth and he tilted his head, deepening the kiss. Trailing his hand from my neck down my back and pulling me in tighter, his strength arousing, my body fitting against his sensuously.

His kiss, scorching hot, turned languid. He sucked in my bottom lip before flitting his tongue with mine playfully. Expertly.

I moaned, utterly lost in the feel of his hard body under my palms. Utterly consumed with the spicy-sweet taste of him, like honey and cinnamon.

He pulled back, breaking away slowly, as though he were savoring the contact. My eyes fluttered, not ready to fully open.

"Sorry," he whispered, his gaze roaming my face. "I think I've just needed to hear that for a very long time. I apologize for crossing the line. I lost my grip on that leash."

I ran my tongue across my tingling lips. "That was a good kiss. I haven't been kissed like that since Robbie Timmons out behind the art bungalow."

"I'm not... I didn't mean... This isn't..."

"No, no." I waved him away and shivered pleasantly. Lava flowed through my veins, so extremely delicious. If he was that good of a kisser, just think what else he was excellent at.

...genuinely satisfying night...

I cleared my throat and turned back to my wine. "Just give me a minute here. My ex was the world's worst kisser. Like...really bad, so we never kissed. I haven't actually kissed someone romantically in...over half my life. I used to love it. I loved making out. Thank you for showing me what I've been missing."

His expression was troubled. Regretful.

"Relax." I took a sip. "I'm happy in the friend zone. I know that wasn't romantic, and I definitely will not try to get in your pants. There is no way in hell I am bumping uglies for the first time after the ex with someone I know. It'll be a stranger, just in case I freak out. But that won't be for a long while. I need a little *me* time."

His lips pulled up into a grin. "*Me* time, as in..."

"Not everything people say is dirty, Karen."

He laughed and finished off his wine. I noticed that the room had cleared and our fearless host stood at the very opposite end of the counter, trying to look anywhere but at us.

"You really have thrown that poor guy for a loop," I said as he signaled for the man to come closer.

"You'll see why in a minute," he murmured, moving away slightly to give me room.

A little tension drained out of me. I hadn't been kidding—I wasn't ready for anything intimate. That kiss had been fantastic—easily one of the best I'd ever had—but I needed a while to figure out who I was in midlife before I jumped into anything, serious or not. I didn't want to lose myself like I had in my marriage and after having a kid. I was finally in a place where I could choose my fate, and I wanted to get it right. I wanted to get *me* right before I brought in anyone else.

It made me feel ten times better that he was on the same page, even if his reasoning made me sad on his behalf.

Turned out the tasting guy was a pompous blow hard who thought the sun that grew the grapes shined out of his ass. He described the wine to the point that I didn't even want to try it anymore. He went over definitions I neither knew nor wanted to know. And if Austin hadn't cut him off by pointing at the new people patiently waiting, the guy would've kept talking my life away until I threw up my hands and walked out.

"See?" Austin said. "He's a know-it-all type that puffs up with any sort of authority, real or imagined. I come in, and he is reminded that he isn't at the top of the food chain and needs to pull back the attitude. Usually I'd cut a spiel like that short—he was trying to impress me—but I wanted you to get the full benefit of his knowledge."

"Yes, and I thank you for that. I'm half brain dead." I savored the wine for a moment. Despite the horrible employee, it was much better than the selection at the last place. "Do you read personality types based on their postures or…"

"Usually I read the type of person based on how they carry themselves, how they act, their movements, large or slight. Guessing at peoples' personalities is more from experience through the years. I can be wrong."

"How often are you wrong?"

"These days, not often."

"Ah. So you had me pegged as soon as I walked in the door."

"You ruined a yearlong perfect record, actually. I think you have some dead skin to shed before you'll become who you are meant to be. You know, if we're doing this insightful, honest thing. Sometimes you act like a wallflower, and sometimes an adventurer bored with this life. I wonder where you'll settle."

I shrugged. I didn't know myself.

"Anyway," he said. "I read people in order to know who might make a play for power. Who might get out of line, and how much work will be required to make them submit."

"So that you stay on the top of the food chain?"

"Yes."

"You'll be really handy when I start dating again, then," I said.

His head snapped toward me. A small crease formed in his brow before he turned back to his wine. "Yes," he said, the word almost like a growl, then took a sip. "Very."

"Don't worry, you'll always be my first kiss in this new life. I will remember it fondly. But a chick has gotta fly, man."

He huffed out a laugh. "I would never dream of clipping your wings."

"Except for the whole—don't let the magic endanger the whole town thing."

"Right, yes. Except for that."

"And if I get that magic and become…more powerful than you?" The woman down the counter glanced over. I gestured between Austin and me. "Role playing. He's really into Ren Fairs."

Austin let the silence linger for a moment. "I do not honestly know, Jess, and that's the truth. It might be a problem for my animal. For me. I crave dominance. My beast side will fight for that privilege. Has fought for it, every time someone tries to barge into this little safe haven. I can tolerate being around someone more powerful than me—that's not the problem. I will not tolerate someone trying to rule me. I cannot, even if it is you."

I put my hands up and noticed the woman down the way openly staring at Austin, lust burning brightly in her eyes. The guys were pretending he didn't exist.

"Tone it down there, slugger," I murmured. "You're making everyone nervous. Can you pour the next one?"

"Yeah, sorry." He reached down and grabbed a bottle at random. The worker looked over, and then looked away. He didn't plan to interfere.

"So if I were more powerful," I said as he filled my glass, "but didn't try to boss you around, you'd still be my friend?"

He looked at me for a long time, his expression unreadable. "I don't have friends."

"Not even Mr. Tom?"

He barked out laughter. "I don't have friends because I'm the alpha figure. Not many people warm up to me."

"Except your night-time relations."

"I actually have to warm them up."

"I doubt they need it. Well, if Mr. Tom can spare you, will you have a problem with a supremely powerful friend that doesn't try to dominate you?"

"Dominate me in what way?" he asked softly, and the spice in his tone sent shivers racing across my body. Heat pooled in my core again and my lips tingled in remembrance. He shook his head, as though he hadn't meant to say that, and looked away. "Do you always talk this much crap when you drink?"

"Yes. Answer the question."

"No, that won't be a problem. Just don't try to kiss me."

"Oh-ho! Double standards, much?"

His grin was lopsided and adorable. "Let's get out of here."

I looked at all the wine we'd left untried but slung my bag over my shoulder and stepped away without arguing. Old habits died hard.

"I'd like one of each of the bottles we didn't get to," Austin said to the man. "And two glasses."

"You need more than two proper glasses for your bar."

"This is for right now. We'll take this tasting to go."

Warm fuzzies radiated through me. I should've known to trust him. He'd probably read the regret at cutting things short in my body language.

Lord help me if I tried to lie to the guy.

He paid for the wine and attempted to pay for the few glasses we'd "sampled." The tasting attendant wouldn't hear of it. Austin left forty bucks on the bar, tucked the half case under his big arm, and motioned me to get moving.

"There's a creek down the way." He directed us right, walking down the alleyway that had previously held Mr. Tom. "If we get ambushed by one of the most powerful mages that walks this earth, we can float to freedom. Well...I can. You'll be screwed."

"Sir, please, let me help you." Mr. Tom stepped out from his position against the alley wall. I jumped. I hadn't seen him there even though he was still wearing his weird getup!

"Nice work, buddy," I said, and put up my hand for a high five.

He stared at my palm in confusion. "Is that some sort of sign language?"

"Thanks." Austin handed off the box, then paused. "I forgot a corkscrew."

"No problem, sir. I will be right back with it." Mr.

Tom hurried away, his cape fluttering behind him.

"And see if they have any nibbles," I called after him. I put a hand to my stomach and turned back to Austin. "I'm hungry. Did you see him there?"

Austin motioned for us to keep walking. "See him? No, I smelled him. The sun is going down. His magic is strengthening. It's strongest at night."

"So that's what you meant by blending into things?"

"Yes. He blends into stone, concrete, stuff like that. He's at home in the night, too."

"I don't get it. If he's intent on protecting me, he wouldn't leave me alone with you to go get a corkscrew. He's clearly also parenting me. Or sticking with a butler role, I guess, but they don't follow their charges around, do they? Isn't this a bit...off? I mean, even for him."

"I think being left alone in that big house for so long has been very bad for him. I wish I'd known. I would've...I don't know...sent someone to terrorize him or something."

"Why didn't Peggy bring in a caretaker before now? I mean, it's not like I do anything yet, though I think there's a list coming, but she was quick enough to hire me."

"You still don't get it." On the other side of the buildings, we ducked through a small patch of trees and then wound down a narrow path to the stream. We walked along it, the trees cutting out the dying sun. A nearly full moon hung heavy in the darkening sky. "That house doesn't let anyone live there who doesn't belong. Earl is a protector of the house and its magic. So is Niamh. Even Edgar. They have passes to be there. The magic allows them to stay."

"But Auntie Peggy—"

"Wasn't chosen by Ivy House. She is the title holder, nothing more. She can stay there for a few days at a time, just like your friend and the rest of their family, but that's it."

"But you've been there and you aren't a protector."

"I've only been there for a few hours or less at a time."

"This is insane," I said, stumbling. He offered his hand, and I latched on to it as I stumbled again, the lengthening shadows hiding the rocks and pitfalls. "Why me? I just don't get it. I'm not special in any way. I'm the opposite of special. Just...why me?"

"Often we don't see things about ourselves that everyone else finds apparent. Also, I've already told you. I don't like repeating myself." I could hear the laughter in his voice. "Just here."

He pointed to a path that led up to a little bridge. A few moments after we arrived, Mr. Tom arrived. He'd brought the wine and a corkscrew, plus a picnic basket with fruits, nuts, meats, and cheeses. He laid out a little blanket, gave us a couple of pillows, and set about opening the wine. With everything out, he closed up the enormous canvas bag he'd transported everything in.

"How…" I looked at all this stuff, which one person shouldn't have been able to carry, and certainly not so quickly.

"I'll be close, miss, in case…you need anything." He bowed. As he turned away, I heard, "Like mace."

"How…" I stared at the delicious looking spread.

"He gets *much* bigger in his other form," Austin said, grabbing some nuts. "And he probably had it all ready at the house. He clearly knows you never say die when the wine is pouring."

"The house? How could he have…" I stared off in that direction. "I feel like I'm going crazy. Does he have super-human speed, or…?"

Austin gave me a funny look. "He has wings."

I replayed what I thought he'd said. It still didn't compute. "Sorry, what?"

"He has wings. He's a gargoyle."

"No, I heard you about the gargoyle… Where are his wings? Is that his other form?"

He was still giving me a funny look. "It's those things hanging from his back when he's in human form. They go to his mid-thighs? You mentioned them before,

I know you can see them."

"Wait…" My world was spinning. "You mean his cape?"

Understanding flitted across Austin's expression. "Right, yes. You did call it a cape. Sorry. Yes, they look kind of like a cape in this form." He sucked wine directly from the bottle, those very lush, very kissable lips curving over the lip.

"This is crazy. Wings! I mean…flight is freaking *awesome*! He is ten times cooler than I thought."

Austin put down the bottle, then hesitated. "I'm an ass. Sorry, I forgot this was supposed to be a tasting. Do you still… Um… Mr. Tom can probably—"

"It's fine. Just pour it. You've already put your spit in my mouth."

Shadows chiseled out his striking features, a smile tickling his lips. He nodded and poured me a glass.

"Look, Jess, there's something I haven't told you." He nearly drank from the bottle again, but I moved his empty glass closer. "It's cooler from the bottle," he said.

"No, it is not."

"Says the square." He filled his glass. "The Ivy House magic is like a shot of youth, I've heard. Earl would be restored to his prime. Niamh, Edgar. They'd both get a taste from the fountain of youth. As would you."

I stilled in the moment, feeling my mildly aching back, an off-and-on present since I'd had Jimmy. My stiffening knees from sitting on the ground. Thinking of my age spots, light now but coming in strong, my sun damage, my wrinkles. Thinking of all the things that made me *old*. All the things that millions of dollars of advertisements a year told me I needed to fix.

Right now, these marks of age were slight, but they were building in potency.

Tears came to my eyes. Then sobs bubbled up out of nowhere.

Austin pulled me close. "Look, you need to do what's best for you," he said softly. "We'll work it out. We'll find a solution."

I shook my head, feeling stupid. Hating that I felt stupid.

Because the truth was, I didn't want the solution to midlife to be young again. I wanted to be accepted for being my age. I wanted it to be okay for a woman to have wrinkles. Graying hair. A few sagging areas due to child birth and the passing of years.

As a woman excited to start this new chapter, I wanted to feel…normal. Accepted.

But the truth was, I *didn't* feel accepted. I didn't feel acknowledged for my service in raising the next generation, for my active role in the community, or even for being human sometimes. I felt utterly ignored. I felt invisible or, worse, frowned upon. Most of the time, when I looked in the mirror, I saw only my flaws. I saw all the things that advertisements and social media said was *wrong* with me.

I wanted to focus on what was right about this version of myself, like the way I'd learned to take life a little slower and enjoy each moment. Like my appreciation for people's differences, and for beauty found in unlikely places. For my friendships, new and old. I wanted it to be okay that I wasn't worried about beauty anymore, or worried about looking young. I just wanted to look like me, however *me* looked in any given year.

I sighed, wishing Diana were here. I wanted to complain to a girlfriend. But all I had was Austin. So, in a gush I'd totally regret later, I unloaded on him. I told him exactly what I was feeling.

"Heard," he whispered when I was done, rubbing my back. "I feel age, too, if that helps any. Dicks might get to be distinguished when they're older, but shifters become vulnerable. Many magical types are the same way. Edgar was completely pushed out of his clan for being too old. He wasn't wanted anymore. If I get slower, weaker, less agile, then my position is compromised. Many of us do actually know how you feel, but for me it's less about looks and more about ability."

"Isn't that always the case, though? I mean, I know what you're saying, but people tend to judge women on looks even if we're successful. We're not known for what we're good at, we're known for how we look. What we wear."

"I suppose that is true, yes." He fell silent for a moment. "I'm not trying to one-up you, but when you get older, you are ignored. When I get older, I could be killed."

"You're talking about a job that you can retire from. That you can walk away from. I'm talking about my life."

He brushed the hair from my face and gently tucked it behind my ear. His breath dusted my eyelashes. "True again," he murmured, his gaze taking me in. "But at least you're not cracked like your cape-wearing butler."

I spat out a laugh as Mr. Tom cleared his throat somewhere behind us.

"Sorry," I said, running my fingers across his cheek to get any errant spray. "Oh my God, I'm sorry. I didn't see that one coming."

"Now you know how it feels." His soft lips pulled into a smile underneath my touch. He reached up and slowly took my hand away before placing it in my lap and giving me a little space. "You're not invisible, though. I want you to know that. Here, in this town, you are not invisible. I see you. I see you for what you are, and what you're trying to be. I admire you for both. Download that magic, if you want. Get young again. We can figure out the town."

"I don't want youth to be the solution for something I don't think is a problem."

"Then don't grab that magic and own your life choices. Raise your voice until you are heard. Look however you want, be whoever you want, and demand people pay attention to you. Stop taking what you're given, and demand the space in life you want."

I lowered my head, silently crying. He was right on so many levels. I needed to hear this. Over and over, spoken with the assurance and conviction that came so naturally to him. Because I wanted to do it, I just needed a little courage. I needed to feel like I wasn't alone when I stood up for myself.

We let the night softly move in around us. Minutes came and went, yet I didn't feel the need to fill the gap with speech. It was nice, just being able to co-exist for a moment.

But finally my mouth caught up with my brain.

"Those daggers in the house…those were real silver, right?"

"Most. And the spike you were holding," he answered.

"And...the gold? The gems inlaid in the hilts?"

"Unless Earl has been systematically switching out the stones to pay for his clever disguises, all real."

"Wow," I said on a release of breath. "That's... Some of those stones were huge. And all that silver? That's a lot of money. Why wouldn't it be in a safe?"

"That treasure trove is nothing compared to what you'll be offered if you download that magic."

"You keep saying download—am I like...plugging in? Like a cyborg?"

"I don't really know the term to use."

Honestly, it still sounded like fantasyland talk. It probably would until I got more proof. But there was one thing I was sure of.

"Matt—the ex—and I were doing well. I mean, he was doing well. I was mostly taking care of everything in his life, usually at home alone with Jimmy in the evenings while he worked long hours so he could crush it. We as a couple were financially doing great. Emotionally, though, we were bankrupt at the end. I don't want someone else's money. I want their time. Their good moods. Their jokes. Their companionship. I don't want a cupboard full of silver and gold, I just need enough to get by and great people around me."

"Well if you're going to hang with Mr. Tom, you'd better have enough cash for odd disguises."

I bent over, laughing. "Didn't you hear? He said I could call him Tom now. I'm in."

"Unlucky you," Austin said.

Mr. Tom's disembodied voice came out of the growing darkness. "I can hear everything you are saying. I am not amused, just so we are clear."

I laughed harder. "What does it say about my frame of mind that I somehow don't find it strange that an ex-butler is hanging around in the darkness, listening to everything we say?"

"It does not say good things," Austin replied somberly. "I don't think you should go too far down that dark path."

A *harrumph* drifted out of the darkness.

My laughter increased and my world swam pleasantly. But I knew I was on the cusp. Without Niamh to push me over the edge, I was capable of knowing when enough was enough. I was almost there.

"Let's head toward home," I said, finishing my glass of wine. "I don't want to drink too much and do something foolish."

"Like kiss a friend in public?"

"Exactly, yes. I wouldn't want to do something so foolish as that."

Austin stood and helped me up. He squeezed my shoulders, his face nearly covered by shadows now. "I actually had a lot of fun today. Thank you."

"Don't thank me yet, you're walking me home. I don't know what kind of riff-raff we'll meet on my way."

"I mean, I *could,* but I have a series to binge on Netflix, and it's a couple of miles out of my way..." He chuckled and took his hands away. "Of course I'll escort you home."

"Don't worry, I'll have Mr. Tom fly you home after."

"I take my joke back. It was in poor taste. Please don't ever suggest that again. That's not a man I want to share a space bubble with."

"You don't want to kiss that friend, huh?"

"I am still in hearing distance," Mr. Tom called. "And I find this chatter highly insensitive. Like a bunch of crude barbarians carrying on."

The walk home didn't take long, and as the night wrapped around us, I kept looking back for Mr. Tom to see if I could spot him. In town, it was impossible. I never once caught a glimpse. It wasn't until the wood overtook our route that I noticed him, a dark shadow within the cascading moonlight. Slight of form and old of body, he still glided like he was made of air. His cape—no, his wings—fluttered out behind him, and I remembered various times when they'd fluttered without a breeze.

"This is all still blowing my mind," I said into the hush, peering into the deep sheets of black between the somewhat swimming trees. The wine had a tight hold on me. "Like…it is blowing my mind."

"I imagine. Your perception of the world has changed in the space of a day. I didn't know that you would take to the idea so fast."

"I saw a woman turn into a rat. And I have a lot of genre fiction to back that up. It's just…believing my eyes. Believing something like this is real! It is crazy! But let's face it, magic is a much better explanation for the amount of weird that goes on at Ivy House. I constantly half wonder how long it will take me to end up in an unmarked grave."

I thought back to my first visit to O'Briens, back when I was ten. Even then, the house had spoken to me. I'd felt drawn to its dark mysteries.

"I think all kids secretly hope there's some magic curling through reality," I mused. "That if we look hard enough, one day we'll find it. I haven't ever grown out of that. And I did find it, in books mostly, as I said. In daydreams."

"Now you've found it in real life, and I have to be honest, your situation, whatever you decide, is going to be a lot more dangerous than most."

I blew out a breath as Ivy House came into view, the windows glowing like a beacon, welcoming us home. Niamh's rocking chair was empty as we passed her house, but her rock pile was steadily growing. Edgar was nowhere to be seen, and I made a note to find him at his residence, wherever it was, or maybe his labyrinth, just to check in. If I was going to choose this as my new residence, I needed to work harder at establishing the community I so badly desired.

"Well." Austin stopped next to me on the porch, scanning the grounds. "You made it. No boogeymen."

"Do you want to have a glass for the road?" I jerked my head at the door. "No foolishness, don't worry."

"No." He traced the doorframe with his gaze. "The house allowed me to hang around earlier. I don't want to tempt fate."

"Yes. It did allow you to *hang around* earlier," Mr. Tom said, waiting behind us. "Why, I wonder. Now that I am on independent ground, I will say that I was surprised and troubled by that. You overstayed your welcome by some time."

Austin sighed softly, then took a bottle of wine from the box he carried. He handed it to me. "You're going to need this. Call me if there are any problems with the hired help."

He was starting to sound like Niamh. I supposed

Mr. Tom could bring that out in people. "Just the one?"

He didn't grin like I'd expected him to. His face was bathed in shadow, so I couldn't confirm my hunch that his eyes had turned haunted. "One is plenty for you. I'll need...significantly more."

"If you don't mind me saying so, Austin Steele, with the visitors we had last night, and the ones who are likely to come...keeping a focused mind might be the best thing for you," Mr. Tom said.

"I do mind you saying so, actually." He strutted toward Mr. Tom, his shoulders straight and his head held high. Mr. Tom wisely ducked out of the way. "I need a night off."

"Okay, well...just think about it," Mr. Tom called after him.

"Who were those people last night?" I opened the door. "And how can this house force people out? I get that it has magic, kinda, but...well, what could it actually do?"

Mr. Tom shrugged. "I don't know—I've never felt it. I've always felt welcomed. But I've seen plenty of people go running out of here, so there must be some feeling of repulsion. It's very strange that Austin Steele didn't feel it—or maybe he did and didn't want you to see him run like a coward? He's very guarded about how people perceive him—oh bloody... Hurry, get into the house.

That horrible woman is back from the bar. She'll be all curses and put downs. She really is very trying."

Once in the house, he took the wine from me and directed me to the kitchen.

"Are you hungry? Do you want dessert?" he asked.

"No, I'm fine."

He sat me at the small table and poured me a glass of wine before sitting opposite me. "Listen, Miss, Austin Steele is a great man. He has done a lot for this town. He has some very good reasons for wanting to keep the magic confined in Ivy House. But ultimately, he has an agenda. He has created this town as *he* envisioned it. He is an alpha—he can be very shortsighted when it comes to other people's visions. Ivy House is speaking to you. The magic is calling you. It would be a travesty to ignore it."

I stood, suddenly exhausted. "I hear you M—Tom. I understand what you're saying. I think I'll just turn in now."

"Of course. Yes." He stood and bowed. "It has been a big day. Lots of new ideas."

I hesitated as I turned to leave. "Who were those people last night? You never said."

"In Jane terms, those guys worked for one of the major mob bosses. If that boss wants to own this town, there is nothing Austin Steele could do about it."

I SAT AT the table in my room not long afterward, letting the sweet air drift in through the windows, and thought about the situation before me. A situation right out of storybooks.

I felt like I was in my own twisted sort of fairy tale, only instead of the handsome prince, I had a geriatric gargoyle. Despite all the messed-up things afoot, I was pretty sure I'd traded up.

I could become magical!

Which was the part my mind really couldn't compute.

This sort of stuff didn't happen to me. I'd married young and spent the last twenty years being a wife and mother. My idea of a crazy, reckless adventure had been changing towns without a plan.

I blew out a breath, staring out at the labyrinth, the hedge leaves shining in the moonlight as though they'd just been waxed.

If everything I'd been told today was true, I had to assume everyone had an agenda. Austin had seemed genuinely supportive toward the end, but he'd been drinking. Mr. Tom was right—he had a vision for this town, and he wouldn't want to see me tarnish it, no matter how much he'd waxed poetic.

That being said, Mr. Tom wasn't any better. If the magic would act as his fountain of youth, of course he wanted to activate it. Who wouldn't?

Me.

My heart sank, the sentiments I'd shared with Austin rising to the surface, along with his response.

Stop being ignored. Raise your voice until you are heard. Look however you want—be whoever you want—and demand people pay attention to you.

"That easy, huh?" I whispered.

Magic wouldn't solve my problems. Even if it was real and this town wasn't playing an elaborate, special-effects-laden game of "make fun of the tourist," it wouldn't make me feel good about being me. It would make me a different me. How could I stand up to people's prejudices about middle age if I no longer looked middle-aged? Because I knew this was a fight worth having, if not for myself, then for the younger generation.

No matter what happened, I didn't want to forsake who I'd become or the battle it had taken to get there.

I sat there for a while longer, letting the blissful night wash over me. The last thing Mr. Tom said, right before I'd left the kitchen, rolled through my head and sent nervous shivers racing through me.

If that boss wants to own this town, there is nothing Austin Steele could do to stop it.

Hopefully this was all some elaborate joke, because if Austin couldn't stop it…someone would have to.

CHAPTER 23

I AWOKE WITH a jolt, half expecting Mr. Tom to be standing over me like he'd done every other morning. But it wasn't morning.

Deep night blanketed the windows. The room around me lay quiet, the silence stretching into the rest of the house.

A presence prowled the grounds.

I didn't know how I knew, I just did. A stranger tread on the property, someone who didn't belong. Not a kid up to mischief or a drunk night hiker who had taken a wrong turn, either. This intruder had an aura of danger. My absolute conviction sent my heart racing.

I dropped my head to the side where my phone perched in its charging dock. Austin lay through that technological portal, a big bad alpha who liked to secure his territory. He'd made that perfectly clear.

Except, for some reason, this house was not in his territory. That was the impression I'd gotten from his exchanges with Mr. Tom, at any rate. It was like this house was a sovereign nation, an island within the rest of the town.

The cops would help. They didn't have to know about the magical stuff to respond to a prowler.

Right?

I pulled the covers away from my feet.

It was probably wise to check for a prowler before calling anyone. It wasn't likely the police would believe me if I said I *felt* a prowler out there somewhere. They'd think I was cracked. And if they knew what house I was calling from, they'd be sure of it.

My fingertips tingling with fear, I edged over to the windows and looked out across the grounds. Branches lightly swayed in the breeze, their leaves moving like little bells. Moonlight sprinkled the ground.

If there was an intruder, he or she wasn't visible from my window.

I closed my eyes and concentrated, imagining the magic *was* real, and I could use it to sense the location of the intruder. Almost immediately my sixth sense grew, pointing me to the side of the house, coming around the front.

"God, I hope I'm cracking up," I said, my heart lodging in my throat, nearly choking me with fear. "I really hope I'm having a nightmare. Why did I want to head out on an adventure, anyway? I should've just gotten a few cats and stayed put. If someone breaks in here, I wonder if Mr. Tom can use that third story trap door and fly me out of here."

An *ah-ha!* light flashed in my brain. That must've been the purpose for the trap door. An escape route for fliers.

Heart rampaging in my chest and limbs shaking, I hastily put on athletic sweats and stuffed my phone into my zippered pocket. I lightly jogged out the door and down the hall. My muscles screamed in protest, the soreness from my run a couple days ago stiffening my legs.

My knees cracked as I ran up the stairs to the third floor heading to the attic. Stupid old joints. That was one thing I *would* like to fix with a fountain of youth.

In the attic, I grabbed a crossbow and some arrows. While there, I picked up a spear just in case. I had no idea how to use a crossbow, but I did know how to jab someone with a long stick. It would do in a bind.

Heading back down the stairs, my ankles now crackling like pop rocks, I started compiling a checklist for the fountain of youth. By the time I reached the top of the stairwell leading down to the first floor, the presence felt like it was nearing the front door, its fast pace now slowing. Its goal was clearly the front stoop.

Why would a burglar come around to the front?

And if the intruder wasn't a burglar, what were they here for?

Last night flashed through my mind.

"You are able to sense the greater—"

I jumped, started to scream, and clamped a hand over my mouth to stop the sound from escaping. The crossbow thunked against the ground.

"Sorry, didn't mean to scare you, miss," Mr. Tom said from right behind me. He bent to grab the crossbow. "I thought maybe you would've felt me coming. Obviously you couldn't have heard me, what with all your thumping around. You sound like a stampede of giraffes going up and down the stairs."

"Yes, thank you, Mr. Tom," I said dryly, peeking around the corner and down at the front door.

"You can feel the greater surroundings, now, hmm?" he said, leaning over me to peek as well.

I elbowed him to get him off my back, but I was thankful he was there. It was less terrifying to go through a burglar situation with someone else, especially someone who named his weapons.

"I guess. There's someone on the front porch—" I pulled back around the corner as a shadow loomed through the glass at the side of the door. My heart kickstarted, beating frantically. "You locked the front door, right?"

"Yes, but we have nothing to fear. There is just one of them, and Edgar is monitoring him or her. They don't seem to want to do damage of any kind. Not yet."

"What do you mean *not yet*?"

"If we're living for the present, we have nothing to fear. If we are worrying about the future, this could be a bad omen."

"How do you know?"

"Because I know who we are dealing with, I know what we are dealing with, and if you mix all the ingredients together, it's a recipe for disaster. But rest assured, right this moment we'll be just fine."

I looked over my shoulder, wondering if he could make out my expression that hopefully said *what the hell is wrong with you*?

"Cats. I should've chosen cats," I said, peeking around the corner again.

"But then you would've had to clean litter boxes. What a drag."

The shadow clipped the edge of the window before moving into the frame, directly behind the white, mostly see-through curtain. Its hand came up, as though shielding a glare, and its shape loomed larger, moving closer.

A thump sounded upstairs, directly above us.

I jumped, pulled back, and nearly wet myself.

"What was that?" I asked, clutching Mr. Tom.

He looked up at the ceiling. "I don't know. I'm afraid to go look."

"What do you mean you're afraid to go look?" I whispered urgently. "You can shift to a bigger magical form, you have a weapon, and you can fly. I'd say you are well-equipped to check it out."

"Yes, but whatever that was might have a better arsenal than old bones, weak wings, and a crossbow with the wrong kind of arrows."

He gulped, and fear doused me. I hadn't expected him to be afraid. He'd been so calm a moment ago. A fact I reminded him of.

"We were fine at the moment. That moment has passed," he replied.

Pounding sounded above me, the thump-thumps of someone or something enormous heading toward the stairs.

"Whatever that is, it is in this house." He yanked me back the way we'd come. "Let's get into the walls. The closest entrance is this way."

Which would take us toward the sounds.

"I am not running toward whatever that thing is for any reason. This way!"

I ripped out of his grip, dashed across the open space of the foyer, wondering if the shadow at the window could see me, and darted into the first room on the left. Mr. Tom was right behind me, his breath harried.

"How did they get into the house?" he asked, panic lacing his words. "I can't even feel it in here. That shouldn't be possible."

"Can it get into the walls?" I ran across the room, fear quickening my feet. Loud thumping sounded somewhere outside the space, like someone crashing down the stairs.

"It's louder than you are," Mr. Tom said, pushing me out of the way and fitting his thumb into the side of the fireplace. "That means it is going for speed over stealth. It's trying to catch us."

The edge of the stone popped open. He reached in, turned the hidden handle I'd discovered the previous day, and yanked the small door open. He shoved me in first and shuffled in after me.

As he turned to close the door, I glimpsed a massive human-like shape filling the entryway to the room. The thing had to duck to enter. Its torso was covered in shimmering, deep gray metal, the armor etched with muscles and nipples like Batman's costume. Long gray hair, like strings, hung over its absolutely massive shoulders.

Its roar filled the room to bursting. I flattened

against the wall, dread drowning me, the click of the door not doing anything to block out the sound. I grabbed a suddenly frozen Mr. Tom and ran.

"Go, go, go, go, *go!*" I said, seeing the map I'd drawn in my mind's eye. I'd done that so I could find my way through the secret tunnels. I always remembered better when I put new info onto paper. Thank God, because now I took the turns at breakneck speed, hearing a loud *thump* behind us.

That thing was trying to crash through the wall. I said as much.

Mr. Tom broke free from my grasp, getting his senses back online. "It can't. These walls are structurally and magically fortified. It won't be able to break through them."

"It got in the house."

"That's because it's a shadow wraith with some sort of magical armor that makes it corporeal. It opened a window."

When we reached the first viewing area, Mr. Tom pulled ahead of me.

"What is a shadow wraith?" I asked. Another thud echoed down the passageway. "It sounds strong."

"It does sound strong," Mr. Tom said, hooking both of his hands through a little hole in the wall I hadn't noticed before. "Sorry, Ivy House, but this is dire. I can't let that thing get its hands on her." A hidden door swung open—huh, a secret passage within a secret passage—and he ducked into the opening and grabbed an iron banister attached to a circular iron staircase, leading straight up. He hurried up the stairs. "A shadow wraith is a ghostlike creature that drains the souls of the living."

"Oh my God," I whispered. My stomach flipped in horror.

"That one has some sort of armor that gives it a corporeal body. Apparently it can still float, because that's how it must've gotten in here. They don't float as fast as I can fly, though, and they don't fight well in the skies. The sky is our only hope."

He slowed halfway up, and I realized his stamina was giving out. His age was showing.

Somewhere deep within me, I felt a pulse. Strong, solid, and sure, it filled me with assurance.

That pulse soaked into the walls. Buzzed through the iron of the staircase. Reverberated through the air.

That pulse was Ivy House, I knew, and the beacon that had drawn me in when I was young was calling me back.

I could fix Mr. Tom, I knew. I could turn back the years for him, curing his flagging stamina. Turning his sagging skin and bowing back into muscle and might, like in the days of old. I could boost my own stamina, too. Up my strength, claim the freedom of flight for myself—

The needle skidded off of the record, the first indication my thoughts were not completely my own.

"If I got that magic, I'd be able to fly?" I asked, winded.

Mr. Tom made it to the top of the steps and doggedly moved out of the way, breathing heavily. "The Ivy House magic is the female version of a gargoyle, though infinitely more powerful. Only females can claim the magic, just as only males can shift into the gargoyles you usually see and hear about. Females lead her army of warriors."

"I think you've forgotten who you're talking to."

"Yes, yes, right. A Jane," he murmured, hurrying down a tight passageway.

A warning flared through me—the stranger on the porch was now inside. I couldn't sense any other presences, but I knew better than to think the shadow wraith had left. Mr. Tom and I just couldn't feel it.

"Gargoyles will be drawn to you once you ingest the magic. They'll recognize you as their queen, and everything in them will want to mate with you so as to best protect you. I won't feel the attraction, of course. We're family." He shrugged out of a night shirt I was only just realizing matched his cotton pants, like a child's PJs. Fluffy slippers adorned his feet and an elf-style hat sat atop his balding head, the little pompom hanging down the side of his face.

"No," I blurted. "No on all counts. I signed up to clean a house, not download magic that will make me the queen of a bunch of legendary creatures who will want to mate with me. Get a hold of yourself, man. We all just need to get a hold of ourselves."

He pushed down his pants and I jerked my head away, squeezing my eyes shut.

"What are you doing?" I asked with gritted teeth. "I have no interest in seeing your begonias, Mr. Tom."

A sound like huge boulders rolling down a hill compelled me to squint an eye open to check on him.

Whereas Donna had shifted shape in a warm flash of light and dare I say magic, Mr. Tom's transformation was slow, his skin mottling into what I could only describe as stone. His shape enlarged, the stone-grinding sound getting louder as he grew. Even in this massive form, I couldn't help but notice his muscles were a little stringy, his skin a little saggy. Great wings blossomed out behind him, unable to fully stretch open due to the confining space.

I gaped in shock at this additional proof that magic *had* to be real, watching as he lowered down onto his haunches, an enormous stone gargoyle fashioned like the water spouts on medieval buildings and cathedrals, and froze.

Seconds ticked by. The presence in the house entered my bedroom, making my skin crawl. The stone creature at my feet continued to do nothing.

"Did you just duck out on me without saying so?" I asked the stagnant statue, suddenly wondering how I would get out if I didn't have wings to fly.

CHAPTER 24

"D ID I CLOSE the door to the passageway in my room?" I asked the silence, reaching into my pocket with badly shaking hands. I unlocked my phone screen, found Austin's name, and tapped it without hesitation.

I knocked on Mr. Tom's head. The dense stone thudded under my knuckles.

"You bastard," I whispered, swaying from side to side like I was rocking a newborn baby, the movement comforting even all these years later. "You didn't even leave me at a proper escape route—"

"Yeah," Austin answered, his voice raspy, barely surfacing from sleep.

"Hey. There are people in my house—well, a person and a shadow wraith with some sort of body armor— and Mr. Tom just turned into a stone gargoyle. I'm…" I swallowed, my voice shaking. "I'm not sure what to do. I couldn't think who else to call. Edgar was apparently monitoring the guy that used to be outside but is now inside and in my bedroom. I'm really hoping I closed the secret passageway door in there because—"

"Wait, wait. Slow down," Austin said, the shroud of sleep shredding quickly. "What did you say? Someone is inside Ivy House?"

"Yes. A stranger and a shadow wraith. And despite popular opinion, the house is definitely not doing anything to get them out. It is just a house. A big house with a very long drop from my current location."

"Earl is stone?"

I gave Mr. Tom a kick. Pain shot up through my slippered foot. "Yeah. He looks like a water spout."

"Where are you?" His voice muffled for a moment, then got farther away. "Where in the house are you?"

"In an offshoot secret passageway, up a spiral staircase. Third floor. There is a thread of blue lighting near the ceiling, but that's it. I can't see much. I don't know where exactly in the house we are, but that wraith was really fast, Austin, and if I have to make a run for it, it'll catch me."

"*Shhh, shhh.* It's okay. No one is going to catch you," he said soothingly, a hard growl rumbling through his words. "Edgar probably went to get Niamh. You say that wraith had body armor of some kind?"

He sounded like he was moving, his voice jogging with his steps.

"Mr. Tom said the body armor made it corporeal. When it roared, it scared Mr. Tom. I had to yank him behind me to get him to run."

"You didn't freeze?" Austin asked.

Impatience made me dance in place. "Of course I didn't freeze. What do you think, I want to get caught? What should I do? I don't know what to do. Mr. Tom basically left me. If there's a hatch here somewhere, I'll roll the bastard out. Maybe it'll leave a dent in his head."

"It's okay. *Shhhh*, it's okay. You have to think really hard about what you need from him, okay? When gargoyles shift, they require a purpose to animate them. They must be called upon to act. Otherwise they'll remain frozen until their human form re-emerges. In Mr. Tom's case, that could be years. He's old."

"*What*? But you said he changed earlier."

"Yes. I needed a bottle opener and you needed some food to eat. He had a purpose. You need to give him a purpose."

"Well...I need him to be a living gargoyle, find a hatch, and fly me the hell out of there!"

The sound of boulders rolling across hard-packed dirt made me jerk away and stare earnestly at Mr. Tom. His body shuddered. His shoulders moved.

"Something's happening," I said quietly, the presence of the stranger still in my room. "Why is he so interested in my room?"

"Who?" Austin asked, and his voice cut out for a moment. "That's Niamh calling now. She must not think she can handle this alone. Damn it."

"The stranger, and thank you for not saying 'I told you so' regarding the sundry characters you warned me this house would attract," I said as Mr. Tom uncoiled, standing slowly.

His gray skin lightened to a somewhat purplish tone in the blue light, and his lips opened, giving way to large teeth that hung over his bottom lip on either side of his mouth. Black hair fell around pointed ears. He was just as ugly animated as he was in stone form.

"Mr. Tom is staring at me with his beady eyes. Now what do I do?" I asked Austin.

Mr. Tom grunted, and a foul smell washed over me.

"The gift of flight comes at a steep price," I murmured as Mr. Tom turned, *thwapping* me with a wing. I staggered back, grabbing the banister of the spiral staircase to keep from falling.

"What's happening?" Austin asked. "Is it safe to hang up and call Niamh?"

I almost said *wait*, but I was a grown woman. I couldn't keep using Austin as a safety blanket. At some point, I had to think for myself.

"That's fine. It's fine," I said.

Mr. Tom bent and pulled open a steel door reminiscent of a storm cellar. Cool, sweet air swirled into the stairway. From my vantage point, I could see the steep slope of the roof. It was another trap door leading outside, not unlike the one I had found the first time I was in the house, but definitely not the same one.

"He's strong enough to carry me, right?" I asked, watching as Mr. Tom slowly turned and started rummaging in the corner for something.

"Plenty strong, yes. He won't drop you. Tell him to meet me at the lake. He'll know where I mean. Don't worry, Jess, okay? He'll get you safely to me. I won't let anyone harm you."

But as I hung up the phone, the same string of words that had snagged me last night sent chills over my body.

If that boss wants to own this town, there is nothing Austin Steele could do to stop it.

Another thought wove through it, as crisp and clear as if someone were speaking in my ear.

"If you accept your rightful place as heir, you will not have to rely on Austin Steele to keep you safe. You can rely on yourself. You can enjoy being truly free."

"Everyone has an agenda," I said, feeling that deep pulse within me again. Feeling the thought that wasn't mine slither through my brain. Feeling bodies emerge from the woods way back behind the house. Feeling the intruder finally leave my room and head down toward the front door.

"Get us out of here, Mr. Tom. Austin said to meet him at the lake." I was not about to go looking around the house for magic. I still wasn't sure if I wanted to stay in this crazy circus. Adventure was one thing, like a zip line with safety cords, or sky diving with a knowledgeable instructor strapped to your back, but this was something else entirely. I was about to jump out of a door in the roof in the arms of an old as hell mythical creature who kept forgetting to explain very important magical precepts in moments of crisis. I'd read dozens of fantasy books, and none of them were this weird.

Mr. Tom grunted, stood, and slung the huge canvas sack he'd grabbed from the floor in the corner around my back. "Sh-*it*," he grunted.

I looked at the bag, which seemed empty, then around the space. "What happened? Did you feel the people coming? They're here for me, right? But you can get me out of here?"

He helped me curl my fingers around the edge of the canvas bag, indicating I should hold on to it.

Then swore again. "*Sh-it.*"

"I don't know how to help. I don't know what's wrong!"

He shoved me with one of his clawed hands, the

points pricking me painfully. I stumbled, couldn't get my footing, and fell into the sack.

"Yer-ah," he said, nodding.

"Oh, *sit*." I curled my feet into the bag, remembering how he'd carried the food earlier. Even still, I was really unsure about this. I weighed more than that food. "Is this bag going to hold me?"

"Yer-ash." He grabbed the handles, collapsing the bag around me and lifting me off the ground. "Her-oh-d ah-n."

"Hold on. Okay." I grabbed the edges. Stuffed my feet into the base. Felt fear travel my length. "Oh God, there has to be another way. There has to—"

Colorful swearing accompanied our dive through the opening as I swung wildly below him. My canvas-covered butt crashed against the roof. I skidded down the slope and then swung wildly into empty air. It would've been nicer leaving out of that other trap door that didn't lead out onto a roof before the fall. His massive wings thrummed, curving down around me. He turned back to the trap door and I skidded up the roof again.

"Wrong…way," I said, trying to wriggle for a softer place to take the bouncing.

The heavy steel slammed down onto the roof. He turned again, treating me to a third encounter with the roof. A moment later we were completely airborne, him soaring through the sky, gaining altitude with each wingbeat, me dangling below him, the view of his begonias sure to haunt me.

"The lake," I repeated from earlier, not sure if he could hear me over the roaring of the wind and his wings. "Austin said to meet at the lake!"

I wanted to shift my positioning so I could look out the side of the canvas, maybe see the intruders, but I didn't dare. My luck, I'd pitch over the edge and go splat before Mr. Tom even knew I'd fallen.

Chilled wind froze me to the core. As we got farther away, it struck me that I'd been blocking out that the voice that had urged me to claim the magic was still speaking to me—probably had been all along. My panic had blocked it out. It got fainter as Mr. Tom hastened us away, but I got the final messages quite clearly. "*If you had my power, you wouldn't have to flee. No man could make you run, ever again. No man would need to be your escape.*"

It sounded less like a house, and more like a woman trapped within it.

"*Rely on no man, for it is he who will betray you. Set yourself free.*"

"Yup, everyone has an agenda," I murmured, feeling the darkness in the voice. The bitterness. I wondered how much of it would corrode me if I relented and took the magic. How much of myself I would lose.

Only as much as I allow. And that voice was entirely my own. *Thanks to my marriage, I know the signs, and this time, whether I'm aligning myself to a man or bitter woman posing as a house, I will make sure to lose none of myself.*

A sound drew my attention to the right. Just over the canvas sack, I could see a new shape fall in beside us, streaking through the moonlit sky like spilled oil.

My mouth gaped yet again.

The horse creature had nightmare black scales, a golden mane and tail, and a crystalline horn coming out of its head. The soft black feathers on its mighty wings had a blue sheen in the moonlight, and its shimmering golden hooves clawed at the air. The sallow vampire riding its back waved at me. Edgar.

"Where'd we get the nightmare alicorn?" I asked stupidly.

It struck me that *this* was my new reality. I was being transported through the air in a large canvas sack by a gargoyle, fleeing a crew of invading creatures, beside a black alicorn ridden by a vampire. Only the severely twisted could make something like this up. It was too insane not to be real.

Which left me with a choice: I could either join this magical world with the magic stored in that house or run like hell and never look back.

CHAPTER 25

A S SOON AS all four hooves touched the ground, Niamh bucked, trying to fling Edgar off. She hated having people on her back. She didn't understand how normal horses stood for it.

He held on, his long nails digging into her sides. She neighed and readied for another, but before she could rise he threw his leg over and jumped to the ground.

Austin Steele waited for them near a large clearing in front of a small cabin, pushed back some ways from a lake. A lone camping chair sat in front of a fire pit.

He came out here to be alone, Niamh knew. This was his escape from the town and all the people who knew him, looked up to him, or wanted something from him. He also came out here to heal after he had to turn someone away at the border. The cabin was his sanctuary, a place where he could be physically alone instead of just emotionally alone like he was within the town.

Niamh was surprised Earl even knew about this place. Before Jessie had moved into Ivy House, Niamh hadn't even realized Austin Steele spoke to Earl. Most people tried to avoid the old nutter. Niamh only knew of the cabin because she'd seen Austin Steele running through the trees in animal form when she was flying over the area at dusk one night. She'd gotten curious and stalked him from the air for a few months.

She shifted to her human form, one of three forms she had to choose from, as Earl reduced down to a statue. Jessie stiffly climbed out of the sack she'd been carried in. She rubbed her butt.

"I've had better escapes," she said. She froze when she noticed Austin Steele. Her eyes widened, and then her gaze slowly tracked down his exposed upper body, cut with muscle. He kept himself in pristine condition as befit one in an alpha role.

Loose, light gray sweats covered his powerful lower half. With no Jeep in sight, he had clearly run here in his animal form and pulled on sweats while he was waiting.

"You made it." His smile was still startling. Before Jessie had shown up, Niamh hadn't even realized his face muscles could move that way.

"Yeah." The breath gushed out of her, and she glanced back at Earl, emerging from his stone stupor and beginning the transformation back to human. "Thanks to you."

"Why, what happened?" Niamh asked, poking through the sack for a change of clothes.

"He changed into stone before telling me I needed to think about what I wanted from him," she said, crossing her arms over her braless chest in a futile attempt to hide it. Her face flamed red, and it was clear she embarrassed much too easily, both with her braless-ness and with the nudity of others. "Austin had to tell me."

Niamh put her hands on her hips, waiting for Earl to complete his transformation. When he had, she said, "Well that was pure stupid, now wasn't it?"

He blinked in confusion for a moment before putting it all together. His eyebrows lowered defensively. "I'd used my magic earlier in the night. I thought she was in the loop."

"She didn't understand what she was doing earlier," Austin Steele said. "But it doesn't matter now. She had the presence of mind to call for help. We made it this far."

"Earl, did you not think to put a few pieces of clothing or a towel or something in the sack while you were bungling your escape?" Niamh asked.

"Might I remind you that I am Tom, now. Mr. Tom to you, you awful jackass. Respect my new identity—"

"Identity? It's a name for a nitwit and I don't have

311

to respect anything."

"—and for your information, we were running for our lives. We barely got out of there! I had to lead her to the spiral staircase. Hopefully that doesn't jeopardize her ability to access the magic, but I didn't see any choice. The house should understand. I was acting in her best interest. I couldn't wait around all day for her Royal Heinous to come break us out. So no, I didn't pack a wardrobe for you. Or myself, as you see."

"Yeah, we all see," Jessie muttered, making a point of looking the other way.

"Enough," Austin Steele said, and a current of power snapped Niamh's mouth shut.

She hated when he did that. She could resist the urge to fall in line, but she had to be actively thinking about it. She almost never was.

"Explain what happened. Start from the beginning," he said.

"I'm just…" Jessie eyed the camp chair by the fire pit, then the lake. "I'm just going to take that chair and go think for a while, if that's okay?"

"Yes, of course." Austin Steele's hard demeanor melted in an instant. He left the others waiting as he grabbed the chair and carried it down toward the water to place it for her. Once she was settled, he massaged her shoulders for a moment, his voice reduced down to a soothing murmur.

"He was doing that all evening," Earl said, and his meaning was as clear as his confusion.

Austin Steele was treating that Jane like an alpha would his mate: looking after her, trying to make things easier for her, protecting her. But there didn't seem to be any romantic attachment with it. He wasn't flirting or sexual, like he would be in a courtship. It...didn't make any sense.

"Is he trying to sweet talk her into doing what he wants?" Edgar asked through a mouthful of fangs.

"Put your teeth back in your head, will ye?" Niamh said, rubbing her temples.

"He might be," Earl said. "Though he did eventually say it was in her hands. That might be a tactic, though. He's suave with the ladies when he wants to be."

"Everyone is suave with the ladies compared to gargoyles," Edgar said.

"You're starting to sound like her." Earl pointed at Niamh.

"Speaking some sense, yeah, I agree," she said. "Edgar is right. Austin Steele doesn't try to get the ladies. At least not from what I've seen. He treats them exactly like he treats everyone else—distantly. Almost like strangers. And still they follow him home like he's the Pied Piper. He's not suave about it."

Austin Steele returned, his hard mask clicking into place and his raw power oozing out around them. This was the reason he'd been given his new last name, something a pack chooses for its alpha, once he'd officially been accepted into O'Briens. Austin Steele had tried to deny its legitimacy, but the magical folk had insisted, one and all. They might back down from actually calling him alpha, but they wouldn't back down from that name. It fit, and it was a matter of respect. Even Austin Steele had had to relent.

"Explain," Austin Steele said, not offering anyone else a chair. "Start from the beginning."

Niamh listened quietly to Earl's account of how he had muddled up the situation. A gargoyle, even an old one, should've been able to take that wraith. He should've been able to secure that house with the magic on his side. His fearful attempt to run didn't make sense.

"Ivy House didn't use any defensive measures to cast them out?" Edgar asked, his brow crumpled in confusion.

"No," Earl replied. "Nothing I'm aware of. I couldn't feel the wraith at all. Not in the normal sense. I only felt the magic when it came into the room. And it came fast. Faster than it should've been able to. It had some powerful magic behind it."

"How'd it get into the house at all?" Niamh asked, scratching her head. "Ivy House should be protected against creatures like that. Naturally protected. Are we sure the magic is still in place?"

"It's in place," Austin Steele said. "A door slammed in my face. The magic is connected to Jess. She looked scared, and the door slammed. Later on, she wanted me to help her test the passageway viewing area. I felt no issue from the house at all. It let me into its walls without a problem."

Earl nodded with a grim face at Niamh and Edgar's shock. Those passageways were like the veins of the house. They ran all over, and only through them could one get to the heart. Only those accepted by the house were allowed into that area.

"Jessie accepts you, and the house is reacting, it must be," Earl said.

Niamh held her tongue. They needed the help of Austin Steele. Too many intruders had poured out of the woods for Niamh to battle, even with Edgar's help. Even with Earl's. She hated to admit it, but she got winded too fast these days. She had lost her vicious edge. They needed the might that was Austin Steele.

The problem was, if he learned that protecting Jessie would tie him to the house, he might back off. It was likely the last thing he wanted. He'd made this magical town what it was, but his decision not to step up as official alpha gave him an out. It gave him a hall pass. Niamh didn't think he'd like that status changed.

"So why didn't the house react when those creatures got inside?" Niamh wondered, wishing she had her rocking chair. Old bones didn't like standing around too long.

"Putting Jess in danger to force her to make a choice?" Austin Steele asked, glancing at the lake.

Niamh sucked her teeth in thought.

"Would you stop doing that? It is absolutely disgusting," Earl said with a downturned mouth. "Have a little pride in yourself."

"Pride in meself? You're always on'ta me about wearing a bra—you oughta be putting those sad sacks in a sling or they'll trail along the ground as you're flying." She pointed between his legs.

Austin Steele's warning gaze cut into her. She clenched her jaw in frustrated silence. She hated being dominated. She hated that he could do it so damn easily.

"What's the plan?" Edgar asked, his teeth finally retracting.

"Elliot Graves wasn't there," Niamh said, lowering her voice in case the trees had ears. "He sent one of his black-collared soldiers to lead."

"What's his play?" Austin Steele asked.

"Those creatures in that house were either there to capture her or harm her," Earl said.

"Whatever their plan, it's not safe for Jessie to go back if the house doesn't do its part," Edgar said.

"Agreed," Austin Steele said, his gaze veering to Jessie again. "She said she needs to figure out if she wants to stay or go. I think our next steps hinge on her decision." He paused for a moment, watching her watch the water ripple against the bank. "One thing she mentioned—she ran when the shadow wraith blasted its voice. Is that right, Earl?"

In surprise, Niamh watched Earl's face. His eyes turned distant in thought.

"She must've," he said. "I managed to close the door, but after that, she was in the lead. Yes, she must've pulled me along. I don't like to admit it, but its magic had me frozen."

"That's…" Edgar clearly struggled for words.

"That's courage of steel," Austin Steele said, probably not intending it as any sort of pun or connection. Missed opportunity, that. "She was scared, but she didn't shut down. The house chose well. Now we just need to see what Jess chooses. Our fate lies in her hands."

CHAPTER 26

A LIGHT JACKET dropped down over my shoulders, immediately allaying some of the chill. The sun was just starting to lighten the sky, shooting out streaks of pinks and oranges in bursts.

Austin crouched down beside my chair, looking out over the tranquil lake. Shadowy forms of trees and brush were painted across the glassy surface.

"Some week, huh?" he said, his voice not much more than a hum in the hush.

"I'll say. Welcome to paradise, here's a nightmare scenario. Good luck!" I tightened the jacket around me, smelling soap and the spicy sweetness of Austin. "It's beautiful here."

He nodded, sweeping his gaze to the left. "It is, yes."

"This is your cabin?"

"Yes. It's secret. Don't tell anyone."

"Sharing your secret headquarters with Mr. Tom, huh? I knew you guys were besties."

He huffed and shook his head, the laugh not quite

breaking the surface. "I told him about this place when we were at Agnes's house, waiting for the forgetful potion. I wanted to make sure you had a place to go if things…heated up."

"Oh." I frowned. I hadn't realized he was serious about the whole secret thing. "Thanks. We needed it."

Silence sifted down between us for a moment, broken only by a bird twittering in the new day and Mr. Tom bickering with Niamh about something within the cabin.

"What comes next?" I finally asked, my stomach in knots thinking about it.

"We're all waiting on you for that one. This is your show. We're merely the players."

I didn't waste his time asking why that was. I knew why—that house. That magic. My arrival had thrown everything into disarray.

"Is it so much to ask for a quiet life?" I murmured.

"Didn't you have a quiet life? And yet, you came here. Maybe a quiet life isn't your thing."

"I don't know how to live a loud life."

He settled, sitting cross-legged, his hands entwined in his lap. "I was exactly the opposite. All I knew was a loud life when I decided to settle under my brother's thumb and learn. I was going crazy the whole time, desperate to start a bar fight for no reason. I hunted more than was normal. Or prudent. I kept our whole city and the neighboring town in meat, and it still wasn't enough. I hated to leave my family, but I was happy to be free."

"Why'd you come here? Why'd you come to the town that houses Ivy House? Were you drawn to the magic?"

This time he did laugh, humorlessly. "I didn't even know about Ivy House when I settled here. I was wandering. Town to town, through the wood—I came up over the Sierra Mountains. The cold doesn't bother me. I randomly stopped in O'Briens. No reason for it—it was late, I was tired, and I figured I'd grab a drink and find somewhere to sleep. This town was the closest, magical or otherwise.

"I hadn't even finished my first drink when a commotion exploded in the bar. Yelling and tussling—I ignored it at first, because it had nothing to do with me and I didn't know anything about this town. I didn't want to get thrown in jail or held up by some mage. But it quickly became apparent that the situation was no good. If there was law in the town, it wasn't stepping in like it should."

"What was the problem?"

"A young shifter—a fox—was being used for sport. Instead of being chased by fat men on horses with dogs, he was being hunted by a pack of young wolf shifters in a training exercise. The fox kid ducked into the bar to get help, and the organizers of the hunt wanted to get him out and get him running so the wolves could track and tackle him."

"Tackle him?"

"It's a nice way of saying what they actually do. After tackling."

I grimaced in horror. "That's legal?"

"No, it's outlawed, but some organizations don't want to change their customs and don't much worry about the outside world. As I watched, I recognized the majority of the people in the bar were clearly uncomfortable but doing nothing. They were afraid to stand up for the kid. They were afraid to create waves with the organization. Organizations like that have money and power. Their influence is far reaching."

"You found a way to get out of the slow lane," I surmised.

His gaze found mine, something unreadable in their depths. "Exactly. I found a worthy outlet. And I ran at it with all my pent-up aggression. I...sent a strong message. A message I knew would be received badly. I stuck around, waiting for the organization to come to town and quell my uprising. When they came, they came hard. Harder than I'd expected. Not harder than I could handle, though. I met the challenge. I lost myself to it."

He paused, staring out at the water. I waited in silence, knowing he needed to tell his story. Given he had no friends, and he was a gruff man clearly slow to trust, I doubted he'd talked about this before.

"The fight was vicious. It was brutal. They brought shifters and mages—I was outnumbered twelve to one. But I had a lot of pain I needed to work through. A lot of uncertainty in my past. Hell, I'm unbalanced. I told you. I let my dark side, as you called it, have free rein."

"What happened?" I asked softly.

"I didn't send them to the hospital. I sent them to the morgue. Every last one of them. I made a statement."

"And that ended it?"

He chuckled darkly. "Nope. They sent more for the second wave, asking for my head on a spike. Offering a reward for it. By this time, my name was being circulated around the shifter community. People were talking. Word reached my brother, and he offered to send aid." He shook his head. "But by that time, fire burned deep within me. I'd found…a purpose. I'd found a place where I was needed. But I'd also found some peace. I faced the second wave alone again, but this time I offered a way out. They could go in peace, as long as they left the corrupt organization that employed them, or they could stay and fight and find their own heads on spikes. Half walked away. The other half…"

"Please tell me you didn't actually put their heads on spikes."

"No. I'm not that sort of man. But I did maim them for life. I didn't kill anyone, but I made sure they'd never fight again. The organization they came from wasn't so kind."

"Do *not* tell me they sent more."

"No. That was it. I then made it clear to the town that it was time for change. Be kind to your neighbor, or get the hell out. I got shot in the back a couple of times, but eventually things settled down."

"You got shot in the back?"

"I heal quickly. Because magic."

Niamh's nightmare alicorn form flashed through my head. Rainbow Bright meets Halloween. I wasn't about to argue with his ability to heal quickly. Or any other weird thing I ran into. I was officially naive again, needing to learn this new world from the ground up. If I'd wanted to start over, I was certainly doing that.

"And that cemented your reputation?" I asked. Dawn had lightened the sky to a deep blue color nearly matching Austin's eyes.

"It started it, for sure. Over the years I've cemented

it. People talk. The stories grow bigger and bigger with each telling. It wasn't until I'd lived in the town for a while that I learned about Ivy House. I thought the rumors were tall tales until I met Niamh. Even then I took a lot of it with a grain of salt. Turns out those tales weren't so tall. Barely even did the situation justice, actually, if Elliot Graves is interested."

"He's the magical crime boss?"

Austin's brow pinched. "Yeah, I guess you could call him that. He didn't show up tonight, though." He shook his head. "I'm not sure what that means. I know about protecting a tribe and making things run smoothly, but I have no knowledge about ancient magic trapped in a house looking for a chosen. This has gotten…too big for me. Too farfetched."

"*Thank* you!" I dropped my head onto the chair back. "I realize that I'm in a huge learning curve with the magic piece, but…the house situation seems absolutely absurd. When Mr. Tom and I were running through the walls, this woman started talking to me. I mean, not talking like I could hear her voice, but…getting her message across. That sounds nuts, but I *swear* it's true." I blew out a breath, thought about pulling up my legs so I could hug my knees, and remembered that the ability to do that was long gone. I settled for slouching. "I sound crazy."

"Yes, you do."

I frowned down at him. "You're not supposed to agree with me on that."

He smirked and curled his big hand around my calf. For just a moment, I felt his support through the touch. I felt like he had my back. Shivers crawled up my body. After a beat he took his hand away.

"You're in a situation not many people in the whole world can understand, Jacinta. I don't claim to be one of those few. But I know what it feels like to have your world turned upside down. I can't take your place—nor would I want to—but I can guard your back. I can guard you. *That* is within my power."

"What if I run?"

He shrugged. "I'm your huckleberry. I got nothing tying me here."

"That's not true," I whispered, a soft spot forming in my heart, and not just because he'd quoted *Tombstone* and I loved that movie. "This is your home. This is the town you practically built. You might not claim the role of alpha, but you are the alpha."

"I hadn't expected you to talk about running. I couldn't very well throw up my hands and say, 'Well in that case, hope it all works out for you. Good luck!'"

I laughed despite the seriousness of the situation. "True."

"When you called earlier, panicked and asking what to do, I felt…" His muscles coiled along his body. "I felt the fire of my youth. Like I wanted to wipe the dust off my shoulders before charging into battle. It made me realize that I've been thinking of this town as the place it used to be, a group of people in need of armor. For a time, I found my purpose in being that armor. But the people here don't need me like they did. They've grown into their potential, and they don't shy away from standing up for themselves. From doing what's right. Old enemies have moved on. New issues are few and far between. Non-magical cops are increasingly effective at dealing with lesser problems. The world is more modern, communication is easier, and safe havens are more plentiful—I've outgrown my usefulness. Now I'm just…getting older. Waiting to retire." He sighed. "No one ever talks about what happens when you realize you're not needed anymore, and what comes next when you have nothing else."

"It's not the same, but I have a kid who no longer needs me. I don't have anything besides that."

"You have friends. And a weird, half-mad butler."

"So do you. And there is nothing half about Mr. Tom's madness."

Silence drifted around us for a moment. "That's true," he said softly. "I have one friend. I hope I don't mess it up."

"Me, too. You're the only normal person in this town."

"I'm too young to feel stagnant," he said after a another moment. "I still feel twenty. I don't want to retire or fade into obscurity—it's time to pivot. Like you are. I feel the truth in that."

"Don't make life choices based on my example. I'm not batting a thousand."

"You're about to go into battle, heavily outnumbered, to claim what is yours. To claim your destiny. I'd say that is exactly batting a thousand."

"Am I?" I asked with a grimace. "About to go into battle?"

His brow furrowed. "Aren't you? Don't you want to live in that house?"

"As weird as it is…yes. I do. I feel at home there. For the first time, I feel like I've found a place I'd be happy to stay."

"Then fight for it. Claim the future you want."

"But the battle part, and the danger…"

"I'll handle the battle and the danger. I said I'd guard you, remember? I'll be your armor. Nothing will hurt you while I am at your back. Nothing will get to you." His last words were said on a growl. His eyes burned brightly.

I swallowed, feeling the fire behind his words. Feeling an equal amount of fear because danger was something I usually ran from. Battles existed in movies.

I couldn't help feeling curious about that magic, though. I wondered what I'd be able to do with it. And as for the darkness tinging it…

Captain America was able to stay himself after the transformation. She-Ra. Batman—his past made him unhinged, not the suit. I could think of plenty of imaginary people who'd made sudden powers work for them. Given what I now knew, it wasn't too farfetched to assume those characters were based on real people.

"I'll let you think about it," Austin said, standing. "I will support whatever you choose. That hasn't changed. But realize that if you stay in that house, you are painting a target on your back. What happened tonight should tell you that much. If you stay, you will have to fight. If you do not want to fight, you have to leave."

If I stayed, the house would need to make me its chosen.

CHAPTER 27

"HERE'S THE THING." I edged into the little cabin as the sun climbed in the sky. I'd sat in that chair, looking out at the lake, poring over every detail. Thinking through the possible paths I could take. I'd called my son and teared up when he said he loved me. I'd called my ex-husband, and grinned when he sounded annoyed.

And here I was, on the doorstep of a terrible idea.

The group sat around a tiny table just off the little kitchen, all of them looking at me expectantly.

"Do I have to have the wings?" I asked. Call it vanity, but I didn't want to walk around with a cape the rest of my life. It was a sticking point, and I said as much.

Mr. Tom's nostrils flared. "It is not a cape, firstly, and it is an incredible honor to—"

"Would ya stop?" Niamh asked him. "They look ridiculous. You must know that." She shook her head at me. "The females of the species have smaller and more delicate wings that retract. Females don't shift, either.

Battling in the sky won't be your forte, but the gargoyles you call to you will handle that. Your wings will only show when you actually need to use them."

"Oh." That was okay then. "So how do we do this?"

"Austin and I can clear a path into the house," Niamh said. "Once in the house, you can find your way to—"

"No!" Mr. Tom put out his hands.

"I was goin'ta say the magic, you donkey," she clapped back. "Jaysus, Mary, and Joseph, why for all that is holy did that house pick you?"

"Oh yes, because a rock-toting, one mammary gland crusader makes all the sense in the world," Mr. Tom bit back.

"Enough," Austin said, and the power crackling through that word produced instant silence. He ran his fingers through his hair. "This is our crew. This is what we've got. Jess, does this mean you've decided to fight for that house?"

"Yes. I want to secure the house. I don't want to be chased away from the life I've chosen. I want to fight."

He inclined his head. "And you're ready to claim the magic?"

"Mostly. I just wish I could pick and choose which elements to accept. It felt a little dark—I'm worried it'll change me into something I'm not."

"You're strong of will, Jacinta," Mr. Tom said, nodding at me supportively. "Certain things, like the wings, are a given, but if you hold on to who you are, no magic can change that."

I dragged my teeth over my bottom lip. "And if you're not really certain about the...who you are part?"

"You're certain," Austin said, and even though the others were right there, it felt like he was saying it for my ears alone. "You know who you are, and you know what you want, or you wouldn't be standing here, trying to barter your way into something most of the magical world would kill for. I don't know what in the past made you question yourself, but maybe it was for the best. It made you who you are. The second I met you, I could tell you had your eyes wide open. You were ready for life to come at you. All you need now is to find your confidence, and you'll be unstoppable."

The others nodded their heads in agreement.

The weight of indecision and self-doubt evaporated from my shoulders, making me feel lighter. I'd never really been supported like this in my adult life—I'd always fallen into the supportive role. So I hadn't realized how much it helped. How good it felt to have the people around me lift me up when life was trying to batter me down. No wonder my ex had hit such professional heights—he'd always had a champion in his corner. I now wished I'd relied on true friends like Diana a lot more.

Regardless, I was here now. My path had led me here, and this time, I *did* have support. Weird as they were, I had a team. And a really strange future to grab hold of.

"Okay." I took a deep breath. "How are we going to get into the house?"

CHAPTER 28

W E'D DECIDED TO make our move at night—the darkness would lend strength to Mr. Tom's and Edgar's magic, and the delay would give us time to rest and plan.

The goal, we'd agreed, was to get me into Ivy House. From there, I would find the magic.

I could tell Mr. Tom was the only one who thought it would be a cinch for me to claim the magic. Mr. Tom...and myself. I knew it would call to me once I was in the house. It would pulse deep inside of me, maybe even shout directions in the voice of that bitter lady I'd sensed.

My question had been—what happens after I get the magic?

Everyone had shrugged it off, returning to their scheming. They weren't worried about it.

I certainly was, especially now, as I stood in the darkness swathing the grounds of Ivy House.

"How you doing?" Austin asked, crouched next to

me just behind the tree line. A wall of bushes rose up twenty feet in front of us, the labyrinth I still hadn't gotten around to exploring. It just wasn't on the list of important things I wanted to waste an afternoon doing.

"She's good. We're all real good," Niamh said, at my other side. She had faith in me, which was great. I had no idea why, however.

"I don't know enough about what's going to happen to be scared," I whispered, wishing I could see how many people guarded the house.

"Don't you worry about it, love," Niamh said, patting my shoulder. "There's only a few dozen or so, I bet. It was hard to tell from the air, but I'd guess about that number. And however many are in the house, o'course. We're just going ta clear the way for ye, and you'll be good to go. Just need to find that…magic."

Nervous tremors ran through my body. Even if her math was right, and there weren't more than "a few dozen," there were only four of us. Our odds weren't great.

I also wondered what the fighting would entail. What kind of damage were we talking? Because inflicting harm had always been a no-no where I came from, unless you wanted to end up in jail. Except I had a feeling this wasn't the kind of conflict that would be adjudicated by human law.

"Focus," I said softly, wiping sweat from my brow in the cool night.

"You'll do great." Austin bumped my shoulder, his voice rough and violent and his mannerisms cool and confident. For some reason, his chill attitude was stressing me out.

This whole situation was stressing me out.

A grunt sounded from down the line, Mr. Tom in his other form and ready to go.

"We are vastly outnumbered." There. I said it. Just in case no one else had realized the obvious.

"Nah. And here we go." Niamh stood from the brush, peeled off the clothes she'd borrowed from Austin's cabin, and tied the sweatpants around her waist with rope. That done, she changed into the nightmare alicorn, parts of her sparkling and dazzling within the ink blot of night. Mr. Tom stepped forward, muscles bunching under loose gargoyle skin. Edgar scooted out, more hunched than normal, his teeth elongated and his nails clicking as he waggled his fingers.

"Are you ready?" Austin stepped out next, still in the sweats and no shirt look from the beginning of the day. He'd driven me here on the back of his dirt bike, stashed at the cabin. Given it hadn't had any gas in it, he clearly had other ways of covering a lot of ground relatively quickly. I had a feeling I was about to see how.

"No." Why lie?

"If I have to change shapes before we're near the house, you will ride on my back until we get into enemy territory," he said. "Just hold on to my fur, okay? I won't drop you."

"Okay. What are you, again? Bigger than your brother, right? What's your brother? A donkey, maybe, and you're a war horse?"

"I'm much more effective than a war horse. And my brother is a tiger. He inherited the sexier animal." Austin winked.

Bigger than a tiger?

As a group we walked around the edge of the labyrinth. Some intruders stood around the side of the house, looking bored. They were clearly waiting for someone.

You, you idiot.

Austin took a moment to stop and push down his sweats. His butt was just as perfect and muscular as the rest of him. He turned around to put a finger to his lips, commanding silence. My eyes snapped up and my face heated, both because I'd been caught looking, and because of the size of the second thing I shouldn't have been looking at.

"Slow and steady," he whispered. "No sudden

movements. Earl, out in front. You'll help camouflage. Everyone, follow my lead." He leaned in to me, his face inches from mine. His breath, honey and cinnamon, dusted my eyelashes. "If I get to my belly, that means climb on. I will help you up. I will not hurt you. When it is time to dismount, I'll take care of it. As soon as your feet hit the ground, you run. Got it?"

Niamh made a light neighing sound, and I couldn't tell if it was support or impatience.

We picked up the pace now, following Mr. Tom on all fours. The labyrinth blocked visibility from the left, arrow straight. The right was wide open. Anyone who bothered to look would see four lurking characters and some shimmery horse hooves and golden hair. That was bound to attract attention.

As we moved closer, a warning beat in my blood. Pounding, deep down.

War. Battle. Fight. Find the magic, and fight!

We were jogging now, and while adrenaline was coursing through me and fear was egging me on, I was not in prime shape. My breath started to come fast, my chest burning. My legs aching. Still I pushed on, little blasts of warning lighting up my insides. Strangers were in the house. Looking around, touching things.

Invading my home.

Rage surged up out of nowhere. My blood boiled

with it. I gritted my teeth, carrying on. Moving closer to the five or so loiterers trampling Edgar's beautiful garden.

"Niamh, Edgar, take them out," Austin commanded, making a throwing gesture with his hand.

The two shot forward, Edgar lurching and loping strangely, his clawed hands extended. Niamh was as graceful as he was grotesque. She pranced at first, then moved into a gallop as she got closer, deep shadows streaking in her wake.

The enemy startled as they drew near. Too late.

Niamh lowered her head and slammed her horn into someone's center, knocking two more to the side with her shoulders and sending them rolling for Edgar to pounce on. She threw the impaled man up over her back, sending him flying end-over-end, then rose up and clawed the air with her golden hooves. Two people approached her from behind. She touched down on all fours before she kicked out behind, catching one in the chest. Catching another in the face. Down for the count, fast and brutal.

Bile rose in my throat as Edgar launched into the air, his feet and hands spread, his long jump distance better than that of any gold medalist. He landed on an enemy's back and crunched into his or her neck. I grimaced. I really should've been too far away to hear the sound effects, and yet my brain was now playing it on a loop.

"Harden up," Austin said in my ear, running beside me. If he was winded, it didn't show. "You're in the magical world, now. Things here aren't daisies."

One of the enemy spotted us, lifting a hand to point. He started yelling, his words rolling and flowing, not English.

"Here we go." Light flared all around Austin, so bright I jerked away and covered my eyes. A wave of heat was next, nearly scorching my skin.

With bright splotches laid over the night, I back-pedaled as his size grew. And grew and grew. A *massive* polar bear stood on all fours in front of me. Its paws were the size of my head with enormous claws, and its jaw could crush bones. Intelligent eyes regarded me, and even in the faint moonlight I could tell they were Austin's cobalt blue.

"Holy crap," I breathed, a tingle starting from the top of my head and slithering down my body. Even though I knew it was Austin—just as a kid knows it's a parent behind the mask of Santa—my brain rebelled. My body tried to follow suit. To run away.

He huffed, turned, and flattened onto his belly. A zip of bright blue light flew into the air and exploded like fireworks. It rained down over us, our positions now completely compromised and a pack of people running our way.

"Oh God, oh God," I said, shutting off my brain and hurrying toward the colossal bear, much bigger than its natural counterpart. So big that I just didn't understand the physics behind a human man changing into it.

The fur was coarse against my arms until I pushed past the outer layer. Beneath that it was downy soft. I swung a leg over and felt his paw bump me up. A moment later, the mountain was moving, muscle bunching and coiling under my legs.

He stopped for a moment and bellowed, the sound building as it blasted over the grounds. And then he launched himself forward in a burst of speed so great I nearly tumbled backward off his back. I clutched fur and gripped with my legs, holding on for all I was worth. Wind whipped by my face and tossed my hair, the cold air making my eyes water. Through them, the people organizing in front of us almost looked like they were swimming.

Niamh swooshed down from the air, sending them rolling out of the way. One stayed stuck to her horn, which was not a good look. She beat her great wings and flew farther right before dipping down again. A body flew up in her wake.

Austin did not slow for those rushing us. He did not

alter course. He ran at them, speed and lumbering power. Once close enough, he batted them away with his front paw, almost a lazy effort. The enemy flew to the side, his head now on sideways, his body crumpling to the ground. Two more were trampled, and when I looked back, I saw that they did not get up, probably gouged by Austin's six-inch-long claws.

Mr. Tom swooped down beside us, ripping into an enemy before grabbing another and flinging him screaming to the side.

My stomach swam. The house beckoned, screaming warnings about the strangers inside. Begging me to come to its aid.

Everyone had an agenda, and I guessed I was buying into this one.

Near the back door of the house, Austin swiped someone out of the way and dove onto his stomach. I jumped off, landed on my feet like I was born to this— then tumbled and skidded on my face. I might not be fast or be able to run for a long time just yet, but I was damned good at falling, bruising, and then getting back up.

With me off his back, Austin rose up to his hind legs, his size now dwarfing everyone. His roar shook my bones. Adrenaline coursed through my blood. And then he launched into action, ripping through enemy bodies like they were paper. Batting them away like flies.

A few foolish souls stopped running to cower at Austin, and Niamh swooped down at them, smashing with her sparkly golden hooves and piercing with her beautiful crystalline horn. Edgar dashed in behind her, clamping onto one person, stunning them, and then grabbing someone else, not so great at fighting but very good at a vampire's equivalent of sucker punching. Mr. Tom held up his end of the bargain, as well, but I remembered their ages.

I remembered they couldn't last forever, and there were still many more enemies to conquer and expel.

CHAPTER 29

T HE BACK DOOR should've been locked, but the handle turned easily in my palm. I pulled it open and slipped inside, locking it behind me. The solid pulse of the house greeted me, deep and pure, vibrating through my body like a second heart.

Danger echoed down the hall to my left—no sound or voices, just a presence. To my right, the wallpaper crawled, outlining a pattern. A door. The handle was as clear as day, a little button and a thick groove.

Moments later, I stepped into a secret space and closed the door behind me, the soft click of the door comforting. I hadn't found this particular passageway in the last couple of days, but I remembered it. I remembered scrubbing the cobwebs from my face and telling Diana, "Just a little farther. I think it's just a little farther."

"What is?" she'd asked.

"Just a little farther."

Pressure built against my back, and lightly sucked at

my front. I started forward, hoping my friends were okay. Knowing the dozen people loitering inside the house would probably go out and help. Knowing that at some point, the effort would be too great for my aging friends. Austin Steele couldn't do it alone.

Faster.

I could almost hear the whisper. The urgency. But like before, it wasn't a voice, per se, more of a feeling. The house speaking.

I slowed as I neared the end of the passageway, feeling the pressure change. Feeling that gentle suction—stronger with every step—urging me to slip into a little alcove I couldn't see. One I remembered from the past.

In the past, I had been quite a bit smaller.

I turned sideways and ducked, hoping to hell I didn't get stuck.

The floor sloped downward quickly. The walls jutted outward, the tunnel getting wider, wood turning to stone, stone turning to rock. The jagged edges scraped my arms. The rough floor tried to catch my feet. Still I pushed on, feeling that pressure behind me, pushing. Feeling the pulse ahead, pulling, urging me to take what it was ready to freely give.

"Okay, but here's the thing." I held out a finger as I ducked through the last little bit of tunnel and into a cavern made of rock and stone. The ceiling curved over me in a roughly hewn arch. A wrought iron light fixture dangled from a thick chain directly above a rock outcropping. Within it glowed a blue orb, the same sort that lit all of the house's secret passages.

Large crystals in a plethora of colors rose from within the rock, almost crawling out like a rose bush. The blue orb above me throbbed, and refracted light from the crystals pulsed and danced across the walls in an abundance of color.

"I have some conditions." I had no idea why I thought I could barter with an inanimate object, but I was going with my gut. This would be far from the weirdest thing I'd done lately. "I will stay me. I don't need my age cut in half to be a badass. I am already a badass. But I'd love it if my back would stop hurting. And what's with the crackling joints? What's that all about? Maybe erase the stretch marks, too. I mean, that wasn't my fault—my skin sucks and my son was enormous. Oh! Can I get a magical skin care regime? That sounds like a good one. I hate bothering with that stuff. And oh, if you could put my boobs back where they belong, that would be awesome. I have to date again eventually, and the boob issue was the kid's fault, too, so I don't mind asking for that. Basically…less aches and pains, and the body I would have had if the kid hadn't stretched me out. Sure, I could diet and exercise, but let's get real. I don't want to. In return, I will return the house to its former glory, host your magic even though it'll put me in danger, and…harden up to fighting. And freedom, or whatever."

The crystals pulsed three times in quick succession. Butterflies filled my stomach. I felt like I was making a deal with the devil.

I took a deep breath, and reached out.

CHAPTER 30

T HE GROUND RUMBLED beneath Niamh's feet. A low hum filled the air.

A host of enemy rounded the house, finally clued in to the battle and coming to lend their aid. Edgar, flagging, prepared for them. Mr. Tom, sagging as well, landed for a moment, catching his breath. Even Niamh felt the effects of her effort.

Only Austin Steele showed no signs of slowing. He charged the enemy, brawn and power. Bodies flew with abandon.

"He's the best I've ever seen," Edgar said, wiping a trickle of blood from his chin.

Niamh had to agree, and she'd battled a great many shifters. The best of the best. None of the others could hold a candle to the magnificence that was Austin Steele, even with age against him. He was larger than life, and used every ounce of his strength and power to his benefit.

But this new round of fighters had come prepared.

Silver gleamed at the end of their spears, illuminated by the magical light showering them from above. He could withstand much, but he couldn't withstand silver.

"Hurry!" she wanted to shout to Edgar, but her stupid horse face didn't allow for it. She charged ahead, using everything she had. Silver wouldn't harm her or Edgar.

A shock wave blasted through the air, stealing her breath. Another, knocking her out of the sky. One more, and suddenly her strength began to grow. Her energy doubled. Tripled. Little aches dried up and disappeared. Big aches evaporated. Her heart beat harder, pumping her blood in steady gushes. She didn't even know that had been a problem.

Earl straightened up in front of her, put out his arms, and then snapped out his wings, spreading them wide. They no longer drooped. Muscles filled in his suddenly taut skin. Then swelled to the size they'd been in his prime. He bellowed and thumped his chest, fairly ridiculous.

Edgar straightened up and his eyes lit. His teeth became sharper. Whiter. Much cleaner. He poofed into a swarm of insects, flew ten feet, and materialized back into a vampire, running toward Austin. Midway there, he poofed back into insects, like a kid with a new toy. That was going to get annoying.

The ground bucked under Niamh's hooves. A dark shadow rained from the sky, blotting out the moon. Blotting out the enemy's magical light cascading down.

Except Niamh could see without a problem, and so could Austin, by the look of it. He took advantage of the enemy's floundering, swiping away spears and clamping down on someone with his massive jaws. He stood, shook his head, then spat out the leftovers. His roar froze Niamh's blood, and then an enormous swipe of his paw knocked out three enemies waving their hands in front of them, trying to see with their feelers.

Ivy House had woken up.

Screams emitted from inside. Glass broke on the second floor. Someone jumped out of a window. Another followed. Nets fired into the air from the third floor, catching one flier Niamh hadn't even seen. The creature fell to the ground, struggling.

Another blast emitted from the house, this one from chest height all around the perimeter. Darts, tipped with poison or sleeping draught or who knew what. They sailed right through Niamh's body as if she were a ghost, rematerializing on the other side. The same happened with Austin, Edgar, and Earl.

The invaders had no such luck. They reached around to touch their sudden wounds, confused. One by one, their knees weakened. They wobbled, reaching out for something to hold them upright. One by one, they hit the dirt.

The polar bear that was Austin Steele looked around in obvious confusion. He reduced down into a man, holding out his hands to look at them. Touching his body. He glanced up, and that's when Niamh noticed the windows. Every one of them pulsed blue, deep and steady.

Jessie had assumed the role of Ivy House master. For better or worse, she now held that magic within her.

CHAPTER 31

"**O**H MAN, I feel great. Like I could run a mile super fast." I ran through the passageways, trying to get a feel for the situation inside the house. I had to get out to the others, but wasn't sure which exit to take. I didn't know how to use the magic yet, so I wasn't ready to fight my way out. I still had to sneak.

I glanced through one of the viewing areas. Two legs lay on the ground, the head clearly near the wall and out of sight. Not moving. "Gross."

The next two rooms were empty.

The whole house felt empty. I wasn't sure how that could be. I'd felt the presence of intruders right after I'd grabbed that crystal and felt the really annoying tickling sensation. I hated being tickled.

But now…

The first floor was clear, so I powered up the stairs without even breaking a sweat. Young me would've been grinning like a lunatic. Midlife me was wondering about the butcher's bill. What had I just traded for the ability to take stairs in a single bound?

More "tackled" people upstairs. Many more. And then I figured out why.

"No! Oh my God, no. No!" I scurried back from the viewing orb and paused for a steadying moment.

The dolls were alive. And they were apparently every bit as much of a nightmare as I'd suspected, carrying knives and smeared or splattered red.

"No, no. I should've made a stipulation about the dolls!"

I ran down the stairs again, crossing from one passageway into another, instinctively knowing them like the back of my hand, and exited the house from the same back door I'd gone in. I closed it up tight. I didn't want those horrible dolls to get out.

The night was so dense it felt solid. No stars sparkled in the suddenly moonless sky. No light at all permeated the backyard. Somehow, however, I could still see.

Austin—the human version—stood amid a bunch of prone figures, patting his body like he wasn't sure it was real. Niamh and Edgar huddled together, talking. Other than that, the battlefield lay eerily silent. The fallen did not move. There were no battle cries or moans to be heard.

My stomach churned. I understood what that meant

for the enemy. Niamh had been right—the odds had been just fine after all. My crew was, quite clearly, utterly sensational. Age, to us, meant nothing at all. We could still kick ass and take names.

Except...

Fear bled into me. Mr. Tom was nowhere to be found.

I looked skyward, wondering if he was doing a sweep of the house. A winged shape sailed through the inky darkness, his wings strong and sure, beating at the air. His movements almost lazy. He wasn't checking anything out, at all. From the swooping zigzags to the dips and climbs, it was clear he was joyriding.

A breath I hadn't known I was holding released.

Moving fast—because I could!—I ran over to Edgar and Niamh, needing to double-check the status of things. Then ran around them. Then hopped up and down. And tinkled myself a little.

"Damn it!" I balled up my fists. "I forgot to ask about not peeing myself in everyday situations! That's crap. That should've been a given."

Niamh turned to me slowly, annoyance on her face. She looked exactly the same as before.

"What's the matter?" I asked hesitantly, wondering if I'd started celebrating too early.

She pointed at her chest. "I got the other tit back!

What a load of hassle."

I chanced a glance. Wished I hadn't. "Yes…well, they are nice and perky. So you have that going for you."

"Whoopdeedoo. What do I care if they are perky? They're there. It's annoyin'."

"It seems we have not changed in our looks, but have regained our youth in our fighting abilities and overall health." Edgar grinned, his chompers either a thing of beauty or really scary, depending on how one looked at it.

"Oh so…" I felt my face, unable to help a smile. "Me, too?"

"Yes, you, too," Edgar said, his smile a thing of fright. "It seems you and Ivy House are on the same page. Congratulations, master."

I felt my eyebrows pinch, wondering if he was telling a joke of some kind with the "master" bit, but I didn't have a chance to ask. Austin strode up gracefully, his muscles playing across his big frame like a symphony. His gaze fell on me, traveling my face and then moving down my body.

"What do I look like?" he asked with some consternation.

"We all look the same," Niamh said. "We just feel younger. Better luck next time if you wanted your looks back."

"I have my looks back, I'm sure of it," Edgar said with a gleaming, sharp-toothed smile.

"That's because ugly suits you," Niamh said.

"Why do I feel…" Austin flexed. *Allll* of him flexed, including his currently not-so-private bits.

Niamh flinched away and scowled. "*Jay*sus. That thing has its own time zone. Go get yer trousers and stow it away. Where are they? I'll get them for ye."

"Don't leave me to explain…" Edgar watched in horror as Niamh walked away.

"Why do I feel…stronger?" Austin's voice was rough. "Why am I faster?"

I spread my hands. "We all are."

"Which makes sense, since *you all* are the masters or protectors of this house. You're a part of it. I am not. Why am I reaping the benefits?"

Niamh was back in no time, tossing Austin's sweats at him. "Because you made a show of protecting Jessie. You protected the house's chosen with pure of heart, and so you are now a part of the house. You said you'd follow her. Well, you followed her. Be careful what you wish for."

He turned to her, very slowly. The small hairs on my arms stood straight up.

"I said I would guard her. I did not say I wanted this

magic."

"I don't understand. What's the problem?" I asked. "The magic helps you."

He stared down at me, slightly leaning. His huge hands were balled and muscle popped out all over his body. Power seethed from him. It crawled up my back and threatened to bow my spine. Holding his gaze was physically painful. Nearly impossible.

But I didn't look away.

"I said I would help you. But I did not say I would enter into…" He gestured around me. "…*this*. I don't need this magic. I don't need a fountain of youth. I don't need this trap."

"Then you shouldn't have put yourself in it," Niamh said, nonchalant. "This isn't Jessie's fault. It's yours. If you're too dumb to see that, well then…"

I sensed action before it came.

A solid wall of pink manifested between Austin and Niamh. I was pretty sure I'd made that happen (I'd always liked pink), but I had no idea how. Austin's hand jutted toward it, open to grab, and glanced off. He pulled back slowly, as though it cost him great effort, and pushed it down to his side.

He exhaled, and I could feel why. Again, no idea how. His rage was trying to burst him at the seams. The darkness inside of him was trying to lash out, to combat this perceived slight. To combat the fear he wouldn't show.

I didn't know what was happening here, with either of us, but I knew he was horribly unsettled. He hadn't signed up to protect the house, he'd signed up to protect me, and somehow the wires had gotten crossed. He felt betrayed. His world had just been turned upside down, and he didn't know how to handle it.

I couldn't say I blamed him. I'd entered into this bargain, not him. It seemed he was a spectator who'd gotten sucked into the turmoil.

"Go," I said, laying my hand on his arm. He flinched and I withdrew my touch. "Go," I repeated. "I don't know what's happening, but I'll figure it out, and then I'll figure out how to set you free, okay? There has to be a way."

His gaze connected with mine and held it for a long moment. His sigh was soft, and his nod was slight.

A moment later, an enormous polar bear was running across the garden, trampling flowers. I suspected that was on purpose. I *knew* it was on purpose when he barreled through the edge of the labyrinth and fought his way out of the other side, tearing a big runway down the middle.

"That is completely uncalled for," Edgar said. "I didn't mess up his cabin, now did I?"

Niamh waved it away. "He wanted a new challenge in his life, he just hasn't admitted it to himself yet. Give him time. He'll come around. Come on. We have some serious cleanup to do."

"I'll go start digging graves," Edgar said, then poofed into a swarm of insects.

"*Blech*!" I stumbled backward. "Gross."

"It's fine, he won't run into you." Niamh headed for the back door.

"No, no. There's a doll infestation in there. Let's stay at your house tonight."

CHAPTER 32

NIAMH WASN'T ANY more lenient in my terror of dolls than she had been with Austin. After much name calling and comments regarding my hysterics, we'd worked together to march the dolls back into their room of horror.

And when I say worked together, I mean that I hid behind her and let her talk me through controlling them (to some degree). No matter how hard I tried, I couldn't seem to make them self-destruct It was a design flaw, I was positive.

With the dolls locked in their room, it was time to set the house to rights. Which was gross on so many levels.

The dolls had done their fair share of carnage—which would give me nightmares for the rest of my life—and the house had taken care of the rest, spraying them with darts, dropping chandeliers on them, and disposing of them in a number of other nerve-wracking ways. The body armor of the wraith had been found, though apparently those creatures couldn't be killed in a traditional way. It was probably the only thing that had escaped. I was supposed to be able to control this stuff, somehow, but realistically I just wondered if it was going to turn on me.

Outside was worse. My four allies had created their own carnage. I wasn't complaining, because they'd saved my bacon, but good lord was it gross. Not to mention morally ambiguous. I couldn't keep my snacks in my stomach as we transported the wicked into their new dirt resting place, making me wonder how many others had found their permanent resting places here over the many long years.

"Now." Niamh wiped her hair out of her face, her emotions pleased and content. Turned out, I could read everyone, not just Austin. I wasn't sure if that was a great thing. It made me feel responsible for them. I'd already shipped my kid off, I didn't want to have to look after adult kids.

She walked into the living room—posture straight, steps light and graceful.

"Are you pissed you still look...older?" I asked, following her.

"No, no!" Mr. Tom ran in with sheets. "Don't soil the furniture!"

"Why not? It gives you something to do," Niamh

retorted.

"Insufferable woman," he mumbled, draping a white sheet over an armchair right before she collapsed into it. "No respect for antiques."

"Ah sure, I couldn't give a dog's bollocks what I look like," Niamh replied. "I have the tools to do the job, and that is a blessing, I won't say it isn't. I would've been happy to retire, but now, after getting another taste of life in the fast lane...I don't mind this so much either. I think I have the best of both worlds."

Mr. Tom covered a chair for me, and then two more for him and Edgar—who hadn't come in yet—and walked briskly out of the room.

Not long after he returned, carrying a highly polished silver tray. "Drinks?"

Edgar flew in behind him in the form of the swarm of insects.

"No." I shook my head. "No, Edgar. No bugs in the house. Absolutely not."

"Well, thank God you said it. I was thinking the very same thing," Mr. Tom said as he paused in front of Niamh, handed her a glass of what looked like beer, and moved on to me. I got a glass of wine. Apparently we weren't allowed to choose for ourselves.

Edgar's drink was also deep red, but it wasn't wine, and I didn't want to think too hard on that fact.

"Ahem," Niamh said, and saluted. "Here's to new beginnings."

"I would've liked to see my old beginnings in the mirror, but beggars can't be choosers, I guess," Mr. Tom said with a sniff, then left the room.

"Trust me, even youth wouldn't have helped that mug," Niamh called after him.

"Have you tested your magic?" Edgar asked me, a red mustache from his drink.

I set my glass down, suddenly uninterested in its contents.

"I don't know how to test my magic," I replied. "I...don't feel any different, honestly. I mean, my body feels more youthful, which is incredible, but...that's it. That's the only change I feel."

"Give it time," Niamh said. "You're tired and this is all new."

Mr. Tom re-entered the sitting room with a port-sized wine glass filled with white liquid. "I doubt you'll ever feel any different," he said. "That is why the house chose you, I am sure of it. To feel different would be an illusion. It would be an emotional response to your increased power and prestige. To feel like yourself means you *are* yourself."

"Now we'll just have to teach you how to use the magic," Niamh said. "Too bad only Earl knows anything about it, and the male and female versions are wholly different."

"She won't need a teacher." Edgar set his empty glass on the table next to him. "The house chooses, and the house provides. The magic will flourish within her naturally. She will not need an instruction manual, she'll need an open mind."

"Yes, the transition will be perfectly natural," Mr. Tom said. "Because she is a natural."

"The next time someone says natural, let's all take a shot," Niamh murmured.

The doorbell rang, echoing through the house. A stranger waited outside, I could feel it.

"Please, let me," Mr. Tom said, literally catapulting off of his seat.

"How long do you think he'll act like a kid on a po-go stick just because he can?" Niamh asked as he left the room.

"I can't really talk. It feels good to change into my other form again," Edgar said. "I half thought I'd die before it happened."

"Why did you lose the ability?" I asked him.

"Age," he responded, his fingers entwined in his lap, knuckles as knobby as they'd been before. "It requires a lot of energy, and when you get to six-hundred or so, you start to...fall apart. You just can't hold it together anymore. By seven-hundred my goose was cooked, so to speak."

"Six...ty, you mean? Six..."

"Jessie." Mr. Tom poked his head back in, his eyes tight. "A couple of officers at the door."

"What?" I stood, not even a little stiff. I just stood right up, not needing to struggle to keep everything in alignment, or give a little groan—everything worked in tandem. It was so...weird. And great.

"Officers."

"What do they want?" Niamh sat forward.

"No, no." Mr. Tom waved her away. "Not you. You'll just make matters worse."

"Why? I have a good rapport with Dick cops in this town," she said, indignant.

Edgar started laughing. "You get arrested for drunk and disorderly every other month."

"That's only because Chuck doesn't have a sense of humor. No one else brings me in."

As I approached the door, I caught sight of the men on the porch, their faces hard, mouths grim, and thumbs tucked into their belts.

"Yes, officers?" I asked, terror squeezing my stomach. We'd just buried a bunch of people in the woods. Could they have found out so soon? I didn't have any neighbors close enough to see into the backyard, but maybe someone had been flying a drone around?

The closest cop, a freckle-faced man in his early thirties, nodded in hello. "We've received a noise complaint about this residence, ma'am."

"A noise complaint?" Niamh said from behind me, stationed near the archway under the landing. I hadn't known she'd followed. "Who called it in? Snitches get stitches in this neighborhood. Was it that old blue hair, Betty Turnable? She needs a new hobby, if you ask me. Only crazy people paint rocks."

"What does that say about people who throw them?" Mr. Tom said through his teeth.

"Are you all...having a party?" The officer's eyes caught my messy mop of hair, probably the dirt on my cheek and clothes, and the little rip in my shirt from the place it got snagged on my way out of the heart of the house.

"Oh no. No—well, kinda." I shrugged. "It was a garden party, but we're all done, now. Everyone has gone home. Mostly."

The cop took a step back and looked up. "Seems awfully dark. You might see about getting a porch light."

"Yes, sir, of course—"

"The illumination on our porch has nothing to do with you, officer," Niamh called.

I pulled the door closed a little to block her out and gave the guys a smile. "Sorry. She's off her meds."

"I heard that!"

"Well." The front cop looked around a bit more. The one in back kept his eyes trained to me. "Okay. Just keep the noise down."

"Yes, sir. Of course, sir. Sorry, sir!"

"Don't grovel to them, we haven't done anything wrong," Niamh said.

"Would you shut up, woman? We just buried—"

I kicked Mr. Tom. The two of them needed to be separated at all times. That was utterly clear.

I waved to the cops as they left the porch, one of them stumbling a little, and got into their car at the curb. Before I shut the door, I noticed a figure standing off to the side. He stood so still, I half wondered if my mind was playing tricks on me, but once I'd noticed him, I couldn't help but zero in.

Dressed in a tailored black suit, with a black dress shirt open at the neck, he stood with his hands in his pockets. His black hair was slicked back and a dark goatee adorned his handsome face. The only pop of color on his person was a silver pocket scarf decoratively tucked in his expensive suit.

A sly smile lifted his lips. He brought up his hand, kissed the palm, and then blew it at me. It wasn't the kiss that rode the breeze, though, it was words, as though he'd spoken them right next to my ear.

"Sometimes all a lady needs is a little nudge toward greatness. I look forward to meeting you soon."

With that, he vanished. There one minute, gone the next.

I gulped and closed the door.

"I don't think Betty would've called us in," Mr. Tom was saying, back in the sitting room. "The golem she keeps in her basement has howling fits sometimes. She doesn't want any attention for that. She wouldn't want to get on our bad side."

"Well someone called," Niamh said, outraged.

I had a sinking suspicion it was the tall, dark, and handsome stranger who'd been standing just beyond the Ivy House property line. He'd wanted to deliver his message, but he clearly understood what the house could do. He hadn't wanted to chance his luck by stepping onto my property.

I wondered if it was Elliot Graves. I wondered if I should tell Mr. Tom and the others.

But really, what good would it do in this instance? He hadn't threatened me. If anything, he'd expressed approval for my decision to take the magic. A move he'd apparently helped orchestrate.

Besides which, my eyes had started drooping. I

doubted I needed to fill them in tonight. There was always tomorrow. The man hadn't seemed in any kind of rush.

As I lay in bed not long afterward, unsure of this new life, and unsure of the magic that was now apparently at my fingertips, I couldn't stop myself from reaching out to the one guy who had so far been there for me during all my freak-outs. Niamh had said he needed time, and I probably should've respected that, but I needed a friend who thought all of this was just as messed up as I did. I hoped he was still that friend.

I texted Austin: *I haven't done a good job of hardening up. I threw up three times during the outdoor cleanup. And the dolls didn't just shut off. I had to make them. What happens when they decide they don't want a master and pop back into consciousness and try to kill me?*

I stared at the message screen, looking for the three little dots that said he was typing. Wondering if he'd even seen the message at all.

After a while, I sighed and set my phone in the charging cradle. It had been a long, utterly screwed up night. This new life would take some getting used to.

Before sleep pulled me away, light flashed against my closed lids. My phone had lit up with a message.

Austin: *You'll harden up to the gritty parts of magic, I have faith in that. You're a survivor. Not sure about the dolls tho. You might be screwed there. Been nice knowin' ya. ;)*

I laughed and reached over to put the phone back. On impulse, I felt my back. Were there wings in there? Or had that aspect of the magic not been included in the deal? And what else could I do besides hear the troubled thoughts of the four magical people who'd helped me claim the magic? I had so many questions. There were so many unknowns.

Rome wasn't built in a day. The first order of business was getting some shut eye. Number two was blowing up the doll room. *Then* I would take the bull by the horns and figure out what I could really do. Preferably before that tall, dark stranger came back for his meeting.

THE END.

About the Author

K.F. Breene is a Wall Street Journal, USA Today, Washington Post, Amazon Most Sold Charts and #1 Kindle Store bestselling author of paranormal romance, urban fantasy and fantasy novels. With over three million books sold, when she's not penning stories about magic and what goes bump in the night, she's sipping wine and planning shenanigans. She lives in Northern California with her husband, two children and out of work treadmill.

Sign up for her newsletter to hear about the latest news and receive free bonus content.

www.kfbreene.com